S

C0-BWZ-942

GUN
PLAY

AN ELTON DANCEY MYSTERY

Mystery

R.B. Phillips

SOUTH BRANCH LIBRARY
16TH & FARNAM ST
LA CROSSE, WISCONSIN
54601

A Foul Play Press Book
THE COUNTRYMAN PRESS
WOODSTOCK, VERMONT

LIBRARY OF CONGRESS CATALOGING-IN-PUBLICATION DATA

Phillips, R. B., 1943-
  Gun play.
  "A Foul Play Press book."
  I. Title.
PS3552.R2298G8   1987   813'.54   86-32793
ISBN 0-88150-084-4

Copyright © 1987 by R.B. Phillips

Book design by DeDe Cummings
Printed in the United States of America

A Foul Play Press Book

The Countryman Press
Woodstock, Vermont

SOUTH BRANCH LIBRARY
16TH & FARNAM ST.
LA CROSSE, WISCONSIN
54601

Removed from the Collections of
La Crosse Public Library

GUN PLAY

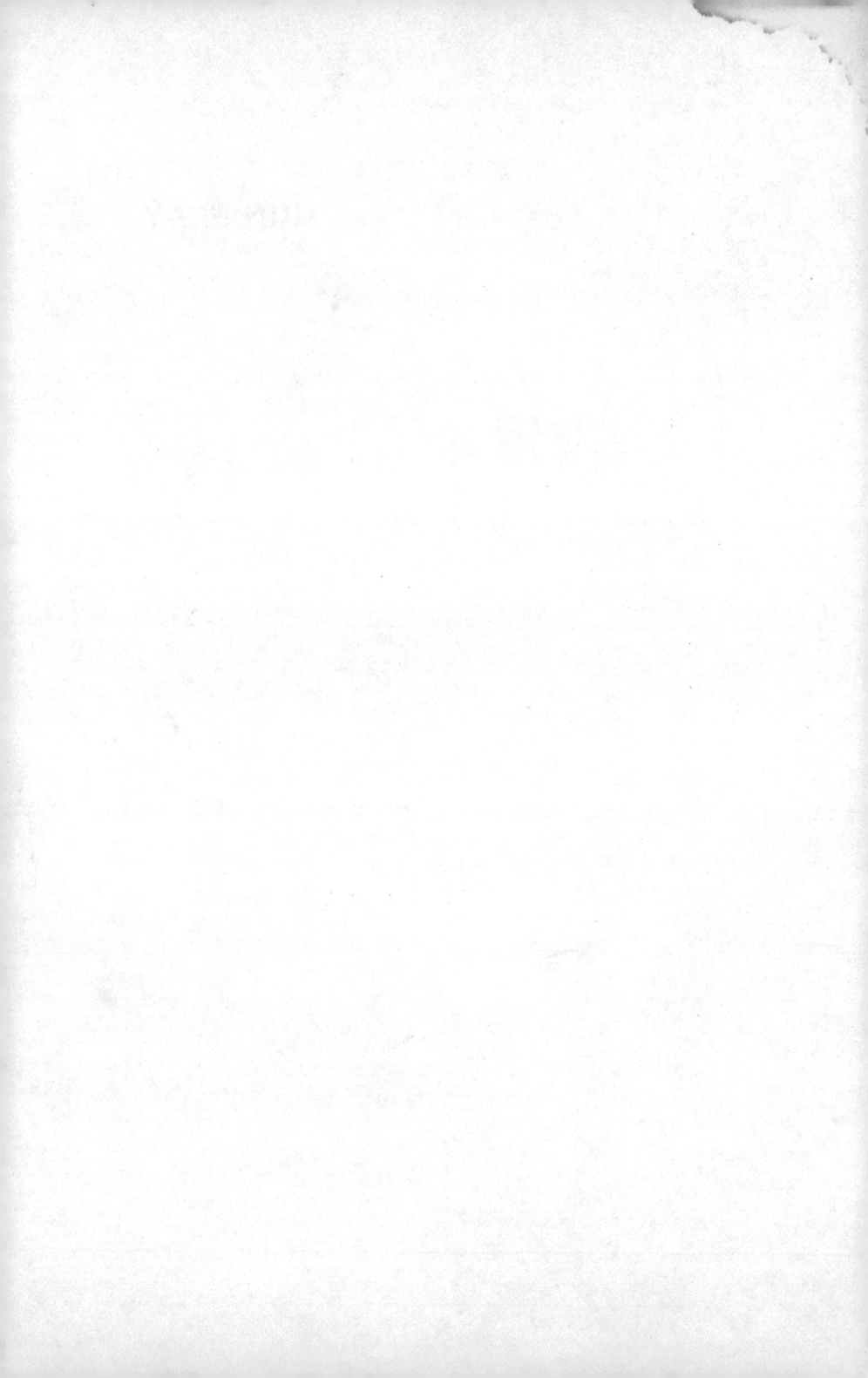

*To all the friends whose faith
kept this from the dark drawer,
especially Joseph Hansen.*

If you listen to every clown around, you're dead. You gotta do what you gotta do.

James Cagney,
advice to a young actor

❧

I T WAS AN ORDINARY SATURDAY NIGHT, and it probably would've stayed that way, but I chose to try and fish it off instead of drink it off. I was missing them. So marriages go bad, I told myself—then something took my bait and started to run. The moment I jerked the rod, I knew I'd missed. My line arced out of the water, stripped clean. Tuss Washington laughed and reeled in another plump bonita. He'd been pulling them in all night. He was still laughing when I dumped the rest of my bait in his pail and climbed to the top of the jetty.

"What you needs, Elton, is a little of the ol' poontang," he called up. Tuss was pushing eighty although he looked a youthful sixty, and when he sang blues he was ageless. He was the only person I knew who didn't pass judgment on my folly: trying to make it as an actor. Our connection was fishing, music, and small talk, the perfect formula for survival in Los Angeles.

"Yeah, maybe I'll rustle some up," I called back.

"An' maybe I'll catch me a mermaid." He slapped his thigh and laughed. It was an infectious laugh, but I was immune, and that kind of immunity was a dangerous thing.

At least my bicycle was still where I'd left it. I clamped on the tackle box and a breeze coasted me down the empty walk toward a row of cars parked just off Pacific Avenue. Most of the occupants weren't watching the boats slide by or the jets take off, but it was a good enough excuse. In another year a neat stack of condominiums would make someone a neat stack of dough, and the backseat romancers would have to move up the coast.

The walkway ended. I eased off the curb and headed for the shortcut through the marina to check the office, which was just one more sore spot. But the ride might clear my head. After two weeks on location in Istanbul, for the privilege of four lines and thirty seconds of screen time, Los Angeles was bound to demand some adjustment.

A flash hit the edge of my vision. Then another. Then a series of three. A female voice let out a scream. The scream was obliterated by the roar of a heavy horsepower engine. A shape began to move. Tires squealed. Lights blinded me. The passenger door was flung open, someone hopped in and the car leapt, twisted, floated broadside. Adrenaline jolted a sound out of my throat. It all floated toward me: the open door, the rear quarter panel, the bright glow of the taillight perched on a ridiculous winged tailfin. Then the impact: metal embracing flesh, taking its impression, tossing it into the air.

A periodic light flashed: green . . . white . . . green . . . The beacon at the end of the jetty. There was a pungent smell, reminiscent of hospital corridors. Under my nose a clipper-ship sailed. It decorated a flat green bottle. I wished it wasn't empty. It wasn't good for me, but I liked scotch. I felt a wet trickle on my face. It was warm, sweet, metallic. There wasn't a crowd, in fact, there wasn't anyone. I was face down in wet sand beside the remnants of what back in the Twenties had tried to live up to its name – The Grand Canal.

She came out of nowhere, seeming somehow familiar: for a split second I flashed back to Becky Tillman in the backseat of an old Chevy in Pennsylvania; way back, too long ago to dare remember.

"You all right?" The voice was wrong, she didn't have freckles, her eyes were larger, more widely set.

"Hey—you okay?" She waved her fingers in front of my face. She didn't dare touch me, and she kept glancing over her shoulder. I tried to say something, but my teeth started to chatter.

All of a sudden I panicked. I wondered where the pain was. Maybe I'd been so mangled it couldn't get through. I patted myself down, took a breath, raised an arm, moved my head. Sensations began to seep through the shock. My left side throbbed, my left ankle felt warm and liquidy.

"Don't move," she whispered. Then she backed away. I sat up and grabbed her arm and her eyes went wide with what seemed exaggerated terror. They were beautiful eyes: dangerously reminiscent. Even in the darkness I could tell.

"I'll get you a blanket," she said. "God, you're bleeding."

The scene replayed itself: the flashes, the scream, the car . . .

"Should I call an ambulance?"

Her face was six inches from mine, her breath quick and bearing a peculiar scent. Wheat germ, I thought—wheat germ and marijuana.

I've always had too much of a nose. I attributed it to my Cherokee ancestry; it was a small part—no better than an eighth—about the only part I clung to with pride. "It's my redskin nose," I'd say, and Joanie would say, "It's your hound-dog nose, Elton." It had been a hell of a marriage. Especially the first couple of years: Italy, Canada, Thailand; taking any job, staying loose. But I couldn't blame her. Women can't stay that loose forever.

"You sure you're all right?" Her voice had a sassy demand I knew I could love and hate all at once. I wished she'd go away.

"Hey, say something."

I couldn't get over the eyes. They were too similar to the eyes I'd looked into for ten years: pale brown, almost amber, with flecks of green.

"You didn't happen to get the license, did you?"

She shook her head, and her hair moved over her face. It was long, fine, and wheat blonde, streaked by the sun. She had a full mouth with a pouty lower lip. Her nose was a little too cute, otherwise her face had an aristocratic poise beyond the wholesome prettiness. It was an odd face, full of extremes. Depending on her mood, it might be inviting or hard. But the eyes would always be lovely because I would never see them as hers.

"Well, if you're really all right, I think I'd better go." The undertow of a smile tugged at her lips. I had no idea what it meant.

"If I let an ambulance take me in, when I report this as a hit-and-run, I'd be a victim of violent crime and the wonderful state might help with the tab. At the moment I'm unemployed and my union dues are in arrears."

A nervous smile pulled at the left corner of her mouth. It'd be a nice mouth for an actress. Or maybe I'd just been around too many so-called actresses. The next time Tuss Washington played the Sundown Saloon, I should go play with him. The thought didn't follow. It did and it didn't. I wished I'd been having a little luck fishing. None of this would've happened.

"I'm sorry," she said. "By the time I looked, they were gone."

"They?"

"The car. It was a big car. With big fins. Dark colored. I couldn't really see . . ."

I decided to stand up. I wobbled and she gave me her hand.

"Was it you that screamed?"

She nodded. "Yes . . . when I saw . . ."

I worked my left foot around waiting for her to finish. "Those flashes?"

"Yes."

"So where were you?"

She turned away.

"Look, if I play it right and we find those bastards, it might be worth something besides the satisfaction."

"I was only trying to help." Her tone said she was sorry she'd ever met me. "I've got to go."

"Listen," I grabbed her arm again. "I don't like getting run over and you're my only witness."

"Would you please let go?" She tried to be distinct, controlled, polite, but it came out a hiss. She was sweating more than she should've been. Her feet were bare. She'd buttoned her blouse wrong.

"You were in that van and somebody took some pictures. Am I crazy?"

She let out a mock-bored sigh, but every muscle in her face was braced. "What's it to you?"

"Maybe you've got some little jailbait badger routine. A friend takes snaps and whoever was in the saddle pays up or gets hit with statutory rape."

I didn't really believe a word of it, but her whole face quivered and her eyes narrowed, as if she hardly knew such a world existed. And, like any upper-class girl, she hated to be reminded.

"I'm twenty. So fuck you!"

Our eyes met, and I knew she didn't like me and doubted she ever would. Unfortunately, I didn't feel entirely the

5

same way although I was doing my damndest.

"Let me go," she said.

"I need a witness."

"Please, you're hurting me." Her whisper seemed to hold a subtle hint of pleasure under the plea. I felt an urge to kiss her, a primitive, perverse compulsion. Maybe it was all that adrenaline reacting to the diminutive breasts, the solid legs, the tiny waist flaring into a plump behind that spoke of moisture and heat and movement; all given a special aura by that peculiar perfume on her breath. And those eyes. Joanie's eyes . . .

"I really do have to go now," she said, mustering an unconvincing whine that did a magnificent job of squelching my amorous impulse.

"As unhappy a prospect as it may prove to be, I think we ought to get to know each other." I sounded like a wiseacre, a kid down on her level. She already wasn't bringing out my best, but I didn't let that stop me. Maybe it was the suspicion that she knew more than she was letting on and the strange feeling whatever it was she was lying about might catch up with her. I'd been in Hollywood long enough to have gained a keen sense of the lie, even the lie that didn't know it was a lie. It wasn't much, but I had it.

"I guess I'm feeling mean." I released her arm. She rubbed it, finishing off her little piece of theatre. For some reason the gesture evoked a familiarity beyond the eyes. "I don't mind getting hit," I said. "It's the hit and run. It seems to be catching."

"Sorry. I just don't like people who—" she cut herself off and tried a different tack. "I don't even know you."

"Maybe we can start with names. Mine's Dancey. Elton Dancey."

She let out a nervous little laugh, "Funny name."

"I've noticed. Get to know me and you'll probably say it fits."

"Your bike looks pretty messed up." Her tone was just apologetic enough to reinforce my feeling that she was hiding something. I hate guilt and I hate taking advantage of it, but some impulse — either self-destructive or self-protective — was urging me to put my principles on vacation. I noted with disgust how easily I was succumbing to the most rampant ethic in town: if it's convenient, use it; if there's an opening, grab it. Despite the self-loathing, I did. I mustered a few tattered remnants of charm and asked her if she could give me a lift home.

M Y BICYCLE HAD SKITTERED into the canal. I slid down the embankment and dragged it out; a sad corpse with a hopelessly crumpled rim, bent fork, handlebars awry. Mangled beyond salvage. I climbed up and shoved the remains into the back of one of those customized vans with an airbrushed Hawaiian sunset on the side, and the interior done in wall-to-ceiling carpeting. It was a very plush deep blue, perhaps meant to be evocative of the Pacific, and there were three tri-fin surfboards racked along the passenger side, each in a custom cover.

I climbed in beside her, and felt the bruises begin to register. The whole business stank of something besides crazies ambushing a lovers' lane for salacious snapshots. Which made me want to ask questions, and would probably just get me more nasty looks.

"You sure you don't want to get checked out?" She sounded as warm as a mechanical doll.

"Emergency rooms scare me."

"I thought you were the guy who wanted to sue."

"Odds are we'll never find the guy, and if we did, he wouldn't have insurance. And I don't like lawyers either."

"What's wrong with lawyers?"

I told her to take a right and head north on Pacific. She drove carefully, those haunting eyes constantly flicking up to the rearview mirror. She would glance up and then she'd bite her lower lip with teeth that looked like they'd been arranged by a master orthodontist. I was glad to see one of them was chipped.

We stopped at a light. She turned and gave me a quick meaningless grin that was almost coy. Maybe she suddenly wanted to be friends. I couldn't tell. But it was the grin that explained the familiarity: Sabrina Trevelyan, six or seven years old, clamping her hands over her mouth to hide the gap in her smile left by missing teeth. The eyes . . . funny I didn't remember them. But then, fifteen years ago there were a lot of things I didn't notice. Especially that summer. I'd been too busy noticing her mother, which was my job. Only I hadn't done my job, or I'd more than done it. It didn't feel very real, that long lost summer.

"What's going on?" she asked.

"Nothing."

All I had to do was ask her name. "Turn left here, then pull in beside that old Buick."

"What a fantastic car," she said with sudden perky interest. "Where'd you get it?"

"There was a lot of money on the table and someone was short. I won the pink slip."

"Oh," she said, as if she had suddenly understood the meaning of my life. "This is your place? It's so quaint. I love it."

I decided to skip my discourse on how the place was even quainter before they fenced it in with condominiums, or mention how all I owned was the shack itself and a lease on its little plot of land that would expire in a couple of years, when Dancey would be forced to move on once again. No wonder I was no good at nesting.

"It's really nice," she said, toning down her youthful enthusiasm to something more appropriate to my age.

"Even the neighbors are nice. They drive nice cars and have nice taste and think everyone should have enough to eat."

"What's that supposed to mean?"

"It means we're both beating around the bush."

I reached over, turned the ignition key and palmed it. She gave me one of her cold gazes.

"This some kind of trick?"

"No trick. I thought an old friend would be glad to be a witness. Maybe a drink would refresh your memory. I even know that you got your name from your mother's favorite movie. And she used to tell me I looked like Bogart."

Her face bore that look of vague, impish terror that takes over when someone knows you and you don't know them. It was a dirty trick but there I was, grinning like a bastard.

"Who the fuck are you?"

"There was a horse named Scotty who threw me and a very precocious girl about seven who was always laughing behind her hand because she was having her teeth fixed. They did a nice job."

It took a minute, and I could see she didn't so much remember me as figure it out. "Are you kidding? You mean you're the one Daddy hired. God, I don't believe this."

"It was the Egleton Detective Agency that got hired. I happened to be the dropout kid on a summer lark they gave the assignment to."

The silence was full of barbs and thorns and one beautiful ghost. Sabrina's face told me she had learned or guessed all the sleazy embellishments of that particular summer lark, and it made me squirm.

"You still playing detective?"

"My passport says I'm an actor. It's more or less the truth."

"I see." She said it as if I'd just confessed to some despicable social disease.

"You've got some nice boards back there."

"That's right, you took me surfing. I remember. God, it's just so crazy. I love it."

She didn't sound like she loved much of anything. I handed back her key. She looked at it and flipped it a couple of times, stalling.

"Might as well come in," I said, "If you feel like it."

"Such a gracious invitation; how could I resist?"

𝒴

THE HOUSE, which I affectionately referred to as the "shack," still had its musty shuttered air. A battered leather suitcase stood in the middle of the main room, along with tubes of rice paper bearing images that had been carved into stone at the time of the Ottomans. Maybe the images would get framed and hung on living room walls, and I'd actually turn a sideline profit from having my walk-on in a modest little forty million dollar epic. The script—an international thriller whose modus operandi was to pack as many stars as possible into two hours of mayhem—had killed me off on a ferry crossing the Dardanelles. I had microfilm of the latest nuclear submarine hidden in a cane. I'd enjoyed the cane and I was proud of the subtlety of my limp, a sinister cliché that I thought I'd managed with finesse, projecting both menace and sympathy.

After the shoot, I'd stayed on a few days indulging myself in forgetfulness through *raki* binges and visits to the first-class state brothels. This was tempered with long peaceful hours in graveyards as old as recorded time, pushing charcoal across rice paper laid against headstones. The timeless and the ephemeral: the eternal conflict; the story of my life.

I gave Sabrina a little run-down of my adventures and she forgot to be aristocratically indifferent. I supposed she saw me as an eccentric throwback, a sort of aging "hippie." She read my mode of existence as "romantic." My dear Joanie had once found it romantic too, but then it had come time to nest down. "Elton, you can't be stumbling along as an unknown actor and/or a piano player and/or a surfer boy when you're *fifty*. Jesus, grow up!" And then she'd added with a sigh, "God, I love you, but don't you ever stop and *think*?" All the time, I'd say to myself. All the time. I'm like my crazy dad, God rest his soul, just another dreamer, babe.

It was a crummy excuse, and after a while I didn't make it anymore, and after a while we couldn't forgive each other.

"I really do like your place," Sabrina Trevelyan said. She was beginning to play the old acquaintance with precocious seductive panache. She sashayed around touching everything, dredging up witty comments, and quite openly trying to figure me out while expressing general delight with the surroundings—subtle flatteries meant to reflect back onto me. She especially adored the sleeping loft and the skylight and the old upright piano where I'd often doubled with Tuss after a night of fishing. Maybe I'd been wrong about her never liking me. I found myself avoiding her eyes. Then I remembered Roger Trevelyan. He'd be late fifties now. Established, important, rich. Filthy rich.

"How well did you know my mom?" Sabrina asked out of the blue.

"Not that well." I was lying and not lying. At twenty I hadn't known anyone very well, but I couldn't say just how I *had* known her. "It must've been hard on you," I said.

"It's funny. I don't remember my mom all that well. I mean, I do, but—well, she isn't very real. I know that's a terrible thing to say."

"It's the truth. The truth is usually terrible—but it's all we've got."

"Cool," she said. "I like that. Mom was beautiful though, wasn't she?"

"Very." And there was plenty of Sophia Trevelyan in her daughter: the athletic build, the small breasts and solid shoulders, the narrow hips and high round buttocks. If I didn't look at Sabrina's face, it was easy to throw myself back fifteen years. Sophia had been softer, more lush, but that was probably just the years. I remembered when she had said, with utter casualness, that she was thirty-eight, then laughed at the shocked look on my face when she pointed out that she was old enough to be my mother.

"You must've been young," Sabrina said with the mindless superiority of those who still think they're immortal.

"I'm not exactly decrepit."

"I didn't mean it that way. I dig older guys. They're more interesting. And frankly, they're usually better lovers." She was bragging now, teasing, throwing out lines she had heard at the movies, saying what she thought it'd be hip to say. And I fell for it. I knew better, but I did. I gave her a drink. She wanted Southern Comfort, neat. I built a fire; we didn't exactly need the heat, but it was pretty and it complemented certain primeval urges. I sat down and played some blues. She loved it. The blues were quaint too. Quaint and funky were the words she conjured up from an extensive and colorful vocabulary. I was a very charming dinosaur. She wanted to know if I had any contemporary highs. Like cocaine. Sorry, I said and began to feel the Southern California nightmare creeping up on me. One of these days I'd wake up from the endless sun and I'd be bald, toothless, drooling and incontinent. This morbid undercurrent ran through my head while I played the charming artifact for a twenty-year-old girl. After this quaint performance, I became even more eccentric. I put some eighteenth-century lute suites on the turntable and took a cold bottle of Corona into the bathroom.

I told her I'd be out in five minutes and to make herself comfortable.

The hot water worked. Muscles loosened, what was left of my mind stretched and quieted, and the pain running up and down my left side seemed to subside, or at least took a back seat. Time slipped away. It was a ten-minute shower, a twenty-minute shower, half an hour. She knocked and stuck her head in.

"You okay?" She was completely coy, keeping her eyes directly on me.

"I like showers."

"I turned the record over. Weird how we met up again, isn't it?"

"Life is full of unexpected charms," I said and was fairly sure I meant it.

"I was afraid you'd passed out . . . I found this joint — I hope you don't mind."

"Help yourself."

"Thanks." She let loose another one of her meaningless little giggles I somehow managed to find completely entrancing.

"I don't like being alone," she said, suddenly sober again.

"Who does?"

"It scares me." She was sitting on the hamper, knees up under her chin, her glass in one hand, the smoke in the other. I shut the water off and gave her time to leave. She sat there with her air of aristocratic nonchalance. I got out as casually as I could and dripped over to the mirror to examine my wounds. Her eyes turned, then they came back. Suddenly, I was acutely aware of my age.

"Feeling better?"

"As long as I don't think. Somebody said: 'Beginning to think is beginning to be undermined.' Camus, maybe."

"You're nuts," she said. It sounded like a delightful discovery. At any rate, she laughed. It was nice having a woman laugh. Even a woman who wasn't really a woman yet. She could laugh all night at anything I said or nothing at all, as far as I was concerned. So I kept trying to make her laugh while I swabbed peroxide on my cheek and dumped it on my ankle. I finished my beer and she took the bottle and blew across the top, playing foghorn. She suddenly stopped laughing and said with the seriousness of someone very young trying to project maturity, "I'm sorry I acted like such a bitch." I looked at her, and then at the ragged beige terrycloth robe she was sitting on. She looked back, then her gaze dropped. I stood there letting her look, face flushed, not feeling any pain at all.

"Your ass is on my robe," I said.

"Oh," she said, but she didn't move. Her eyes were having an effect, a rather ludicrous effect. I was standing there dripping wet as a completely irrational and unwarranted erection began to point at her, then swooped upward like a wet setter zeroing in on my belly button. The beast embarrassed me. It probably embarrassed her too, but she was managing to look reasonably dignified despite the smirk on her face. I dropped the towel, and it caught and hung there, and she laughed. Then I was laughing with her and before we stopped our mouths had come together. I had a last sober thought, which was that I was out of my mind, but by then I didn't give a damn. The ephemeral had gained the upper hand.

༰

I WOKE TO THE MELLOW LIGHT of a day already ripened and beginning to fall. She'd folded my clothes in a neat pile and left a note on top.

Mr. Dancey,
Please don't get the idea I do stuff like this with just
anyone. Maybe it was the full moon. But I really do
like you.

Sabrina

P.S. I plan on calling. Okay?

Every part of me was stiff and bruised. Every cell so agonized I couldn't believe I'd managed to perform at all. On top of which I felt like a heel. Maybe I'd taken advantage, getting a little carried away with my tough-guy act and letting her know that one summer when she was a little girl I'd gone to bed with her mother. But Sabrina wasn't naive, and the seduction had been mutual. I was one more episode in her book of a wild summer. And she? I wasn't sure. I wanted to think she was just a lithe, lively female who had a reciprocal lust, who saw the moment and seized it with joy, and maybe with sadness too. And she probably had, because the truth was that she'd tried a little too hard to please. Was it just vanity? I'd tried as well, wanting to make sure she had hers. And a far worse vanity — wanting her to remember. It had been a hard night's work for both of us.

But worth it. Yes, worth it and memorable because it was work and because at least she had not had to fake it: the sounds quieter, less dramatic, yet more open. And she'd cried; the tears silently streaming down her cheeks. All told, it had been a good night, but a night with enough awkwardness to tell me it probably would not happen again.

I told myself to shut up and swung out of bed. When I stood up my left ankle crumpled and I let out a yowl, excruciatingly aware of the half-dozen bruises I had somehow overlooked the night before. This made me mad enough to start thinking about why Sabrina Trevelyan was so reluctant to be my witness when she was willing to go to bed with me. Of course it was two different matters. Her going to bed with me had nothing to do with anything. She was a member of that new breed of women who at least tried to act as casually as men. But I never really believed the ones as young as Sabrina. A thirty- or forty-year old woman can let her lust truly blossom, but it usually took the threat of beauty dying, the knowledge of mortality, before it did. Like Sophia Trevelyan fifteen years ago.

I hobbled out to the beach for a salt-water cure and stretched out in the late sun, trying not to think that it had been over a year since I'd been out to surf. When I woke up the sun was gone, and there was a clear indigo sky that made me feel small and unreal. I made myself a solitary meal, put on some Billie Holiday, trying to ignore the jet lag until Turkish time caught up with me a few pages into the script of a low-budget, youth-gang picture called *Bloodbath Blues*. I was up for the part of a taciturn, cowardly Indian with lines like "Holy shit, it's the Avengers. I'm splittin', man."

Then it was Monday. I drove to the marina and climbed the stairs to my tiny office above the Near East Gift Shop.

The office was left over from another enterprise that had never gotten off the ground. But that was circumstance, I reminded myself, not failure. The idea had been noble, perhaps even viable: low budget films with class.

Tom Silver had believed in it, and he knew people in Texas. People get killed in automobiles all the time. It didn't mean anything except I'd lost a friend and maybe the key to making a living doing something I loved. There were five months left on our lease. I could run out on it and let them take me to court. They weren't starving. Why sit there with heavy memories and pay the rent because you signed a paper — be convenient, I told myself. This is Los Angeles, convenience city.

I leafed through *Bloodbath Blues* again. Maybe it wasn't so bad. It'd be a week of work, maybe 1,500 if Max drove a hard bargain. Of course, for a lousy 150 bucks, how hard was he going to drive? And how could I say those lines and pretend to be twenty?

I wrote a polite note saying I loved the part, Blackfoot Pete was a "profoundly challenging" character, but I was only an eighth Cherokee, I couldn't play twenty anymore and I'd be doing them a disservice if I accepted the role. Then I picked the junk mail off the floor and took the wastebasket down to the trashbin. I sent off a couple of rubbings to Joan and Angelina, feeling a little sorry for myself, and then felt disgusted for feeling that way. I should've been feeling fine. I was broke but I *had* rustled up some female company after all. Or had it rustled me? Either way, Tuss wasn't going to believe it.

The phone rang. A wrong number. I took a chair out to the roof and watched the boats parade by, reminding me of how much money there was in the world and how little of it I had, and then I reminded myself of how four-fifths of the world lives on an annual income amounting to less than what I spent on gasoline. I locked up and drove home thinking it was the meaningless tasks that eat up ninety percent of your days.

I heard it as soon as I turned off the engine—that ring that for no logical reason transmits panic. I knew it was Sabrina Trevelyan, and I knew I didn't want anything more to do with her. So why was I rushing like a madman, tearing through the locks and diving over the sofa?

"God, I thought you'd never answer!" It was her all right. My sweet little one-night stand. This wasn't about last night's indiscretion; she was too suave to even mention it.

"It doesn't sound like you called to ask me to dinner," I said, panting.

"They called Hal! Dancy, you have to help me!"

I didn't like the sound of that. I was having a time trying to help myself. I was an aging bohemian actor with no money, no career, no prospects.

"Who's Hal?"

"Don't you remember?" She sounded miffed. "I was staying on his boat, the *Corlinda.*"

She paused as though expecting me to say something to acknowledge my recognition.

"What's so important about them calling Hal—and who in hell is *they*?"

"Dancey, I'm scared. I guess I thought it'd go away. But if Daddy sees those pictures—not that *I* really care, I just don't need any hassles. And he's been so on edge lately."

Her breath drew up. I couldn't read her any more. She was theatrical, but then again she was a Trevelyan.

"Tell me about Hal," I said, "Or have you got company?"

She said there wasn't any company, and then she told me a muddled tale about how she'd met him quite by accident when she went out to her folks' house, and he was there for some big social gala and he'd asked if she was the daughter of the house and they'd got talking and it turns out Hal used to be quite a surfer too, even won some competitions and maybe Sabrina would give him a call and he'd give her some pointers; he had this little floating palace parked down in Marina del Rey, just a hop-skip and he was very attractive, very charming, very mysterious— "and I'm human," she pleaded. I didn't tell her I'd once been halfway decent on a wave myself and I didn't know any Hal Fitzgibbons, but there were a lot of guys I didn't know.

"So why weren't you doing your romancing on the *Corlinda*?" I asked. "Is there some kind of kick to the back of a van I don't know about?"

"You don't have to be nasty," she said.

"Maybe I'm just jealous." The truth was that I wasn't sure. Last night I had somehow managed to forget he had even existed, although now it occurred to me with vague distaste how it must've been the interrupted amorous heat generated by playboy-surfer Hal that I had, in the crudest sense, cashed in on.

"If you want to know, we usually do," she said with a snide brag. "Listen, I really do like you, Dancey. I know what you're thinking."

"That he warmed you up for me."

"You're cruel."

"You're right; uncalled for. I'm just a sucker, Sabrina. A sucker for anybody's woes. They don't even have to be beautiful, great in bed and very flattering to an aging dinosaur who still retains certain illusions."

"I never called you a dinosaur. You're not even *old.*"

"I like the way you say that. A sort of malediction."

"Dancey, please. I know I was crazy. I know. I don't

really care about Hal that much. But . . . I don't know. It was just fun. Anyway, if you don't want to help."

"I do, Sabrina, it's just I'm worn out."

"I thought it was good. For me it was. Really good."

"Like older guys usually are."

"Please. Just listen. I need somebody to listen."

"You must have friends."

"Flaky kids. I need someone . . ."

"Mature?" I laughed. "I'm not, kid. I've just attained the years where I should be."

"Don't call me kid. I hate that."

"Okay. Just trying to get impersonal, Sabrina. I'll listen, but I don't want to like you."

She made no comment, she just launched off on her tale: "Hal loaned the boat to a friend, so when I called he said maybe we could go out, and . . . he liked doing different things . . . you know . . ."

She trailed off. It was getting to be a habit. I tried finishing for her. "So it was a kinky little thrill to blow a couple of joints and get it on in the back of your van."

"Fuck you," she hissed, and then there was a long strangled quiet. She was right. I was being nasty for no reason. All she wanted was some help in a blackmail case. Right up my alley. About on a par with *Bloodbath Blues*.

"I'm sorry," I said. "The whole business makes me edgy."

"You just act so rude," she whined.

"Sabrina, I'd like to help, but I can't. Maybe I like you too much. I guess you remind me a little too much of your mother."

"You two had an affair, didn't you?" she said. It wasn't an accusation so much as a triumphant declaration. "I knew it, I just knew it!"

I began to get an eerie feeling that last night had meant

more to her than I had suspected; something twisted yet touching, something neither of us really cared to talk about.

"Tell me about it," she asked. She asked sweetly, really wanting to know.

"There's not much to tell. I was a dumb kid. Why don't you tell me what happened last night instead. Maybe I can give you some advice. I presume they caught you in the middle of . . ." Now it was my turn to leave something hanging.

"You don't have to try to be so fucking delicate," she said. "I was going down on him, if you want to know. God, what's with you?"

"Who are they? Can you take a guess?"

"I don't know. I mean, I suppose they know who I am and that Daddy's rich, and they think I am too. But all I get is my allowance until I'm twenty-one."

"When's that?"

"Nine days."

"Maybe they know that."

"They called Hal about four hours ago and he's gone to collect the negatives."

"What?"

"Collect them, the pictures!"

"This kind of stuff doesn't happen anymore. What's it matter? Everybody's screwing everybody anyway and everybody knows and people are publishing their own pictures in swingers' magazines — christ."

"You're behind the times, Dancey. Monogamy is back. You're showing your age."

"Well you don't sound too worried. Hal'll pay them and that will be that. I'm curious, how much?"

"The thing is, he wasn't going to pay them. He said he

was going to bash heads. And he's not back, that's what has me worried."

"So call the cops. They'll get a kick out of this one."

"Please, Dancey. Just go and see if he's there. I'll pay you."

Her voice had a whiney beg that didn't become her. I preferred the facade of ultra-liberated cool. Or the sass. The smell of her came back and the way she'd moved, trying so hard to impress. I reminded myself she was more than this desperate voice in my ear. True, she was a spoiled little rich girl who had a taste for dinosaurs because she probably thought she was too sophisticated for twenty-year-olds, which was also probably true. What I liked most was the way she seemed to have herself in perspective sometimes, that hint of self-irony in her back talk. Maybe I was reading too much between the lines.

"Dancey, you still there?"

"Tell me, how come I turn up as your last friend in the world?"

"I don't know," she said, then she added with a little too much sweetness, "Maybe it's that under all the cynical stuff, you're very sensitive."

"You mean easy to manipulate. Besides, I don't like being sensitive. It's too much in vogue. I like being tough. If you want to flatter me, tell me I'm tough."

"All right, you're tough."

"You don't sound like you mean it."

"I said I'd pay."

"Hire a professional."

"Please, Dancey. There isn't time, and they'd charge too much and laugh up their sleeves. Listen, you knew me when

I was just a kid. And besides . . ." She stopped short, but I could fill in the blanks: *you screwed my mother and you screwed me*. That didn't mean I owed her, but guilt isn't logical. I didn't know why, but I suddenly felt like I did owe her.

"Please, I'll give you five hundred. It'll only take an hour."

"You must get quite an allowance. Any pro would do it for three."

"Please. Just go."

Suddenly, I'd had it. I gave in, more or less just to get her out of my ear. "Okay, give me the address. I check it out and that's it, right? Five hundred." I tried to pretend it was the money. It was true that I needed it. I needed it so much I hated it.

"But we're still friends okay? I mean once this is over."

"Just give me the damn address."

She did and I wrote it down. I crumpled the paper and hooked it into the fireplace. After a while I fetched it out again. I told myself that I needed to get out anyway. Soon I was making the long, overly familiar drive east up Venice Boulevard trying not to notice the mini-malls stuffed with franchise haircuts, fast food, fast videos turning the world into something cool and efficient. And profitable beyond any reasonable doubt.

꒰

THE SUNSET PALMS MOTEL was at the eastern end of Sunset Boulevard in a limboland where it was easy to get the impression that every tenth citizen still had dreams about making it in movies, and the way to do it was to watch a lot of television. A cursory glance at the place said more than likely the management had discovered disinfectant was the cheapest form of upkeep, and a three-hour quickie rate at least meant survival.

It was a two-story square stucco fortress built around a blacktopped courtyard guarded by lifesize plaster nymphs. The pink neon over the arch sputtered in the twilight: SUN ET ALMS. The only palms around were depicted in a peeling fresco of a South Seas landscape gracing the outer walls. It was an early work done by a friend of mine who sometimes took a job as an extra to get by.

I cruised past and parked on a side street. The old Buick had never been inconspicuous, and by now simple endurance gave it the glamour of a near classic. Two kids of around eight or nine, some beautiful Latin-Indian mix, gave me the high sign and stared at the car. I bribed them a buck apiece to stay on my side.

It was after seven, but heat still welled up from the sidewalk. I inhaled lingering fumes of rush hour; each breath shortening my life a week. There were no other pedestrians. The drivers of passing cars looked like cardboard cutouts. The motel was a projected backdrop to conjure up the cheap sleaze of Hollywood in the Fifties.

I went around to the back and stepped over the chain that blocked the alley exit. Sabrina had told me Hal drove a brown, late-model Jaguar sedan, but there weren't any cars anywhere close. And nothing like the old hulk that hit me, either. I found number 13 in the rear on ground level. There was no car in front. I knocked and waited, then knocked again, trying to make it sound firm but not threatening. I glanced across to the office. There didn't seem to be anyone there, but a tightness in my gut said I was being watched.

On the third rap the door opened very slowly, about an inch. "Hello," I said, not liking the voice. It should've been a lot more sure of itself. "Anybody there . . .?"

I couldn't tell if the silence read emptiness, or was the held breath of ambush. I reminded myself that easy living tends to corrode the instincts. I pushed the door open, and since nobody objected, I stepped in.

Nothing hit me except a stench of sweat not quite drowned out by cheap perfume. The walls were cigarette-smoke beige. A sofa and two chairs with orange vinyl covers crouched in the reddish light of smog-filled dusk. The sofa was flanked by two oversized table lamps with cylindrical shades three feet tall. The bases were headless plaster Venuses, distant relatives of the statues in the courtyard.

To the rear was a doorway with a beaded curtain veiling a small kitchenette which served as a vestibule for another door. The door was closed, vibrating faintly from the insistent bawling of a televised sporting event. I listened. It was a wrestling match between Hulk Hero and The Arab. For some reason I wished I carried a gun. Then again, television always made me jumpy. I reminded myself this place was just a set, that nothing real could happen. If there was anyone alive, they'd wink and prompt me with my lines.

The television noise stopped. Very abruptly. My breath

stopped with it. Three seconds later the TV racket snapped back on. Some glitch, a faulty wire in the vast network of wires. A voice intoned a cheerful sermon about a pill that would make your tensions bearable. The voice had doctors and statistics for proof. The voice was collecting a lot of money for sounding good. Then the voice changed to a thousand voices shrieking for Hulk Hero.

I pushed on the door; gently at first, then with more force. It opened the width of my hand, stopping against something heavy that reminded me of those hundred-pound sacks of rice hulls I'd carried one summer on the San Francisco docks. I looked down. The edge of the door was blocked by someone's head. A large square head with its face buried in dirty gold shag carpet. Whoever it was wasn't interested in Hulk Hero tossing The Arab across the ring and jumping on his back.

I knelt down and eased my hand through the crack. Nobody told me to mind my own business, but I wished somebody had. When my fingers made contact, I shivered. He was still faintly warm, but he wasn't going to be warm long. His temple didn't have the hint of a pulse.

Suddenly I was shaking. This was a real corpse. Very real. But she was paying me. Sure, she was. That made me a professional. A professional what? Snoop? Seeker of sleazy thrills? Or, just another unemployed actor who'd gotten laid and thought it meant something because the rest of his life had turned to shit. Simple as that.

꒜

I CROUCHED THERE A LONG MINUTE trying to decide whether to leave. Maybe I was waiting for somebody to decide for me. I don't know if it was blind curiosity or the part of me that has always courted what I called reasonable danger. I would usually look back on the courtship as sheer madness. This would undoubtedly prove to be one of those times, but whatever was driving me was sufficiently strong to overcome common sense. When my nerves settled I squeezed through into the adjoining room.

A cheer went up as Hulk Hero pinned The Arab's shoulders just as they had rehearsed. A man with a vinyl voice started to sell cars. I turned the voice down to a fly buzz, then the knob wouldn't turn any more. To shut the set off you had to pull the plug behind a big bureau with a swivel mirror. The vinyl voice with the "million unbeatable deals" droned as I studied the man on the floor.

He was short and solidly built. Somebody had hit him on the back of the head with something unforgiving. There wasn't much blood, not even enough to wend through his thick and unfashionably slick black hair down to the ugly carpet. Possibly whoever had hit him had intended he should wake up.

I pulled his right arm out from under him. His hand was already stiffening around a short-barreled revolver. A .38 caliber Colt that smelled like it had been fired.

I eased him over. There was a mean, irritated grin on his face, as if he'd known he'd been stupid but was enraged he hadn't been able to kill whoever had outwitted him. This look was setting into a heavy face that probably carried a big smile in a barroom. I guessed the face had smiled on and off for more than fifty years. He had a lot of scars. His right ear was ragged at the edges. He might've been an over-the-hill fighter. I was sentimental about fighters. My father had tried and failed. One of his many tries — and one of his many failures. He was just Indian enough to have trouble with the bottle.

For some reason as dubious as the original impulse that had led me into the room in the first place, I decided to take his picture. The sun had set and about the only light was the blue glow of the television tube. I took out the little clamshell Olympus I always carried and snapped on the overhead. It was a dusky 25 watts. I had to try to hold steady for an eighth of a second. I braced myself and took four shots, hoping I'd get one sharp enough. Then I tried to find out whose portrait it was I'd taken. Maybe I thought it was my duty. But I wasn't thinking anymore. Something had grabbed me and I was on automatic pilot.

His driver's license read Tunney Ray Mackey and gave an address in Inglewood. He was fifty-eight. Whoever had knocked him on the head either hadn't been interested in his wallet, or didn't like money. He was carrying five one-hundred dollar bills and three twenties. No credit cards, but there was a business card from an insurance broker and a hockey schedule. There were two cigars, not too cheap, not too expensive, and a lighter with a see-thru case containing a girl who shed her little red dress when you tipped her upside down.

I didn't find any pictures of Sabrina. There was a photo of someone that might be Tunney Ray Junior, and hidden away in a secret compartment of his wallet was a snapshot of an expensive-looking blonde holding a pair of toy poodles. It was autographed on the back: *"To Tun, the greatest, love, Doris."*

The last thing I found was a roll of quarters. He was a long way from the slots. Maybe he had a collection. Or maybe the extra weight felt good in his fist. Mr. Mackey might've known all the tricks of the persuasion trade, but this time he'd gotten himself outsmarted. I wondered if it was going to make his widow sad.

I stuffed everything back in his pockets, careful to smudge any prints, and eased him back over. He didn't look like he'd be a playboy's bosom buddy, but then maybe Hal Fitzgibbons was putting something over on Sabrina. Hal might have paid Mackey to go after the pictures but pretended to go himself to show off for her.

But even if Mackey *was* Hal's muscle, why didn't the blackmailer go for the wallet? Maybe five hundred plus isn't worth stooping for anymore these days. How about a Colt with no serials?

Sabrina thought she'd overheard Hal mention the name Larry as he read back the instructions over the phone. Hal had even scribbled it all down on a notepad, and she'd done the trick of lightly rubbing a pencil over the next sheet to bring out an impression. So she'd been sure of the address, but maybe it was unit 3 or 8, not 13. Maybe this was the wrong can of worms.

A lot of things didn't make sense. Why hadn't the blackmailer hit on Roger Trevelyan who was rich enough and proud enough to pay to keep his daughter's image pure? And why had Hal been so hush-hush with Sabrina about meeting this guy? And why did he give a damn about a few snapshots, he wasn't a politician for christ's sake?

I told myself to take a quick prowl and get out; this wasn't the movies, and it wasn't my business. The man with the vinyl voice agreed. The only important event in the universe was the sale of a used car. He went about it with the enthusiasm of a dictator. He intoned his promises across the unmade sheets that clung desperately to the violently sagging mattress. The sheets were grey, rubbed thin by nerves and desperation and furtive sex. A damp spot was drying into a yellow stain that would soon blend with all the other stains that had held the possibility of life.

The ashtray didn't contain any slim cigar ends of the type Sabrina mentioned Hal Fitzgibbons smoked, only lipstick-stained menthol filters spilling over onto the bedstand. Beside the ashtray were two plastic glasses half full of diluted whisky. One of them had a hint of pink lipstick and a faintly bitter smell.

On the way to the bathroom, I kept thinking about the still fresh semen. I found myself considering the drying time of male reproductive fluids in relation to the rate at which a body cooled. Had whatever happened on that mattress occurred before or after Mackey got his skull beat in? Maybe Mackey had accidentally interrupted something somebody else was watching, and that someone happened to keep a blackjack in his hand.

The more I thought, the worse it got. I told myself I could think about it on safer ground, but I kept on prowling. I was beginning to like it. Just the way I had gotten to like Sabrina's silly coy laugh. Joan would've insisted this stemmed from my self-destructive impulses: subconscious, non-conscious, unconscious predilections passed on by my self-destructive father. And I'd say, maybe—but I'm having fun, Joanie, it gives me a kick. It's like being on the set and the cameras are rolling and you're carried by the flow. Or great sex. Sex with you, Joanie. It isn't just sex, it's . . . christ, I don't know, it lifts the spirits. And for whatever perverse reason, this was beginning to lift my spirits. Or maybe it was just the best distraction available. Troubles that're not really my own to help me forget. Maybe that was it.

For a minute I hovered, half-disgusted with my own curiosity and paralyzed to the point of near-tears by the thought of Joanie tucking Angelina into bed. I was a long way from Manhattan; a long way from anything. I needed to piss, but it seemed uncouth in the presence of a corpse, so I closed the bathroom door. Afterward, I kept snooping. Most of the bathroom gear belonged to a female: disposable razors, tampons, a spray can of feminine deodorant, and a repertoire of make-up. There was a hamper of dirty clothes, half of which looked like they belonged to a hooker in the same movie as the Sunset Palms Motel. The other half was just your casual contemporary-young-lady-about-town: nothing outrageous, but with a certain flair.

I went back to the kitchenette. The refrigerator was noisy, cramped and looked like it'd done time on the set of *Grapes of Wrath*. Inside was a bunch of wilted celery, two cans of no-name beer, a jar of instant coffee, and some powder that theoretically could become milk. There were two ice-cube trays in the freezer with half a dozen fifty-dollar bills stuck to the bottom of one. Crammed in a corner was a small formica-topped table featuring a full cup of coffee skimmed over with mold. Stacked beside it was the library: a weekly astrological guide for Libras, a book of crossword puzzles, a TV guide, some recent fashion magazines, and a tabloid called the *Hollywood Star*, which sported page after page of anonymous bodies. The few faces that showed either looked bored or sported ecstatic grimaces. The hams of pornoland. A nice-looking Asian girl almost distracted me from an interesting item on the opposite page: a section torn out of the middle of the classified ads. The issue was three weeks old.

I found some paystubs from a place called *ECOSKIN, Inc.* stuck in the astrological guide. They averaged between eighty and a hundred a week, and ran from May to June, the last being a week old. Whatever the job, that kind of pay seemed reason enough to turn to heavenly bodies for guidance.

So far, there were no signs Hal Fitzgibbons had ever walked into the place, and the closest I'd come to a file of dirty pictures was the *Hollywood Star*. I'd done Sabrina a favor. Her boyfriend wasn't here, her pictures weren't here. Just a man named Tunny Ray Mackey.

I went back to check on Mr. Mackey. Opening a drawer in the bedstand, I found a Volkswagen key and a loose bunch of printed business cards:

COLLEGE OF INTERCOURSE
837 Western Avenue
Hollywood, CA 90038
838-6969 Ask for: Sally Swann

The name was written in script so small and close to textbook that I had to look twice to be sure it wasn't stamped.

The bedside wastebasket was made of real leather, old and cracked, maybe an artifact of the original decor. I emptied its contents onto the *Hollywood Star*. There was a flattened tube of surgical jelly, a couple of wheatstraw paper roaches, an empty prescription bottle for Librium, several wads of bubble gum, a bouquet of gunky Kleenex, and hundreds of red pistachio shells. The prize was a note pencilled on the back of a sales slip from an outfit called Surplus Sales.

Somebody had paid $198 plus tax for a 16mm surveillance camera. The note was in the "Sally Swann" script:

> *Larry sweet, got the late shift tonight. Call from the canyon or stay over. I got the day off tomorrow. Let's do something nice. You got any more of the good stuff?*
>
> *Love,*
> *S.S.*

I pocketed the note and slid the rest of the junk back into the basket. Mr. Mackey kept staring into the yellow shag carpet. I sat on the bed feeling like I'd been there half my life. The thrill of discovery had lost its glitter. I sat and couldn't think. I was staring at the stain again. It was almost dry. Nestling in the wrinkles of the grey sheet were several black hairs, one of which held a straigher blonde one intertwined. There were also what looked like crumbs. And the scent of something subtle, about a hundred a half ounce. Something far too elegant for eighty dollar paystubs, something that didn't belong at the Sunset Palms Motel, a mirage. . .

I flopped back on the bed and noticed that the mirror on the bureau gave an angle on the closet door in the corner. The mirror's angle made sense. There was a peephole in the door. About the right height. A small box had been hung on the tie rack with its eye to the hole. About every ten seconds the eye winked with a tiny *ping, click*. A cord ran down from the box to a power-pack. All this was what had cost $198 and tax at Surplus Sales. An antiquated surveillance machine at a bargain price. More than likely compliments of a Pentagon cost overrun back in the Sixties.

The camera door was open, the film magazine gone. Somebody hadn't bothered to shut it off, or hadn't had time.

What in hell was it intended to record: the intertwining of hairs? Ex-boxers getting their heads bashed?

A low mournful growl, some indeterminate mix between terror and pleasure, came from the alley. I lifted the shade and spotted a battered old Siamese and a cauliflower-eared calico moving in wary crouching circles. The window was open. The screen, opaque with accumulated grime, was unhooked. The black dust on the sill had been smeared. Someone had taken the back way out. I did the same. As the calico gave me a sidelong glance, the Siamese attacked and a yowling ball of fur tore through the trashcans.

ᕁ

TWILIGHT HAD LET GO, night had taken hold. A tired breeze tried to push the dirt of a million engines over the mountains, but the evening rush was killing its progress as a whole new army was arriving to man the machinery. The dishwashers and projectionists, the waitresses and bartenders, the valets, the hustlers, the naked dancers and not-naked dancers. One of the more glamorous recruits figured to be Sally Swann.

The Buick's guards had doubled in number. All four of them were armed with what looked like torn pajamas, and despite the darkness they were wiping the tired grey paint like this was the dictator's limousine. A small crowd had gathered to stare, strangely quiet, like witnesses to a holy rite.

I passed out change and the band of pajama lads chased me to the intersection of Sunset, yelling *"adiós, hombre,"*

and *"buenas noches,"* in a way that told me they must've
mistaken me for somebody important and I figured who.
I waved and smiled back, not much flattered by their mistake. I'd once done stunts for the son-of-a-bitch in an in-
sipid little feature before he'd kissed his way into the big
time.

I felt tired, dangerously tired. Tired of bribing kids to
protect my dilapidated car; tired of putting on a half-assed
detective act to wheedle information. The world was being
carved up: dangerous few getting the choicest pieces; the
others learning to be grateful for scraps. I didn't want to
be one of the grateful others, and I didn't particularly want
to carve. I should light a cigarette and try not to think, and
the cigarette would tell me that I'm killing myself. Maybe
Joanie was right. Self-destructive. I should go home and
go to bed. It was the commonsense thing to do. It might
indicate a certain maturity.

It was good advice, but I didn't take it. If I had, I would've
had nightmares about a man named Mackey and intertwined
pubic hairs, and I'd have wondered for a week how Sally
Swann fit in. I imagined her as a redhead from Omaha with
a detachable heart who would make that heart sob right before your eyes.

A horn blasted. A car full of teenage girls, firm, nubile
and bursting with aimless energy, pulled up beside me. They
blew giggles and kisses. It was my night to be a star. Too
bad I wasn't getting paid. Too bad certain casting directors
couldn't witness my innate appeal to teenage America, which
now constituted ninety percent of the audience. Christ,
Bloodbath Blues.

They honked again. I managed a smile and a wave. They
were even younger than Sabrina Trevelyan. Too young. But

enjoy, enjoy it while you can. Forget the men in high places, forget the murders, the bombs. Give yourselves another couple of years thinking the world is full of movie stars ready to fall in love with you. I smiled again, tooted the horn and watched them giggle, thinking: god, how soon it's over, how all too soon.

꙳

T HE COLLEGE OF INTERCOURSE was tucked between a *Great American Burger* and a two-story, yellow-brick building that housed a Thai restaurant, a porno movie arcade, a *Pizza Quickie* stand, and a competitor in the higher-learning racket called *Wild West Massage*. The particular scent of each enterprise wafted out as I walked up Western Avenue from where I'd parked.

I didn't need to look at the numbers. A dark, slender man with mirrored glasses and a black paste-on moustache stood out front as a sort of doorman-barker. He handed out fliers the size of dollar bills, printed on hospital-green paper that advertised the curriculum: "Wrestling, Painting, Peeping, and Private Seminars." The instructors were promised to be young, nude, female, and alive.

He waved flamboyantly at the stairs that led to the second-floor balustrade of one of those apartment buildings that imitates a motel and looks ready for demolition two months after it's built. The stairs were carpeted in dirty red, and as I walked up I could feel my gait change. I was trying to act tough again. Practice for my next paying role. It would be for a tough, taciturn Italian. A hood, a short mean hood "trying to compensate for an inferiority complex," the college-educated director would explain. But one day, I might get to play the "sensitive" hood in a real movie. There'd be residuals. I could send Angelina to college. I could help Joanie be a painter. I could make amends. Meanwhile, act tough. Act tough or somebody's going to mark you.

When I got to the top of the stairs, a giant cutout of a finger pointed me through a black curtain into a dingy lobby. An electric buzzer woke a peroxide blonde with a glossy crimson mouth, three-inch lashes, and painted eyebrows. It seemed to take all her strength to lift those lashes. Not that it mattered. Her eyes looked right through me into some private emptiness. They were an odd color: a sort of demented turquoise; hard or if not exactly hard, just empty and alone. She had probably been pretty before she'd discovered that the quick road to a little cash was to paint on a face and tell the right lies. She could've been twenty-five, she could've been nudging forty. She'd probably taken enough downers so she didn't care anymore herself.

"You want the menu, or you got something special in mind?"

An old pro, she'd be wary even nodding out. The vice could look like anybody these days, but even in bangles and beads they always hinted of something arranged, on parade. I wondered if I looked like I was in costume myself, the way everyone was waving.

"I came to see Sally," I said, and I thought my voice was good, just tough enough, but not forced, leaving a little room for imagination.

"Sally's busy, hon. My name's Leila. I'm sure I could help." She fluttered her lashes. Very slowly. Like little engines were behind them working pulleys.

Something stirred in back of me. I whipped around and Leila squealed. It was only a man slouched in a chair. His fists were folded across his chest; his mouth worked and smacked under a bushy black moustache that had all the appearances of being real.

"You're awful jumpy," she said.

"I've been hit from behind a lot."

She raised half an eyebrow half an inch and stifled a yawn.

"Well, three nights ago when George was out getting an ice cream, somebody got hit right on the stairs. The lousy bastards didn't get my tips, but they took the rotten TV. Can you imagine?"

"That's George in the corner?" It was a nice dark corner, the perfect spot to hide the bouncer.

"Yeah."

"And the lousy bastards?"

"Guys with nylons over their heads. Been hitting all the parlors. They came in with guns and told me to get my clothes off. I said not for any of you lousy bastards. Then this customer came in. They wanted his wallet. The poor bastard ran and they panicked, I guess. Anyway, they shot him. He rolled down the stairs. Died right there on the sidewalk. The bastards took off, and one of them grabbed the TV. Can you believe?"

"Sounds like a class job."

"You got to sign in," she said. "It's twenty a half hour, thirty an hour."

"What do I get?"

"I put on a good show, hon. Believe me."

"That's all?"

She sighed and dredged up a ragged smile. "Watcha want? You tell me how much you got, I'll tell you if it's enough."

"I want to see Sally."

"She's booked for another half hour, hon, I swear it."

"I'll wait," I said. Her turquoise eyes squeezed out small grey knives. "It's personal business," I added. "Nothing to do with the curriculum."

"Yeah, tell me," she said, but she stopped the knives. It took too much energy. "You still got to sign in. No visit without paying. You can use any name you want."

"You don't sell names to affiliates, in case I use my own?"

"You being wise?"

"My sense of humor's always rotten. Blame it on the smog, I don't know, maybe it's premature senility."

She gave a tired laugh: "Yeah, it's lousy that smog, and that premature whatever you said, it's all lousy. But you get used to it. I wish they hadn't grabbed the lousy TV."

"When'd you come on?"

"Four this afternoon, off at midnight, yes I've got a date, hon. I'm not that kind of girl."

She rattled it off, a pre-recorded loop she punched up a thousand times a day. I shrugged with resigned disappointment, then asked if Sally came at on the same time.

"Yeah, we do this shift together, any objections?"

"You're right," I said. "This isn't even as good as TV."

"You always so funny?" She gave one last snarl and chunked her chin in her fleshy little hand. The bouncer belched, then resettled into big, even snores. Traffic rattled the plate-glass window where the miniature marquee with the running bulbs and the changeable red plastic letters hung behind tangerine drapes. Nobody came and nobody went and nobody found anything worth saying. I tried to sit "tough" and breathe "tough." My thoughts buzzed like monotonous flies around the body of Tunney Ray Mackey. I had to decide whether to tell Sally Swann about the surprise in her room at the Sunset Palms Motel. Presuming it was a surprise. And later, when I woke up from this dream, I'd have to call Joan and tell her I might be late with the Angelina fund this month, but I'd make up for it.

❧

T WENTY-SIX MINUTES LATER Sally's customer went through the lobby like he was stealing something he didn't really want. His shirt wasn't tucked in, and neither was his belly. He looked like he'd worked all his life for the privilege of a couple credit cards. The electric eye tripped the buzzer and one of the bouncer's eyes opened.

"It's the last one on the left, with the yellow curtain," Leila told me.

Behind the yellow curtain was a yellow shag carpet, the same dirty yellow as in Sally's bedroom. In the middle was a big waterbed; the sheets looked clean and cheery, bursting with big stylized sunflowers. Tacked on the ceiling above them, a sheet of mylar made watery sunflower reflections. All the shabby dead smells that must've been hiding there were choked out by a terrible jasmine sweetness. In fifteen seconds I had a jasmine headache. A little jasmine on the lung along with some lead, strontium 90 and marijuana. The coroner could do a geological study of the layers; cause of death would still be jasmine asphyxiation.

Sally took about two minutes to clean up between customers. She came in with a big smile in the middle of a lot of freckles, and I thought, damn I knew it, I just knew a girl named Sally Swann would have freckles. The freckles almost made her look innocent, though not completely innocent. Maybe it was her body, the way it was a touch too lush, and the way all that lushness stretched a yellow leotard that zipped down the front. Only the zipper wasn't closed, and it was hard not to notice she had freckles all the way down. And when you got down you couldn't help notice her only underwear was a thatch of curly red hair that matched that on her head. Christ, if she turned out to be from Omaha I'd have a use for my useless office. I'd hang out a sign "Authentic Cherokee Psychic."

"Kind of stuffy in here," I said, still trying not to look at all those freckles.

"There isn't a window in this whole darn place that opens." Her voice was a flirtatious soprano singsong with a hint of brass.

"I imagine they wouldn't appreciate you leaning out into the sunset, getting whiffs of that dreamy Hollywood air."

"When was the last time you saw a sunset in Hollywood, mister?"

"Couldn't 've been more than seven years back; at that drive-in down on Third. The one they tore down."

She laughed. There was still innocence in her laugh at least. Then she asked, "Did I have you before? No, I'd remember you. You're kind of cute. Listen, the deal is anything more than talk is extra." She stretched out on the waterbed and patted the edge, indicating I could sit down and take a closer look but couldn't touch.

"I appreciate it, hon, but the truth is I'm looking for Larry."

At least the name was right. It hit the bright damaged innocence of her face with something cloudy and suspect. Her easy-going customer just sprouted the stubble of a bounty hunter, or some sort of law that could get by the blond cop-detector named Leila.

"Listen, I don't know him so well. We're kind of casual."

"I'm a friend of his from way back. The way things've been, it's hard to stay in touch."

"Larry's like that," she said. "How'd you know I knew him? From Nam?" I nodded noncommittally. "Boy, that is a long time. I was hardly born."

I told her my old buddy had mentioned Sally Swann with more than passing affection and had said we could meet at the Sunset Palms, but if something happened, to leave a message at this address. I explained I'd got hung up so we'd missed meeting. It was important we get together because we had certain mutual interests that couldn't wait. I kept it as vague as a newspaper horoscope and read her face: the paranoia faded. I was on a roll.

"You know this isn't my usual line of work . . . but you got to make a living, right? While you're waiting for a break." She winced out a little smile.

"Yeah, I know how it is," I said, feeling the weight of truth in my voice. "So what's Larry doing these days? Waiting for his mythical ship to come in?"

"How'd you know? Something to do with stocks. Larry's weird. He knows all kinds of stuff."

"You don't think it's all talk?"

"Well he can sure kill you with charm. I remember once he got all dressed up. It wasn't the same person. I guess it's sort of a disguise, huh? Going around the way he does? But in this town everybody's strange. You kind of get used to it."

"I'm still trying," I said and she laughed. It was a free

girlish laugh reminding me of the kids in the car. If she went back to Des Moines or Cincinnati or Urbana right now, she might stand a chance.

"You're nice," she said. "Nicer than Larry in a way."

That killed me. She was either the best little actress in the world, or there was no way she could've known about Tunney Ray Mackey.

"Larry hasn't let out his real name, has he?"

Her face hung there, a pretty puzzled mask. I reminded myself she wasn't much over twenty, and she'd been weaned on TV. She was trying even harder to be cool than I was. Finally she said: "He told me his name was Loper."

"Hey, don't worry. He's not trying to fool you. An alias is like a pair of shoes."

She didn't quite follow, but she smiled bravely and a bit excitedly. "What are you guys into, anyway?"

Somehow I had a hunch it was more than a sleazy blackmail job that didn't make sense. Then again, maybe it was meant to look amateurish to disguise what was really going on.

"You guys aren't . . . you're not like terrorists, are you?"

I didn't even crack a smile. I put the gentle, intimate hand on her shoulder and gave the deep, searching gaze. If I could've seen myself, I might've puked.

"Nothing like that. I just wanted to make sure he hasn't gotten careless."

So easy. Much too easy. A little sugar coating of intrigue, and she starts to drool. A rare one, Dancey, a truly trusting creature, and here you are taking advantage because it happens to be convenient.

"Drugs?" she whispered.

"Is that what he told you?"

"He does a little dealing, but I never thought he took it all that serious. Course, I've only know him a few months. Sometimes he hints around about working for some sort of organization. But it's only when he gets high. I figured it was just talk. He kind of likes me, see? But you're much nicer. I'm sorry. I'm a little high myself. Do I sound silly? I hate to sound silly. I know I'm not too smart."

"Hey, you're fine, Sally. I like you too."

"Really?"

"Really," I said. And I did. But she scared me too. I didn't want to like anything so close to ruin. Not that young. I wanted to quit. But I didn't or couldn't. I was thinking maybe I could send her home, or at least get her a job at the Lafayette. She'd make a great waitress. She'd cheer people up. She'd make great tips.

"Hey, you still here? I don't even know your name."

"Dancey. Elton Dancey."

"I like it," she said. "It's so unique." She was proud of the word unique. I wanted to hug her, to take her back to the shack and clean her up. I'd call Mel at the Lafayette tomorrow. I'd give her Sabrina's five-hundred dollars and put her up at the Star. Damn, Dancey, you can't save the world, not even a small red-headed part of it. You can't even save yourself.

"You sure he hasn't mentioned who he's working for? Nobody named Fitzgibbons?"

Her eyes seemed to get bigger. They were cobalt blue. With the right kind of agent those eyes could promotes a lot of dreams. They were clean blue slate: you could label them secretive or seductive; pick any cliche in the book.

"Or Tunney Ray Mackey?"

"Is he a producer?"

"Not the kind you think."

"Oh," she said. I realized that she really did have a detachable heart, and it was in my hands.

"He hasn't seemed kind of down, like he's depressed?"

"Of course he's got his moods. Sometimes he just isn't *there* any more, you know what I mean? But basically he's a fun sort of guy. Loves to joke. Like once he rented this gorilla suit and rode around with that guy Baba Ridiculoso. You know, the guy with the Rolls-Royce and the llama."

I'd heard of him. The son of some salad-oil magnate. He'd come into the family fortune and was busy spending it in peculiar ways.

"The guy with the temple at the top of Topanga?"

"Yeah, but I think he went to India, or something."

"Would Larry still hang out up there?"

"I think they got in an argument or something. Larry's got a trailer at the bottom of the canyon near the beach. There's no address or anything, but I could draw a map."

"You think he'll show up at your place?"

She shrugged. "It's loose, you know? When he shows, he shows. But I do kind of miss him. He's fun. I'm not exactly ready for a steady relationship, you know? But you're nice. Nicer than Larry. I guess I said that. I'm sorry."

"It's okay. Sal, I was wondering, does Larry have a key to your place?"

She didn't bat an eye. She wanted to tell me, tell me everything. "Yeah, he does. I'm moving out real soon. It's a dump. You know, I'm not even sure I want to see him anymore. You don't seem like him. I mean it's weird you're friends, you know?"

There was a pause filled with music droning out of a tiny transistor radio lost in the corner behind the incense pot. The waterbed rocked us. There were cosmic charts on the walls. It was a perfect little church for trying to piece together the soul of a shabby blackmailer with what seemed like complicated wiring.

It wasn't hard to get Sally Swann to tell it, not hard at all. I heard about how Larry had decided to help her with her "Career," how he knew important people in the "Industry" and was going to get her various introductions. I heard about The Sixty Second Academy that made you a star in TV commercials; after you made a fortune, you went on to "Serious Work," meaning movies.

Every so often the buzzer on the lobby door would complain through the walls. Sometimes there were voices, and once a mangled groan that had to be one of the strangest exclamations of ecstasy I'd ever heard. Twice Leila yelled through the curtain about "expired time," and Sally told her not to worry. Leila whined about "customers waiting" and how Maxine hadn't showed.

I bought another fifteen minutes and tried to figure if I was on Sabrina's time or my own. We hadn't talked about expenses; there weren't supposed to be any.

"You sure you just want to talk?" she asked. "I mean, this is costing you. We could talk later. You could meet me after work."

"I really don't mind," I said. "I just hope you're getting a decent cut."

She gave me a darling little smile and for some reason she made an attempt to pull the zipper up, as though covering her charms had become the real act of seduction. The zipper stuck about an inch above her belly button, then gradually worked its way back down as she told me everything she knew about Larry Loper.

She said he'd come up from Mexico a few months back and told her how you could rent a big villa on the ocean for practically nothing and live like a king. He seemed to speak fluent Spanish. He liked marijuana. He liked cocaine. Sometimes he flashed wads of money, but twice he had touched her for loans. The thing that she found so fascinating was how he could seem to be different people on different days, how even his age seemed to change. Once he had taken her to a party in Malibu and had introduced her to a producer. Nothing had happened except the producer had wanted to go to bed with her. Yes, he still liked pistachios; ate them all the time. As far as she knew he didn't have a gun. No, he never mentioned parents or relatives, and when she'd asked he'd told her he was born in Rhodesia, that his father was English, his mother Dutch. He did seem to have a sort of accent, but that seemed to change, too. He'd been everywhere. He knew everything. But he scared her sometimes. He made her laugh, but sometimes he just got this look in his eyes.

Yes, he did have a beard, but when she'd first met him — she confessed he'd picked her up on the beach near Topanga — he was just starting to let it grow.

I asked her about Mackey. I gave her a vivid description. Nothing. Nothing at all. Finally she came out of her trance and pulled in the reins. "Listen, Mr. Dancey, you're real nice, but I feel kind of strange talking about him like this. Why don't you tell me where he can get a hold of you."

I felt like a heel again, but I climbed into my best hang-dog, soul-searching gaze. Out in the lobby, several voices were doing battle. "You don't trust me, do you, Mr. Dancey? You think I'm just a flaky kid. But I'm quite responsible. I'll give Larry the message, just the way you want." She'd suddenly fallen out of love with me.

"It isn't that. It's just he might think it was a trick."

She nodded. "You're right about that. He's totally paranoid."

"I've got to catch him in person. You see there's other people involved . . ."

I watched the pretty freckled face of Sally Swann whisk back into the realms of intrigue. She was scared, but part of her loved it. Just the way I did. Maybe Larry Loper was all he claimed. Maybe she would get introduced to the right important people. Maybe she would live in a villa in Mexico.

"It's all so mysterious."

I almost forgot to swallow my smile. "Yes, it is . . ." I unfolded a pocket spiral notebook, handed her my pen and managed to persuade her to draw a map to Larry Loper's canyon hideway. She'd just finished when Leila poked her head through the yellow curtain. "Hey, sugar, Roger just came in and wants to know how come all the extra time with this guy isn't on the books. We got three live ones waiting."

Sally Swann sighed: "Give me a minute, okay?" I laid out another ten. It was all I had.

Leila grinned, then ducked out with "Sure sugar, I'll give you a minute." I imagined her ticking off the seconds with her big lashes. She'd certainly come to life since the boss jumped on her tail. All over town orders were coming down: the guy below was getting kicked; the guy on the bottom was running his butt off toward an early grave; and the guy on top was counting his cash.

꒱

I WENT DOWN THE STAIRS past the doorman-barker's smirking salute, thinking that Sally Swann didn't deserve the trouble the unfortunate visitor in her bedroom was bound to cause, but I didn't know what to do about it. The door of the Thai restaurant was open and a small dark-eyed man with bronze skin and a beautiful posture was looking out, his hands fluttering in a towel whiter than the whitest snow. His shoebox eatery was empty. A half a dozen people would've made it look bustling.

The man took my order, then went in the back and prepared a soup: light and pleasantly spicy; full of shrimp and vegetable, lemon and coconut milk. I knew the minute I left this place I'd be back in the real world, or maybe it was the unreal one. At any rate, the flies would start buzzing. So I sat and drank another beer and tried to ignore my bruises, my broken marriage, and Sally Swann and Tunney Ray Mackey.

It was 11:05. The man smiled, bowed, and a bill appeared in front of me on a glass dish. The bill was much too small. I opened my wallet. I'd forgotten it was empty. I offered my one credit card and he gave a puzzled shrug. I agreed. The little man didn't appear alarmed, only interested, as I took off my left shoe, stripped off the sock and peeled my last twenty off the bottom of my foot. In broken Thai I apologized for its being soiled. Slowly shaping the words in English, he replied: "In my country, money is all the time walked on."

We laughed. I wished I knew more of his language. He seemed like a good man to tell your troubles to.

I left half my change on the glass dish. He picked it up and tried to put it back in my pocket. We argued until we agreed to a split.

By the time I left I was smiling; the traffic on Western Avenue hardly bothered me. I'd even forgotten I was carrying around an unreported murder. I wasn't worried about being a man with a handful of nonexistent careers and an ex-wife he missed more than he cared to admit.

After two out-of-order pay phones, the smile was fading. The third generously buzzed once, then a machine answered in a brisk cultured tenor, presumably belonging to Hal Fitzgibbons. The voice told me to leave a message.

Either Hal wasn't back, or maybe he was and was busy with Sabrina rocking him to sleep, a reward for his daring dealings with tough-assed extortionists. Being a considerate girl, Sabrina would call me in the morning: gee thanks, Dancey, you really put my mind at ease. Sure, kid, anytime. Here's my bill.

I stood there with a dial tone in my ear. I started to call downtown, knowing cops like to get a quick start on a murder. I hung up. Coins jingled in the return drawer. I put one back in and dialed. After the sixth ring my own machine picked up. It was human, female, fifty-five, and named Agnes. "Phoenix Productions," she growled.

Just to test her, I used my best voice-disguise.

"So sorry," she said. "Can't accept no messages from imposters, Mr. Dancey."

"Can't fool you, can I, Agnes? By the way, forget Phoenix Productions. It's just the number now."

"I didn't say you didn't get any calls, Mr. Dancey. A girl. Real young. You watch yourself."

"Did she say anything?"

"She just said she'll call back. She sounded in a hurry. She stand you up?"

"I'll tell you later."

"I bet you're on a case. Anyways, welcome back. I was a little hurt you didn't come by and kiss me personal. How was the part?"

"Small, Agnes. But I won't end up on the cutting room floor."

"You going to keep me when you get famous and can pay your bills on time?"

"If you live that long, Agnes."

"Good-bye, Mr. Dancey, she said in a long, lush drawl.

Part of my little world was still intact. Agnes would undoubtedly be there after I'd reached the state when all I needed was a neat pine box and my own little plot of earth. She'd live forever, of that I was reasonably sure.

I called the *Corlinda*. After the first ring, just as before, the cultured tenor said he'd call in for messages within a few hours. I hung up and called back. After a while I got the voice down pretty well.

Tunney Mackey's number was listed. It rang twice before a woman answered with an irritated, "Yeah, whatcha want?" There was a television in the background, with lots of bullets flying.

"Sorry to bother you, Mrs. Mackey."

"Who's this?" The voice was snarly, and a little desperate.

"Hal Fitzgibbons, Mrs. Mackey."

"Well, he ain't here. You the one with the boat?"

"That's correct, Mrs. Mackey. He ran a little errand. He didn't leave any numbers—"

"We don't want no trouble, mister. Everything's legit, ain't it?"

"Certainly, Mrs. Mackey."

"Well, he ain't here. You wanna leave a message?"

"He hasn't mentioned if he may be working for other interests, has he, Mrs. Mackey?"

There was a pause filled with television racket in one ear, angry traffic in the other.

"He don't tell me much."

"How's the boy, Mrs. Mackey?"

"Tell that lunkhead that Junior won tonight. Only gave up two hits. You tell him."

"I sure will. Goodnight, Mrs. Mackey."

I hung up. I still couldn't tell how Mrs. Mackey would take the news. Maybe she'd just be relieved to know her lunkhead of a husband wasn't going to get into any more trouble. If she was lucky, Mackey wasn't in debt. Apparently he did believe in insurance.

I used my last change to call the College of Intercourse. Sally Swann answered and I told her I'd be waiting outside at twelve if she needed a ride. Her voice bubbled its bright soprano, how happy she was I'd called back, could I make it ten after, she was booked for an hour, but she'd just love a lift home. I said I'd be honored.

I walked back to the car praying for rain. I wanted to sit and listen to the patter on the roof and watch the world get washed. I prayed, but I knew the first rain was at least five months away.

I stretched out, hung my legs over the seat and closed my eyes. I kept seeing Tunney Ray Mackey. After a while I got the flask out from under the seat and took a hit. Then I drove up Western toward Sally Swann, biting on the sour taste in my mouth.

彡

S HE WAS PERCHED HALFWAY UP THE STAIRS like some giant exotic bird. She wore a white blouse tucked into skintight jeans, and was draped in a long green cape with an electric orange hood. I pulled to the curb and opened the passenger door. The interior of the Buick fluttered with taffeta rustles and was drowned in jasmine. Before I could get a word out, she was bubbling over with gratitude, in love with me again. She just hated paying for taxis, but since she'd sacrificed her car to The Sixty Second Academy, she had to take a taxi every night or there'd be someone following her. She took a breath and added what a shame it was I'd got soaked for all that money just to talk, and hinted if I was in the mood, well, after all we were almost friends, and I seemed like a nice guy that wouldn't forget a favor sincerely offered.

By then there were only three blocks left between us and the immobile visitor that was going to put a damper on any romantic intentions. Of course the cops might already have come. They'd want to take Sally in for questioning, and she was going to feel even lonelier than the lonely that had prompted her to latch onto me.

I kept postponing telling her. Finally there was no space left for further postponement. I couldn't figure a way to do it delicately, so I just told her flat out. I had to repeat it half a dozen times. When it finally got through, she let out a single sharp laugh.

"You got to be kidding," she said, "You got to be."

"You sure you don't know the guy?"

"Never. I promise."

Nothing told me to doubt her. Sally Swann had a long way to go as a liar. I doubted even The Sixty Second Academy could teach her.

"Oh god, I'm scared. I don't need any more hassles. Please stay, okay? I hate cops."

"You think Larry had something to do with it?"

"No, I mean—I don't know. It's all so weird."

"You realize they're going to ask you about him. They're going to be tough. They may even decide they've got enough to hold you."

"But it's not fair! I didn't do anything. Honest! Only, I think my father's looking for me. I just hate cops!"

I pulled over. Her tears streamed. Her red hair, nestling against my shoulder, smelled of jasmine. Everything in her life had gone bad. Everything. Larry hadn't really helped her. The Sixty Second Academy was a ripoff. She didn't have any friends. She hated her job. She might as well be dead.

Then suddenly she stopped crying. Something had dawned on her. And before she could ask how it was I knew about Tunney Ray Mackey, I told her. Only I hedged on the time. I told her I'd gone back to wait for Larry after I'd visited with her. Then I asked who knew she lived at the Sunset Palms and if the management knew where she worked. Nobody knew except Larry.

"And you," she added, then burst into sobs. I didn't want to trust her with the police. It'd take them about five minutes to get her to spill how a certain Elton Dancey had discovered the body, and how he was a bosom buddy of Larry Loper.

I helped her decide. Since no one was expecting her at the Sunset Palms, she might as well take a small rent-free vacation at a little dive in Venice I was looking after for a friend in the hospital. On the outside it was called the Star Motel, but we jokingly referred to it as the R & R. I added how the air was cleaner in Venice. She could walk to the beach and earn her keep caretaking the garden in the adjacent vacant lot, and maybe there'd be a waitressing job at the Lafayette. If the cops did get hold of her, there was no law about taking a vacation, even a suspiciously convenient one. Let the cleaning lady discover Mackey next week.

I cruised by. The pink neon of the Sunset Palms still sputtered. There were still no official cars out front or under the courtyard goddesses. I parked in the same spot I had before. We went by way of the alley.

"Let me go first," I said. "And don't turn on the lights in the front room. By the way, you ever see any bodies?"

"Just my mother's," she whimpered.

"This one isn't fixed up. Don't let it throw you." She gave me the key and we went in. Nothing smelled any different, no ghosts of interim visitors. The refrigerator rumbled. The TV buzzed. Mr. Mackey lay with his nose to the floor. Sally Swann made gulping sounds and clamped both hands over her mouth.

"You going to make it?"

She nodded.

"Where's your suitcase?"

She pointed to the closet, then she started to shake. I sat her down on the bed, got out the suitcase and started to throw things in. First the stack of printed cards. Then about half of what was hanging in the closet.

"Don't take that," she said. "Not the flowered dress."

I gave it a toss and it settled over the TV where the vinyl

voice was selling cars again. I told her she'd better sort it out herself, that it shouldn't look like she'd moved out, but that she'd never been back.

She had the suitcase stuffed when they announced themselves with burning rubber and rapid-fire door slams. Feet slapped the pavement and knuckles pounded the door. I doused the overhead, leaving us in the cold blue of television light. It was going to take about fifteen seconds before the front door popped. I checked the back window. A trashcan lid fell and someone cursed. The battered old Siamese scampered between uniformed legs.

I dragged Sally and the suitcase over Mackey and into the bathroom and locked the door. The long, narrow window was hinged on the side. The outside screen disintegrated with one swipe.

The passageway between the motel and the deserted roller rink next door was about two feet wide and blocked at either end by a wooden fence better than ten feet high. I saw the whole grand escape in a flash: the cops get in and half a minute later they stumble over Mackey and head for the bathroom door. They'd kick it down and in another thirty seconds flashlight beams would blaze down our little cul-de-sac. There might be a drawn gun behind the flashlights. There might be an itch on a trigger finger. We'd raise our hands, admitting guilt. Still, there was a chance. Maybe an open window to another unit. Or maybe they'd all be in the courtyard and we could vault the fence in front and calmly stroll away. Sure, and there was a chance of rain in Hollywood in June.

I boosted her through the window, handed down her suitcase.

"What if they shoot?" she said, and oddly, she sounded more excited than panicked.

"Usually, they tell you to freeze. And you freeze. Very fast. Hands up, the whole bit."

I pulled her toward the front fence. Our feet clattered in broken glass. There weren't any open windows.

"You know anyone in this place that might let us in?"

She shook her head. I heard the report of the front door bursting open. A car backfired on Sunset and we both jumped. I swore I could hear hard official voices.

I cupped my hands and she stuck in a pretty foot wrapped in a pretty gold sandal. She pushed off my shoulders and scrambled up peeling ochre-painted boards. I guided the pretty gold sandals onto my shoulders. She stepped on my head, caught the top and edged her chin over.

"God, this is crazy."

"Just go!"

She hoisted herself, got one leg over, teetered. I heard a tiny fluttery yelp and the sound of her landing as echoes of the bathroom door's destruction crackled down the passageway. I heaved her suitcase, moved back half a dozen steps and ran. My fingertips caught the top edge, my feet scrambled, my right arm stretched another inch and I found a grip. Flashlight beams found my hands, my face, and men were yelling "Freeze!" Just like in the movies. Almost instantly, there was the sharp crack of a shot.

ﾑ

I HIT THE SIDEWALK half-expecting to feel a warm sickening trickle, then the agonizing burn as pain penetrated fear. Sally had a five- or six-second start and was running east, her green cape fluttering behind her. I grabbed the suitcase and the latches sprung, clothes avalanched, white cards fluttered.

I dropped the whole business, nabbed her hand, jumped into the traffic, and catapulted off a front fender. The iridescent cape caught the miniature silver eagle perched on a hood and the pretty head of red hair jerked back. The cape tore as she fell forward, leaving a tiny green tag on the ornamental eagle. As we tripped up the north curb of Sunset, I caught a glimpse of two men racing out through the motel archway, weapons drawn.

I slowed to a brisk walk, took Sally's arm and steered her towards an old three-story stucco apartment building called the Cornish Arms. We walked down a corridor lit by 15-watt bulbs and went out the back. A narrow walkway led to a wooden gate that opened onto a compound containing four miniature bungalows with peeling paint and overgrown lawns. In one of the bungalows lights glowed behind stained, yellow shades. Another held the yellow dance of candlelight. The wet grass smelled clean. For a second it seemed we could knock on one of these doors and sit down for a friendly game of rummy.

"What are we going to do?" This was the kind of excitement she'd dreamed of back in Omaha, it was her kind of movie. Only there weren't any cameras and the only pay-off was the thrill. At least the cops hadn't seen her.

"Can you drive a shift?"

A calmness entered her face, a calmness that must have been rare. She nodded, and I handed her the keys, told her where the car was, that she should walk very calmly, then drive back and pull in the alley. She turned to go, and I grabbed her arm.

"That damned cape. You're wavin' the flag, hon."

"Oh," she said, and slipped it off.

I watched her move down the alley, gold sandals clicking, hips rolling in luxurious swings. I began to wonder if I wasn't wrong about the cape. At least it would've kept her rear under cover.

~

I T WAS A LONG WAIT, long because it was filled with careful listening, speculation about dented fenders, lost keys and lost redheads circling endlessly trying to remember which alley it was, as the police bands chattered a description of a certain unemployed and perhaps unemployable actor.

The thirteen minutes it took her to make it back equalled a week of wear and tear on the system. When she finally arrived, I slid behind the wheel and laid the cape in her lap. Suddenly her face trembled and tears began to fall. I figured she'd tell me soon enough, so I just said she'd done a great job, put the car in gear and rolled down the alley crunching glass. After a few blocks of meandering with an accompaniment of sirens and Sally's sobs, I blended into the traffic heading east on Hollywood Boulevard. In a few minutes we were downtown, sailing past the extravagant, brightly-lit citadels of corporate success.

"I forgot all my money," she said and blew her nose.

"Maybe we can get it later."

"It's three hundred dollars," she said. "You know where it is?"

"No," I said, not wanting to wound her innocence any more than I had.

"In the freezer." She laughed a choked, snuffly laugh.

"Clever," I said, and for some reason she started to wail again. I made the interchange to the Santa Monica freeway, wondering if I should give her a tired lecture on how the world tortures us all, how she'd be smart to stop basing her life on $300, an astrological forecast and Hollywood dreams. Instead, I tuned in some music, a nineteenth-century symphony as we were transported down a twentieth-century freeway.

I pulled into the courtyard of the Star Motel where there were no plaster nymphs and the neon was even more exhausted than at the Sunset Palms. But there was a pool. You couldn't swim in it, but you could wade, or watch the frogs and goldfish as well as a mermaid who bathed all the day under showers spouting from various sea creatures, mostly mythical, that crouched at her feet. Felix Greene, the night manager who'd fashioned this sculpture, his own little Tivoli Gardens, was sitting in the office, as usual. He peered out, gave a wave, and went back to reading what was probably either Kierkegaard or what he would blushingly refer to as erotica.

In a few minutes, Sally was installed in the "Guest Suite."

She thanked me profusely, said she'd pay it all back. I told her to get some sleep, then drove home to get some myself.

⁊

I LIKE TO SLEEP, and once I get there I like to stay there. A full eight hours. So I wasn't in the best of humors when I picked up the phone and the clock read 2:45 and it was still dark.

"Dancey! I'm so glad . . ." Her voice wouldn't stop. She had to tell me what had transpired. She told it all in great frenetic detail. She'd followed a phone message she wasn't meant to get out to a bar on the Pacific Coast Highway, where of all things, Hal Fitzgibbons shows up and meets Sabrina's stepmother, Angie Trevelyan. "My father's third wife. A primo bitch. Totally irresponsible!"

I thought about telling her I'd had a pretty crazy time myself, and I didn't give a damn about her boyfriend or her stepmother and not much of one about her.

"You're not going to believe it," she said. "It was weird. Weird!"

"You're going to tell me they shacked up."

"They sat there and got drunk, and then they went down to these cheap little cabins. The bastard didn't even call to tell me if he got the fucking pictures!"

"Sounds like a real loverboy."

"He's a complete shit. He's just using me. He uses everybody."

I didn't have much to say. It sounded like a pretty fair assessment.

"You don't give a damn," she said. Then she added, "I guess I asked for it, didn't I?"

"If you want it to get weirder, I stumble into a corpse and just about got my ass shot off checking on your boyfriend's health."

"He's not my fucking boyfriend. He's an asshole. I just want those pictures."

"Sorry, no luck."

"Did you say you got shot at? What corpse?"

"Where should I send the bill, Sabrina?"

"Dancey, are you putting me on?"

"About the bill?"

"No! Come on, Dancey, I appreciate . . ."

"Then get out of my ear for eight hours. And maybe it's time to get a professional. No matter what Daddy says."

"What did you mean . . . ? You're so fucking uncommunicative!"

"In the morning. At my office. Nine-thirty." At least, the place would be good for something. Neutral ground: no drinks, no bed, no temptations.

"You sound so cold," she said.

"I'll give my report. And I'll expect a check."

"Dancey," she said, and her voice took on an enticing purr, "I'm really spooked, Dancey. I was wondering, would you mind if I came over?"

"I need to get some sleep, Sabrina."

"You're not taking anything I say seriously."

"Try me at 9:30 a.m. I'm usually more serious in the morning."

I hung up and waited, half expecting her to call back. But she had more class than that. Self-indulgent maybe, but she had pride. Or so I wanted to think. It was amazing how a single night in bed with her had blasted my judgment.

I congratulated myself on resisting her offer. I'd take her damned check and give three hundred of it to Sally Swann. Then I'd be free and clear.

I lay there, and my mind wouldn't stop. I kept seeing Tunney Ray Mackey, and when I got my mind off him I saw that tailfin slamming toward me again. After a while, I managed to convince myself that the last twenty-four hours had just been a bad dream. Then I was thinking of Joan, Angelina, and the cost of airline tickets. Finally, I got up, poured myself a brandy and fumbled around on the piano. I caught myself wishing that Sabrina would call back. I drank another brandy, read a few chapters of *David Copperfield* and finally fell into a fitful, sweaty sleep in which men wielding blackjacks chased me down alleyways choked with hordes of raging felines.

A T NINE I CLIMBED THE OUTSIDE STAIRS to the office, considered taking down the brass sign that read "Phoenix Productions," and tried not to think what folly my life had been for the last month, or year, or five years. I distracted myself by throwing away about ten pounds of junk mail, then pulled the canvas chairs out onto the flat part of the roof and watched the catamarans nip back and forth across the harbor and an eight-man hull jump on eight synchronized legs down the channel. The hull was manned by the UCLA rowing team. UCLA had been a long time ago for me. I'd made the wrestling team, but I hadn't made graduation, more to my old man's disappointment than mine. Still, it had given me three good years. And, a few years later, it had given me Joan at a private screening of a desperate film made by a graduate student in which a certain Elton Dancey had a starring role. A long time ago, high ambitions — and you didn't do *that* bad a job, I told myself. But the whole thing was pretentious and muddled and self-indulgent. Losing causes, Dancey. Maybe this was another one. Chasing dirty pictures had to be more honorable than *Bloodbath Blues*.

I tried to relax. The first busload of tourists had begun to browse the overpriced mementos in the prefabricated village stretching along the harbor. Behind me jets took off to anywhere you might or might not want to go. It was all working. Civilization at ease. There weren't any wars you could see. Even the water was cooperating: it sparkled with illusions of purity.

A few minutes later I watched as Sabrina Trevelyan came bouncing up the stairs two at a time. The few moments of her ascent seemed frozen in time. Her wheat-blonde hair was blown across her face, her white shorts snug against her thighs, and a gold chain linking delicate gold coins graced a hard brown belly below the flimsy silk blouse tied above her midriff. She plunked down into the chair I'd put out for her and seemed oddly cheerful, as if the insanity of the previous day had evaporated without a trace. She seemed content to bubble commentary on my luck in having such a neat office with such a neat view. And absolutely no purpose, I thought, only a five-month obligation.

"What's the matter?" she asked.

"I guess I just realized everything's so neat around here, I wonder if I fit in."

"Must you always be so morose?" she said. She took joy in the word.

"I got shortchanged in the gracious sportsman department."

"I'm sorry about last night, if that's what you mean." She impulsively stuck out her tongue, another cute vulgarity I converted into touchingly innocent charm. Then, just to make sure she had me, she hoisted her legs into the chair and crossed them with sultry lassitude, leaving a spacious, provocative view of crotch-hugging cotton and bare thigh. I tried to keep my gaze on her face, but the sassy mouth was just as aggravating as the minimal shorts. A strictly temporary cure, I reminded myself. And how would you like somebody looking at your daughter like that? In another five or six years, somebody would be. A lot of somebodies, and she might be liking it just the way Sabrina was.

"Are you lost somewhere?" she asked.

"Completely," I said, enjoying my private joke. It was time to grow up and stop playing detective and stop dreaming a great part was going to come my way if I didn't play the Hollywood game the way it had to be played.

"Sometimes I don't get you, Dancey." Sabrina let out an exasperated sigh; she acted as though we'd been on intimate terms for years.

"So where's Hal?"

"The slimy bastard," she hissed.

"Still with Angie?"

"I don't give a fuck where he is. But I would like those pictures. I'll give you two thousand if you can get them. And what's this about you getting shot at?" Her voice was a touch too casual to disguise the underlying thrill.

Maybe she wasn't so different from Sally Swann. Only she wasn't truly innocent. A Trevelyan probably never could be. They'd had too much of the good life.

"What makes you think the pictures really exist?" I asked her.

"Why would somebody call Hal and say he had them?"

"The question is: Why should Hal give a damn? And why do you give a damn? None of this makes sense."

She chewed on her lower lip with those near-perfect teeth. I read it as more calculated charm and tried not to fall for it. I was trying hard.

"I don't, Dancey, not for myself. But it would kill Daddy. He has certain old-fashioned ideas. And I respect him."

"What you mean is: There goes the inheritance."

"Sometimes you're mean." It was too theatrical, and for once I didn't bite.

"Whenever I say anything close to the truth, I'm mean. Let's presume the pictures exist and they arrive on Daddy's desk. He's old-fashioned; I'll even buy that. But some part of him must've figured you're no virgin by now. He's a tough man. The whole thing is just too small-time for someone like him to bother with. Let him pay the money and forget it. He'll slap you on the wrist, and he can deduct it from the pile he's going to leave you down the road."

Her gaze drifted over the channel. I couldn't tell if those eyes were hunting an answer or dodging the question. One thing was for sure, there was only one other person with eyes like that and she was painting pictures in Manhattan.

A couple of gulls glided overhead, riding the on-shore breeze. Rivulets of sweat trickled down her brown belly. A thin girlish voice that had suddenly lost its sass told me Roger Trevelyan wouldn't exactly take it in stride, that it wasn't the money and it wasn't her doing whatever nasty thing she was doing with Fitzgibbons. It was the idea of getting caught. Even though five grand wasn't all that big a deal, Daddy wasn't as flush as his life-style implied. His latest wife was costing a fortune, and he'd been taking a beating on the market. She babbled on, milking my sympathy for the cash flow problems of the rich, until I told her I was about to bawl.

"I'm sorry," she said. "The point is that I hate hassles."

"Maybe it's time for you to learn to deal with a few. Think of this as a golden opportunity."

She was about to tell me I was being mean again, but kept quiet instead. There was a hole in the conversation, and the ghost of Sophia Richardson Trevelyan drifted into the bright blue day, a day like the one she'd slipped overboard and nobody had noticed. She hadn't left a note, hadn't uttered a threat, hadn't even left a faint trail of despair. Only glittering, gay conversation. A week later the body washed onto a beach. The verdict was accidental drowning.

"Why do you think your mother tied up with your father in the first place?"

She shrugged in a way that said she didn't want to talk about it.

"You blame him for what happened?"

She shook her head noncommittally and murmured, "He used to be so different."

I imagined that when Sophia Richardson had fallen for him, Roger Trevelyan had been a handsome charmer. Not unlike Hal Fitzgibbons. At some point it had gone stale, then bad. Then there were the affairs, the indifference, the drinking, the false gaiety and the maintenance of all the pretenses the aristocracy seems set on. The mystery was why she hadn't simply bailed out. She had her own money; she still had her looks. And potential for something more than her knack for cheerful decadence. All I could figure was she'd been steeped in the social code that said you didn't make mistakes, and if you did, you pretended you didn't, grinning all the way. Maybe Sabrina, who thought she was running free and naked, still bore clinging remnants. And if I looked at it with cold eyes, Dancey wasn't sticking his neck out just because she had a nice ass and a check for five hundred bucks. I had some clinging remnants of my own. "Guilt is always messy," as Sophia Trevelyan had said fifteen years ago.

"What are you thinking now?" Sabrina asked as if our contract included instant access to my thoughts.

"That's it's all pretty strange."

"I want those goddamn pictures back, Dancey!" she stated with sudden vehemence.

"Why don't you buy them back yourself? Five grand, right? Any problem?"

"Not next week. I could collect what my mother left on my birthday." She grinned, proud and sassy again. Of course, there was always a trap: five thousand could escalate.

"Seriously, Sabrina, you ought to get yourself a guy with a license. It doesn't seem to register there's been a murder."

"But what does that have to do with it? Listen, I give up. You're my friend. Please, Dancey. I'm good for the money. Are we going to sit and argue?" She tightened that full alive mouth into a hard line that aged her by ten years. I turned away. A forty-foot cruiser plowed the channel, breaking the harbor limit. Its wake pummeled a dinghy with a five-horse outboard. It made me think of Mackey, how maybe his dream was to make enough of a killing to have a boat like that, wear a captain's hat, chomp a fat cigar and have a couple of chunky blondes on the overnight payroll. But all he'd managed was to get his head bashed in.

"It gives me the creeps when you get quiet," she said. "I keep thinking about yesterday. I'm in over my head, Sabrina."

"I told you I'm willing to pay you. How about two hundred a day? Isn't that what they get?"

I didn't like being bought either. But that was purely principle. It was either work for Sabrina or call Max and tell him I'd changed my mind about *Bloodbath Blues*.

"The little guys, yes."

"Is it enough?"

"Yeah, it's enough."

"But we're still friends, okay?"

"It gets messy, Sabrina."

"You're so, I don't know — old-fashioned."

"I thought that's what amused you. A bohemian who hasn't got a potbelly. Shit, I'll introduce you to a real one sometime."

She looked at me and shook her head, then said with odd delicacy, "You're exasperating, you know? Now tell me about this body, and how he shot at you and stuff."

I had another flash of Sabrina as a sophisticated upperclass version of Sally Swann. None of this was real. Not even close to real. But the thought of it excited her.

"The body belonged to a guy named Mackey. He was working for Hal. He didn't shoot at me except in my dreams."

"I never heard of him," she said. There was an edge to her voice now, but I believed her. I gave her a description. She still hadn't heard of him, but she began to look a little more worried. Maybe it had begun to register that this wasn't just a game to liven up a summer vacation.

"I'd like to take a look at the *Corlinda*," I told her.

"What if Hal shows up?"

"Tell him I'm a private detective called in to protect the Trevelyan family's virgins."

"Real fucking hilarious."

"You already knew I had a lousy sense of humor. So why don't you want me to see his boat?"

"I don't know. He'll throw a fit."

"Maybe you don't hate him anymore."

"I don't hate anybody. I just quietly despise people who don't give me what I want. Of course, they're the only people I like. Paradoxical, huh? Like you—you're good for me." She said it all with a superb sense of irony that made me like her again. She was a bit too clever for me and too clever for her own good.

"Pretty sophisticated self-assessment. Meant to bring me around."

She bristled, smiled, then stuck out her hand in an oddly masculine posture of conciliation. "Friends?"

I shook her hand. "Provided I can make a few decisions. I may have a nose, but I'm not a dog."

"Okay," she said, and we walked over to Pier 6.

ᚤ

A N OLD TOP-SAIL RIGGED SCHOONER was being duti-fully photographed by a gaudy flock of tourists. We slid past the bright shirts and hats and cameras, taking a shortcut through the boatyard as Sabrina filled in the details of last night's adventure. She'd waited on board the *Corlinda* hoping to hear from Hal, but at around six she'd gotten hungry and walked over to the coffee shop on Lincoln Boulevard. When she got back, the answering machine had a message from Angie Trevelyan asking Hal to meet her at a bar called *The Shipwreck* at eight.

"When did your father hook up with Angie?" I asked her.

"About four years ago. She's a singer. Or so she likes to claim. She wasn't much good, I mean she was never going to make it, but he used to go to this piano bar. I guess he thought of it as romantic slumming or something."

"And Angie saw your father as a convenient retirement fund."

"I guess."

"How old?"

"Around thirty. It's weird."

"What's weird?"

"She isn't even his type. I mean real rough at the edges. And those tits. My father never went for girls with tits like that. Men are weird," she said.

"He took your mother's death pretty hard. Maybe he didn't want anything to remind him . . ."

"Yeah, he did kind of flip. Maybe it was middle-aged crisis." She cocked her head and for a minute I thought she was going to demand a progress report on mine. "Anyway, if you want my opinion, Angie's a total slut. I think Daddy's punishing himself."

"You a psych major?"

"Minor," she beamed. "But I'll tell you one thing. She isn't a dummy. I thought she was, you know, just a piece that he could kind of demean himself with."

"You care about your father?"

"Why do you think I want to spare him those pictures? You think I enjoy this shit?"

"You seem pretty contemptuous."

"All I was trying to say is Angie would do anything to better herself. As far as I'm concerned she's totally amoral. And she doesn't give a shit about him."

"Just the money."

"Yeah, the fucking money. Sometimes I hate it."

"Tell that to the maid and ask for sympathy."

For a second she flashed her aloof aristocratic disdain for the uppity peasant who'd dared an unapproved wisecrack. Then she suddenly smiled. "I guess I deserved that."

"So, Hal is having a rendezvous with your father's wife. And he's been enjoying certain other favors. What's his secret, anyway?"

She dismissed the question with a quick sneer and went on with her story, which didn't reveal much more than the 3:00 a.m. version. There was the touching detail of how she'd snuck up to the back of their hideaway, gotten herself perched on an old orange crate and was about to get a look inside, when two kids crawled out from under the cabin. She hadn't heard them because of the traffic noise and they'd scared her out of her wits. She'd taken off, a voyeur ambushed by other voyeurs.

"Then what?"

"I drove back to my apartment. I called but I guess you weren't home. I got some clothes and came back here. Don't ask me why. I guess I'm a glutton for punishment."

"Or maybe you're really gone on him."

She didn't answer. I felt like reminding her that she had indulged in her own indiscretion a couple of nights before, that maybe she shouldn't take Hal's betrayal so personally, but I kept my mouth shut. A rolling derrick revved its engine and a thirty-foot cruiser was lifted clear of the water. We stood and watched it levitate. I didn't know what was so fascinating about watching a half a million dollars worth of boat float through the air, but it was. The kid on the rig saw us and elaborated his performance. I could see him thinking the only way an ancient creep like me could catch such a knockout chick was to have a shit-load of dough. The crane rolled the big white Chris-Craft off to a cradle, where it would be coddled and pampered at great expense.

"Then I called you again and you hung up on me," she yelled cheerfully over the noise.

"Why does your father tolerate Angie's extracurricular activities? Or doesn't he know?"

"Of course he knows," she said with that arrogant haughtiness that seemed a Trevelyan family trait; then she became suddenly human, almost apologetic. "As long as she doesn't advertise he doesn't care. I think it's all part of his weird guilt trip. Actually, I don't give a damn. Half the time she's on speed, and when she is, she'll do it with just about anything that moves. I feel sorry for her," she sighed, playing the insightful, empathetic, superior young lady.

"What's Daddy doing all this time?"

"After all, he is president of a major corporation," she said with some pride.

"Armco?"

She nodded.

"They've got a few Pentagon contracts that've turned sour, if I remember right."

"Yeah, major bullshit scandal. Daddy and I argue all the time. Or we used to. He says people have always made war, so they'll get the stuff somewhere. I feel guilty about the money too, you know." She was becoming self-righteous again and I didn't like it, even though I was on her side.

We stopped at a chainlink gate blocking the entrance to

Pier 6. A sign welcomed you if you were an owner or a guest. A spiral of razor-wire across the top emphasized the point. Sabrina brought out her key with a flourish and we walked down a corridor of yachts to the end where the *Corlinda* was docked.

It was a fancy piece of boat, maybe forty-five feet on the water, with a high bow and a long bowsprit sporting the traditional bare-breasted mermaid. She had a wooden hull and was gaff-rigged, which made her a charming anachronism.

"Hal designed it himself," she boasted.

"Where'd he bring her in from?"

"Mozambique, can you believe? He was in Mexico for a few months just before he came up here. She sleeps eight."

"Sufficient even for Mr. Fitzgibbons' ample appetites," I said, and instantly regretted it. She pouted with supercilious contempt so broad it was charming. "Just my morbid jealousy," I said. "Try and ignore it."

She grinned triumphantly, "It's pretty damned hard."

"But you'll put in your best effort."

"Of course," she said, with her pretty little nose sailing high.

There was plenty to be jealous of, if you liked teak, and polished brass, the finest available audio gear in the master stateroom, as well as the mirror over the bed. It wasn't hard to see why most any twenty-year-old would drop in the sack with a guy who owned such a boat. Even if he had a hunchback. From the few snapshots around, Hal Fitzgibbons had the sort of rugged handsomeness that was always emerging from some daring feat — scrambling up a cliff face, or climbing on deck with a man-eating shark slung over his shoulder. He'd always be smiling with a hint of virile arrogance as he informed you that he drank only the most expensive booze.

"Nice looking guy," I said. "Looks like he knows it too."

"He's confident, if that's what you mean," she responded defensively.

"How is he in the sack?" I said, trying to joke. I got what I deserved: a quick slap out of nowhere. Talk about old-fashioned. She even looked a little surprised herself.

"You want to fire me for being a wiseguy?"

"You'd like that, wouldn't you?"

"I've decided I need the money. I'll try to keep my mouth shut."

Sabrina stood with her arms crossed and fumed while I fiddled with the answering machine. She hovered with a proprietary zeal, as if I was expected to ask permission before touching anything. I did my best to ignore her, and kept fiddling long after I'd found out someone had taken the precaution of erasing all the messages. Finally she stamped her foot.

"Ain't life grand?" I said.

"You're impossible."

"Thanks, I've seen enough." We walked back up the avenue of yachts. The breeze was ripe with sea-scent; the day, the air itself, so benevolent that Sabrina forgot to be mad.

"He's sailing for Europe in a month," she said. "I was invited to go along."

The chainlink gate clacked shut like some hidden hand had snatched it.

"I hope this doesn't upset your plans," I said, and proceeded to remind her about the unique doorstop named Mr. Tunney Ray Mackey. This time, I was determined to get through.

⅄

SABRINA SEEMED TO HAVE A KNACK for expressing disbelief. She made me repeat everything three times. She
cross-examined. She scowled. There couldn't possibly be any
connection between Mr. Mackey and her playboy aristocrat
Hal Fitzgibbons. No, it just wasn't possible. Which I read
to mean she couldn't admit that Hal had taken her in. I
reiterated the substance of my chat with Mrs. Mackey and
offered to show her the pictures of Mr. Mackey.

By the time we'd trudged back up the stairs, her face was
slack and numb. We sat down on the roof and finished the
thermos of tepid coffee. Flies buzzed in our thoughts. There
wasn't any reason to sit there except the sun and the view,
though we didn't notice either. All we could do was wait
for Hal to show. And wait for the man with the pictures
to contact whoever he planned to contact. Sabrina patted
her flat hard belly in a nervous little rhythm, "I don't want
to think anymore."

"Leave word when Hal gets back," I said.

"I wonder if there's any surf," she murmured.

"Maybe it'd do you good," I said and for a second I
almost pitied her. I didn't like myself for it, and it betrayed a rule I had made about never pitying anyone. Pity
was too close to contempt. It was a sign of how badly I
wanted not to like her. "You'll have to clue me in on the
latest sometime." I said. "I'm getting pretty rusty."

"We could go right now," she offered, but there wasn't much sparkle in her voice.

"I should hit up my agent for a loan," I said, dropping the heavy hint.

"Can I write you a check?" She breathed with easy superiority, her eyes still fixed on the mountains to the north.

"Sabrina, we should get one thing straight. If I get in over my head, I have to bail out. It's not a question of betrayal, just competence."

"Oh, you're competent. I know you are." She was playing the double entendre for all it was worth, being seductive again. She wrote out a check and I reminded her she could trust Agnes with any message. She smiled, her troubles over. All you had to do was pay. Every Trevelyan had learned it from the cradle. If it stinks, hire a servant. "Thanks Dancey. I know I'm a terrible bitch sometimes. Just slap me, okay?" she said gleefully.

"I go for more salacious persuasions."

She smirked and stuck out her tongue and mimicked those persuasions that had worked so uneasily for both of us, and for a moment I wondered if she was authentically crazy or just young. She bent over me, and a tiny gold medallion swung out from her throat and grazed my chin as she gave me a kiss. A chaste, almost daughterly kiss at first, becoming more friendly, then abruptly, too friendly, making my blood surge, directing my hand to slip over that perfect hard little rump, then between her thighs where I could feel the damp right through her shorts.

"Go surf," I heard myself croak. I slapped her bottom, but she didn't move. Her lips seemed to quiver and I was swallowing for no reason other than to keep from biting her.

"I like you, Dancey," she said with such sudden complete

simplicity that a wave of authentic affection swept through my lust.

"Go—before I take you over my knee."

"I wouldn't mind," she said with an ingenuous cock of her head. "I bet you're gentle, even with the rough stuff."

"Sure I am," I said.

She grinned and tucked the little gold St. Christopher back into her blouse. I remembered how she'd removed it that first night and seeing my questioning look, she'd explained with nervous emphasis that she wasn't Catholic, not anymore, all the Trevelyan's were lapsed; but her grandmother had given it to her, and she regarded it as her lucky surfing cross. Then why take it off, I'd wondered, but I'd lost the strangeness of the gesture in the larger strangeness of the evening.

"You sure you want me to go?"

"Maybe I'll stop by later. Where're you going?"

"Malibu."

"Maybe it would embarrass you. A lot of them still know me out there."

"Jesus Dancey, you aren't *that* old."

"Thanks for the vote of confidence."

"Part of you especially," she said and again her mouth worked the naive gestures that seemed to know well they could get the better of me any time they wanted. What a strange girl. A little crazy, just crazy enough. And her lucky medallion. But then, most everyone had some inexplicable, contradictory ritual. I had plenty myself. I didn't know where they came from or why I held onto them, but I did.

"That's the part that gets me in trouble," I said.

"You aren't unhappy about it, are you? About what we did."

"No, but let's leave it at that, Sabrina."

She was feeling very bold now. She knew she had me. Her voice purred, "You know I've never even seen your office. And I've never been fucked on a desk."

She whispered it with such completely playful innocence that I had to laugh. She *was* strange, but I'd always had a bit of predilection for the little quirks life seemed to produce with great abundance in Southern California. Perhaps because I'd somehow become one myself.

"My only inviolable principle is not to mix business with pleasure. Go ride a wave. Call me if it's good."

"I will," she said, and somehow I thought she sounded relieved that I hadn't accepted her challenge. What a funny girl, I thought again as I watched her dance down the stairs, her trim behind bobbing above the strong legs — pretty as a deer, the way she moved. I had a feeling somebody was sighting in on her after far different pleasures than those I was doing my best to resist. I wished I could ignore the feeling. I looked at her check, at the bold inviting loops of her signature, and realized I was scowling. Fifteen years ago it was a lark getting involved in the troubles of the rich, but I was younger then. Now it felt like pure desperation.

ᕕ

I SAT GAZING OUT AT THE CHANNEL for another half hour before I drove inland. It was clear as a bell except for the dense air hanging against the mountains like the trivial thoughts hanging in my head I wondered why the *Hollywood Star* had its offices in Beverly Hills. Did the publisher have the city attorney in tow? Did the fancy address scare off perverts?

The traffic on Wilshire Boulevard progressed at a violent crawl. It was hot and getting hotter. I grabbed the first parking space I saw and walked, passing traffic that had held me captive. My eyes smarted, and my body submitted to the subtle agony of trying to evolve into a creature that would run on carbon monoxide, sulphur and lead.

I got to a door that would've been more appropriate on a mausoleum, rode an elevator oozing Muzak up an ordinary glass building and arrived at an ordinary plush suite on the top floor. Across the corridor was a lawyer named Zahn who had incorporated himself. Maybe he was the reason the *Star* was here: a convenient location for a lucrative hobby that provided a supply of enlightened females like the smooth brunette with the dramatic make-up and the even more dramatic figure spilling out of a froth of filmy translucent black studded with rhinestones. She had on black stockings, silky black shorts, no shoes. She had black outlines around her eyes, and another black outline around her silver-tinted lips. As I came in, she made a show of bending busily over a desk papered with photographs of the sort that might make the *Star*'s front page.

I gave her the date of the back issue I was interested in. She got curious, so I told her I was doing a thesis on American erotic folk art. She thought that was fascinating. She said they could always use fascinating material that a fascinating person such as myself might come up with. The back issue was on the house.

"Thanks," I told her. "By the way, they ever raid you up here?"

"They used to," she said wistfully. "Now we're kind of old hat."

"Fascinating," I said and she didn't bat an eye.

"What's your name?" she said.

I handed her one of my cards. She thought I had a fascinating name. Hers was Ellie Duncan. We had the same initials. She might be able to get me an invitation to an orgy if it would further my research. I told her I was the shy, scholarly type, but I'd keep it in mind.

"It's fascinating just to watch," she said, then fell back to her photographs, as if I'd suddenly disappeared. I told her goodbye and she looked up. A tiny lost smile twitched across her face. In the elevator I found the two-inch square of the *Star* that had been torn out of the copy at the Sunset Palms:

PHOTO DISCREET. We Process Anything. Absolute Privacy Guaranteed. 1669 Cherokee Ave. Suite 210, Hollywood, CA 90056

As I fought my way into Hollywood the radio told me it was the hottest day since the record set in 1898. I believed it. One of the many luxuries that hadn't been tacked onto the Buick was air-conditioning, so I rolled down the windows and breathed hot exhaust.

I found a place to park about eight blocks from the address. According to my calculations, I produced about a pint of sweat per block. The old yellow brick building wasn't air-conditioned either. Right up my alley. Another dinosaur like the Buick; like Dancey. I felt right at home. I followed black arrows with white numbers painted inside them up two flights of stairs that hadn't seen a broom in a decade or two. I proceeded down a long echoey corridor to a pebbled-glass door, and met another real-life cliché.

She had close-cropped hair and thick lavender-tinted glasses and a cigarette in an ivory holder. She was sitting behind a counter, sorting mail into pigeonholes. She was very thin and very small, and she appeared as brittle and fragile as a glass cat, although she probably wasn't a day over forty. Her hands were too large for her wrists, and she seemed to be lost inside a green sequined dress. Her voice, asking if she could help, was as deep and throaty as any man's.

"This Photo Discreet?" I asked.

She swung around in her chair and stood up. Her chin barely reached the top of the counter. She didn't appear to be sweating.

"I've got a rush job," I told her.

"You'll have to leave it. They only do pickups," she said, sitting in her swivel chair and swinging her back to me.

"Elsie Duncan over at the *Star*, said you'd be able to help."

"Don't mean a thing to me," she replied, and blew a cloud of smoke as if to emphasize the futility of further discussion. The smoke swirled and darted into the pigeon-holes, drifted around her tiny bat-face, and slowly dispersed. She took another drag.

"I realize you're just doing your job . . ."

"You got anything to offer besides tired talk, mister?" Smoke streamed from her nostrils. Where did she get a line like that, I wondered.

"Not much." I uncrinkled a ten dollar bill and laid it down gently, even a little tenderly, on the counter. In a blink it had disappeared.

"You better be legit," she said.

She snapped out the address as fast as she'd snatched my money. I asked her to repeat it. She laughed a dry smokey laugh. I asked if she knew anyone named Mackey. She picked up an emery board and fiddled at her long mauve claws. It was her way of saying she was busy, that the only thing that might make her unbusy was more money. I decided I couldn't afford it.

꽃

THE ADDRESS I'D CAUGHT, and hoped I'd caught right, proved to be a modest Spanish-style stucco house at the end of a clean quiet street in West Hollywood. The kind of street where the lawns were overseen by Japanese gardeners, where the sprinklers always worked, and any acts of desperation took place behind well-kept facades. The house was barely visible behind bamboo and honeysuckle and a rampant kumquat tree. The front lawn wasn't as well kept as it should've been. There was no gardener here.

I parked on the opposite side of the street across from a big black Cadillac about a dozen years old. Somehow it looked familiar, especially the menacing appeal of the front grillwork. I sauntered around it, trying not to look like I was looking, and then I was smiling at a long longitudinal scratch on the right rear panel about pedal-high. Then I smiled again: the driver's door wasn't locked.

The car was registered to a George Paskus at the same address the baritone bat-lady had sold me. I decided to poke around. I didn't know what I expected to find: maybe an envelope with the negatives of Sabrina and Hal would be tucked between the back issues of the *Star* sliding off the back seat. They weren't. They weren't in the glove compartment either. Just some old maps, crumpled repair slips, two made-in-Taiwan screwdrivers, and a couple of broken plastic forks. I did find something that made it all worth it while. The ashtray was choked with red pistachio shells.

A door banged and a tall lanky fellow, who looked like he'd earned his late twenties the hard way, came storming towards me. He was clean-shaven, completely clean-shaven, even his head. At least he didn't appear immune to the heat; his faded Rolling Stones tour t-shirt was soaked through. He had a camera strapped to his chest. It was a narrow chest, almost concave, so it seemed to need the camera to protect itself. The camera's shutter went off three times in rapid succession and his face twisted in a sort of demented triumph. I smiled. He hit the shutter again. The motor whirred and he had five more shots of a very unknown actor.

"I always knew I was going to get discovered," I said. He didn't even crack a smile, and I didn't really blame him.

"May I inquire what the fuck you're doing in my automobile?" His growl was high-pitched, adenoidal, pitiful. Even I could growl more convincingly.

"Looks in great shape. Except for that nasty scratch. How about five hundred cash?"

"It's not for sale," he said, sounding relieved enough for me to know he'd bought my line.

"Too bad. I've developed a feeling for it, George. It comes from intimate contact. I can still feel it all up and down my left side. Like to see the bruises? No charge. . ." He backed up a couple of steps and stammered, "I told you, it's not for sale."

"Sure you wouldn't like to change your mind? I've got a witness. Hit-and-run is a felony, George."

He did an abrupt about-face, marched up the steps and slammed the front door. I walked up the overgrown walk and rang the bell. He didn't answer. I rang a few more times, then I fished around in my pocket, found a paperclip, jammed the doorbell and sat down. I was relieved that George Paskus had turned out to be somebody I could handle, but I experienced a certain ambivalence about how much I was enjoying it.

After the bell had rattled the windows for five minutes, George yelled through the door that he was calling the cops. I told him to go ahead, I'd be glad to see them since I hadn't made my report yet. After another minute or two the bell stopped. He cracked the door, and as soon as he saw me he slammed it shut again. I felt another rush of nasty pleasure.

"George, this is just a bad joke. Larry sent me with some film." I could feel him listening. "He wanted me to test you. You've got to learn to take a little heat, George."

"I never saw you before in my life," he whined through the door.

"Listen, Larry's got bigger possibilities than you probably know. If you play along you could be in for some real bucks."

"What's your name?"

I slipped my card through the mailbox slot. After a minute the door opened.

"So what is it you want?" he asked, still trying to sound mean.

"I need a proof." I took the film out of my Olympus. He immediately felt more at ease. Undeveloped film was something he could cope with. "How long?"

"Half an hour. I'd have to charge rush. Twenty minimum."

"Too much."

"That's the price," he said.

"How about fifteen?" I asked, and then took the long shot. "And we need a couple of more prints on that couple in the van. That was nice work. Real nice."

He smirked. For the first time he wanted to like me. "We got them good, didn't we?"

"I haven't seen the prints yet."

"Oh, we got them. Believe me."

"I don't know how much he's told you about his operation. We're sort of silent partners. I'm private, got my license and everything. I handle mostly divorce work, tail jobs, you know the scene."

He hovered in the doorway, his camera over his heart, little spasms of distrust flickering on his face. "Well, I never really did anything like this before. I mean, once in a while is okay. You had me scared."

"Yeah, Larry said you'd hit someone making the getaway."

George backed up a step. "He was driving, you know."

"Now about those extra prints, how long would it take?"

"I'd have to confirm this with Larry first," he said. "I mean, he never mentioned anybody."

"Sure, I've been trying to reach him myself."

I followed him through the house and out into the backyard where a flat-roofed double garage stood at the end of
an overgrown drive. Stands of bamboo grew along the fence,
and a mammoth Chinese elm spread a green umbrella over
the entire yard, including the garage. Under the tree a naked cherub held up a broken birdbath. Photo studio bric-
a-brac littered the two-foot high grass: old mannequins, rolls
of backdrop paper, cardboard tubes, unraveling wicker
chairs—a strange collage of decay.

I followed him down the cracked concrete drive and
through a door. I felt my way through the curve of a light
trap and brushed by a black curtain into an breathless air-
conditioned darkness heavy with the pungency of hypo.

George switched on a light. My eyes adjusted and took
in a well-laid-out darkroom, an island of order shut off
from the chaos of the yard. A nice little lab for turning
out passport photos to whatever form of dissipation made
you jump.

Another doorway with a light trap led into an area about
eight-feet square that served as an office. An ancient safe
the size of a bureau squatted in one corner. Next to the safe,
an old round-edged refrigerator painted Day-Glo orange la-
bored away beside a bottled-water cooler—all derelict arti-
facts of Fifties technology.

George sat down at a small oak desk and disarmed himself of his camera, placing it squarely on a velvet pad, a
hunter putting his gun in its rack. He set my roll on his desk
and pressed "L" on an old pop-up phone index. I walked
over to the cooler, pulled a decidedly antique paper cup off
the top, and tried to look fascinated by the bubbles chugging
up inside the blue glass, while I watched him dial. It took a
few seconds to realize why the number was familiar: it rang
the dispatch center for the major paging system in town.

George left his name and cradled the phone with the same delicate pickiness with which he'd set down his camera.

"You know," he said, "I wish you'd tell Larry I don't like to keep doing this all on spec."

"Sure George, be glad to. Larry does get behind in his bookkeeping at times. Anyway, you got the negatives, right? So you hold all the cards, George." There was a silence. A fly buzzed around George's shaved head. Another joined the first and they did a little dance about his furrowed brow while he thought whatever it was he was thinking. His long nervous fingers fiddled with his camera. His head reminded me of a Paleolithic skull I'd studied in Anthro. I was glad he liked cameras. Now there were three flies buzzing around his head. They seemed to be waiting. Or maybe it was just we were all waiting for a call from Larry Loper who wouldn't remember any bosom buddy named Elton Dancey at all. The camera went off with a sharp clack, and the motor whirred the next frame into place. The noise seemed to startle George as much as it did me. We stared at each other for a few seconds, each wary, each trying to get the jump in figuring the other. Then we both smiled.

The longer I stood there the more I got the feeling I was playing it all wrong, that it was pointless to try to negotiate or wheedle or trick. I might as well just strong-arm Sabrina's pictures. Mr. George Paskus wasn't likely to report a little robbery of some blackmail negatives. And if Larry Loper roughed George up, well, all the world's innocents that got in over their heads couldn't be protected.

"George, I'll tell you what. You give me the negatives of that guy Fitzgibbons with his girl, and I'll give you two hundred in cash and drop the hit-and-run."

This really threw him. First I'd been the victim of Loper's driving, then I'd been Loper's partner testing him, and as soon as he'd adjusted to that, I'd flipped back and was offering him some crazy deal that scared the hell out of him.

"Just who are you?" He was trying to act tough again, but the harder he tried the more pitiful it became.

"I'll level with you, George. I'm Mr. Loper's friendly competitor. I don't like guys horning in on my territory."

He thought this over, or pretended to. He was probably too nervous to really think or to come to a decision. But the idea of getting out of this jam a few bucks ahead appealed to him so much it was killing him not to smirk. Then reality took hold.

"Larry'll have my ass."

"He's that nasty, huh?"

"I can't do it. I can't." It was almost a plea for help.

"George, let's face it, I can be just as nasty as Larry. Maybe nastier. I'd like to see you get something out of this, George."

He cringed away from me. "I can't."

"Just tell me where. A neat little robbery. You'll be off the hook."

He reached for the phone. "Get out," he ordered. "You're trespassing."

"Sure, George, sure. I've got a witness on that hit-and-run, you know. Listen, three hundred or nothing."

"Loper was driving," he pleaded.

"Your car, George. Owner responsibility. It isn't fair, but it's life."

His look said he wanted to break down. I took a step towards him. Then I felt something in the room change. The hairs pricked the back of my neck. George stiffened, and his eyes widened ever so slightly just as I started to turn. A faint wind whisked over my head. For a fraction of a second I saw beard, dark eyes, a powerful frame. Something like a curse started to form in my mind, but it was cut short. My arms thrashed upward, following an instinct to leap for his throat. I struggled against the shockwaves, but darkness was already drowning me. Better to let go before he raised his arm and hit me again. Suddenly it was easy. I was going down. Down into another world.

ᆺ

A SOUND LEAKED INTO THE DARKNESS. Smothered organ music came from far away as though it had seeped through cracks in stone. The air tore my nostrils with an elemental pungency. Almost inviting. Thick, hot, strangely like hashish. It *was* hashish. I was in the backroom of a gambling club in Cairo. My mind scrambled, shifted, laughed; then I remembered a photographer in a West Hollywood garage. There had been a man with a beard, dark eyes, his mouth wrenched in exertion.

The back of my skull throbbed. A needle pushed its way in. I struggled against the pain, then I was lost to another darkness. After a time that might've been a minute or an hour or a day, I saw a dim light. Sweat stung my eyes. My mouth was stuffed, my tongue frozen in a Kleenex straightjacket. If my nausea got the better of me I'd drown in my own vomit.

My arms were laced behind my back, my hands numb. My fingers groped, and I pulled my wrists upward only to discover they were lashed to dead useless feet. A demented vulture seemed to peck at my skull, and the world started a slow, sickening spin.

I opened my eyes. Light danced and blinked, little comets shot through a miniature void. There was a faint scent of lost attics. Then it registered: he'd taken the blanket from the trunk and tossed it over me.

I worked myself off the floor onto the back seat and nudged the window button. Nothing. I shoved the front seat forward against the horn. More nothing. Eventually I wrenched myself upright and worked the door handle. My stomach made a fist, my scalp prickled, my forehead broke out in sweat that wouldn't fall. Framed in the Buick's rear window, six gilded patriots marched with Old Glory, fife and drum. The six soldiers spun, faded, then merged into three and stood motionless and golden on their mammoth pedestals. Behind them, rows of history-book Americans stared from the cornice of a square windowless cathedral. The raised gilt letters over the portals read Patriotic Hall.

I pushed the door open and was greeted by a faint chlorinated freshness. Automatic sprinklers whooshed water over the bronze grave markers. A gilt scroll announced *Freedom Hall* in bold Georgian script. Far down the slope a mower chugged, blades raised, the driver riding over the acres of identical markers engraved with names and dates. Soon he would punch a clock and drive home, maybe to one of the two-bedroom stucco tract houses down below in Glendale. I kept telling myself: yes, this is Forest Lawn. No, Dancey, you're not dead.

A stench of stale sweat tickled my throat. I slumped back on the seat shaking, chills racing up and down my back. A tired evening breeze carried a perfume of rotting flowers. Suddenly the pain took me away again. When I came to, the sunset had eased into deep lavender, and the mountains stood in hazy purple silhouette. I had neighbors. About twenty yards west in a yellow Toyota at the end of the lot. They were busy kissing. Passionate, cannibalistic kisses, youthful and sweetly obscene, the kind of kisses that mean you're in love. I worked at my knots and thought, gather ye rosebuds, kids, it's all over too soon. I remembered Sabrina and I had almost kissed that way. Almost, but not quite. It had dredged up something within me. Yes, the kissing had been the best part.

Whoever had tied me up had done an admirable job: lamp cord cutting off the circulation on the inside and, for good measure, some quarter-inch nylon, wrapped turn upon turn. The gag was top notch, too: a half box of Kleenex and a nylon stocking.

At the worst, I figured the security patrol would find me before I got loose. There'd be the lingering scent of hashish, and no telling what other little surprises my friend had planted. No telling at all.

My neighbors were moving from the front seat into the back, their mouths still joined. Dancey the trussed voyeur, the yearner, youth spent. The symbolism was as heavy-handed as the gilded patriots.

I worked and worked at it, but nothing loosened, nothing gave way except my spirit. Finally I rolled out the door and thudded onto the blacktop. It was still warm. I lay there feeling the urge to laugh, afraid that I'd choke if I did. I was waiting for them, my lovers, my rescuers to complete their pleasures. I didn't want them to hurry. There were too few pleasures of the kind they had found. The pleasures that were happiness. Joanie and I had had it. Why hadn't we held on; what happened?

It was quiet. I heard the tiny motions of the car, the muffled whimpers, the far away organ music, the crickets. I saw an arm, I saw feet braced on the back window. Hurry, I thought. *Don't*, I thought. I tried not to listen, but it didn't work. The rhythm inside the little car increased and I could hear her — the laughter, the shyness, the astonishment all mingling in her cries, and she said *yes* Davey, *yes* . . . There was that brief silence when the world seems to stop for a fraction of a second, followed by a long cry of affirmation. Then only crickets and organ music. I had an erection. There I was, half dead, nauseous, needing like crazy to take a leak, and the beast had reared its ungainly head. Take your time, I thought. But not too much. You don't want the security patrol to catch you. But don't separate, not too quickly. When you do, go gently, and promise to come back together soon, very soon. Christ, I was crazy.

The organ drone broke off and a gigantic breath was expelled from a nearby tree, followed by the amplified ruckus of someone clearing his throat. A polished, solemn voice informed one and all that the grounds would close in twenty minutes, please kindly proceed to the front gates.

I caught glimpses of arms climbing into clothes. She rolled her window down, and a faint human perfume found my nose. I growled through my gag but they didn't hear. She whispered she had to pee. Yes, I thought, yes, I know the feeling. The door swung open. Bare feet, dark hair, a surprised face, her mouth opening.

She squealed once, then lapsed into a sort of hysterical quivering. I closed my eyes. When I next looked they stood side by side a safe dozen feet away and gaped while my head wagged and twisted in movements meant to be gestures of good will and prayers for release.

I watched the debate. Should we or shouldn't we? Let sleeping dogs lie. But she, soft-hearted, generous and in love, persuaded, "No, we can't leave him like this, Davey. We can't."

I tried to smile through the gag. They couldn't get the knot out. I tried to tell them there was a knife in my right front pocket, but I couldn't get through. Finally she fished in her purse and dug out a thin gold pocketknife, opened a blade the size of a toothpick, and Davey cut through the stocking. I spat out a pound of wet Kleenex as the loudspeaker crackled out another warning.

Another voice, familiar but somehow remote, assured the staring couple he was grateful and suggested perhaps they had some wire-cutters, or if they didn't there was a pair in his car.

They didn't seem to hear. They were too busy shooting out questions. I kept mumbling that it was a long story. I promised to tell it, drinks on me, if they'd only help a private investigator who'd gotten a trifle careless out of his predicament. Namely, several yards of lamp cord and nylon rope.

Maybe I was incoherent. Maybe the words issuing from my mouth had no relation to what I was saying. Finally, I just gave orders. I told them where the spare key was hidden inside the left taillight, which they could remove with the help of the screwdriver on my pocketknife. Nancy's hand timidly slid into my pocket, fished around and found my knife. The trunk was opened, the toolbox brought out, and tools were wielded with frightening ineptitude. Eventually, I was loose. I stretched. Then my stomach clenched, the world began to spin, and nausea clutched at my throat. I closed my eyes and swallowed.

"Are you okay?" they asked in unison. "You want us to take you somewhere? A hospital?"

I assured them I was fine and suggested we'd all better leave before the gates closed. We shook hands and they got into their little yellow Toyota and waved goodbye. I dashed behind the nearest tree and, muttering apologies, let my stream flow onto the fields of the dead.

Nothing happened when I tried the ignition. The fuse-box was empty. I put in spares, but the engine still refused to catch. I opened the hood, pulled a plug wire and made the long stretch to the starter button. No spark. I pulled the coil wire and cranked again. A fat yellow spark arced against the block. Then a floodlight hit my face.

"Having troubles, mister?"

I apologized, explained how vandals had sabotaged my car, maybe thinking I'd leave it overnight, so they could sneak back and strip it or drive it out in the morning.

He pushed the spotlight away from my eyes, stepped out, and looked me over at closer range. He sniffed the air "We'll keep an eye on it."

"They nabbed the rotor. I'm pretty sure I've got a spare."

"It's god damn aliens," he said. "The whole damn country's going to hell."

He walked back to his car and turned off his spotlight. When I took the distributor cap off, a neatly folded square of paper fell out. The officer continued to tell me why the country was going to hell while I installed the spare rotor and regapped the points. The engine caught at the first touch of the starter and I started to smile. Then I was hunching over and vomiting with as much dignity as I could muster between "Beloved Wife, Loving Mother" and "Faithful Husband, Devoted Father." The man who understood the country's ills didn't seem concerned, didn't ask any questions, or offer advice. He simply waited for me to recover, then gave me a squealing escort to the gates where a devoted fountain showered waters of hope over a cornucopia of angels.

꙳

ABOUT A MILE DOWN San Fernando Road, I knew I
wasn't going to make it. There were too many phan-
tom headlights, too many splitting and merging road reflec-
tors. I checked into an old stucco motel lost in an indus-
trial warehouse limboland, "VACANCY" its only visible
identification. Next door was a rowdy cantina featuring a
feisty four-piece mariachi band. I walked over to change
my last dollar into coins. Getting change took a long time.
A girl with two ruby smiles and four dark almond-shaped
eyes offered a cure. She made the offer in beautifully
fractured English, then added something in Spanish about
a laying on of hips. I told her I was broke. She said for a
gringo I talked nice Spanish. I responded with something
about *la inspiración de la hermosura*. I hoped it came out
right, and I guess it was right enough because she laughed
and said she liked me.

About then I caught the doorknob to unit #8 and hung
my head down between my knees and saw this kid I knew
when I was fourteen that got his head rapped in a street fight.
His buddies carried him up and down the streets of that small
Pennsylvania town all night, afraid his mother would get
him sent up the river again. Around dawn we realized he
was no longer breathing. That kid had been my first body
at close quarters. Death. It registered, but in the remote
way things register with youth. It was still an abstrac-
tion.

The sweet little whore who'd walked me back to my room was really a dove named Paloma. Or so she said as she helped me inside. She was half my height and twice my strength. She got me onto the bed and took off my shoes. Maybe company wasn't such a bad idea, and what better company than a girl with big dark eyes, a full painted mouth that was always smiling and a chunky body with black hair down to her waist who at least pretended I was still alive enough to do the age-old act of affirmation? I needed the illusion, but there was no way. I thanked her again, told her I really was broke, and I really wasn't in any shape to play.

"*No puedo amare esta noche,*" I tried. "*Tu eres muy simpatica.*"

"You want me I go away?" she asked.

"No, but if you stay, it's just for company. *Para compania solo. No amare. Es verdad, no tengo dinero.*"

She laughed. It wasn't just my bad Spanish, she simply didn't believe me. I let her examine my wallet for secret compartments. She looked crushed with disappointment. When she came up empty, she looked so disappointed I told her if she'd stay I'd pay her later. She asked if I meant to pay her even if we did not do what men and women do, and I said yes, I just didn't want to be alone.

"You scared from something?"

"Yeah, a little. I got hit on the head. Nothing catching."

"I am not worried from this. I am very strong, you understand?"

I took off my watch. I said she could keep it until I came back with the money to pay her. I'd trust her to hold onto it for at least two weeks. It was a very sentimental possession. Yes, the letters etched on the back were an inscription from my wife. My ex-wife. She was named Joan. Yes, I still loved her. She was a painter in New York.

I had one child, a daughter, eight years old.

She didn't ask any more questions. Not even when I asked her to take me out to the pay phone and help me dial the numbers.

First I called the *Corlinda*. I had another interesting story to tell Sabrina but she didn't answer. Nobody answered, not even the answering machine.

The next call was Sabrina's apartment. No answer there either. The coin rattled down. My dove made a joke I didn't quite get about putting my ear to her receiver. She laughed and I loved the laugh; lush and bawdy as the relentless Latin trumpeting that ricocheted around the courtyard. When she finished laughing I gave her the number for my answering service. No messages. Next the Star Motel. Felix picked up, his voice wavery with quietly sipped bourbon and the ebullience of Kierkegaard. I asked if there was any money in the till. About fifteen bucks. I told him I might need a loan, and if I didn't show up for it sometime tomorrow, he'd better send the coroner out to the VACANCY Motel on San Fernando Road. He didn't even ask if I was kidding, he just informed me that Sally Swann had departed and he wondered if he should rent out the room.

Then I asked Paloma to dial the *Corlinda* once more. I let it ring and ring, shuddering as if a signal I couldn't quite tune in was spewing bad news essential to my survival. The only brightness was Paloma. She still didn't believe I didn't want to sample her real talents and made another joke about being able to dial something besides telephones. The more I looked at her, the more I was tempted, although she appeared uncannily young when she smiled. The older my daughter got, the more the ancient taboos seemed to take hold. But Paloma wasn't my daughter, she was someone else's daughter.

"You like me now?" She smiled, and I thought she was sad, but she hid her sadness well.

"One more call," I said. County General Hospital. For a Dr. Malm. I felt queasy just being connected to the place. Dr. Malm was in surgery, could someone else help? I said I'd catch him at home.

The dove then told me not to worry, she would be my *enfermera*. I asked if she could loan me the price of something strong; preferably whisky, not tequila. She called me *loco* in a kindly sort of way, and her laugh trailed after her as she headed toward the cantina.

I went back inside my room, sat down on the bed, and read the message that had fallen out of the distributor cap. It was neatly printed in block letters with a red felt-tip pen:

MR. DANCEY, IF YOU PLEASE,
YOU CAN'T SEE THE FOREST FOR THE TREES
STAY OUT OF MY WAY, AND YOU'LL STAY OFF YOUR KNEES,
OR YOU'LL BE STAYING HERE PERMANENTLY!

—LL

The dove came back with a pint of Wild Turkey. She kept saying funny things, but every time I laughed my head hurt. After a while it didn't matter, and after another while I couldn't speak Spanish anymore, but that didn't matter either. I lay with my eyes closed and felt her hands pull away my clothes and when she bent over me, I stopped. "*Me baño*," I said, then crawled into the shower followed by her sleigh-bell laughter.

When I got back to the bed, I told Paloma to find herself a real customer. She said she didn't want to, and I didn't fight her anymore. I let her do her dance. First with her crimson lips, then with her plump little bottom. I asked with my hands for the slow, easy dance. The throbbing in my head began to ease. I felt very long and light, and I was floating inside a very soft, fluttery mythical bird. She was sweet and not too showy. The last thing I remembered was her emphathetic coo when I came, and she pretended to come with me. It was a nice pretend. Subtle and almost believable, not at all what I'd expected.

ᗰ

MY HEAD HURT LIKE A DYING TOOTH, and when I tried to sit up the room started a slow sickening spin. I lay there a long minute listening to the morning rush by. People on their way to work, people locked in, some loving it and some hating it. Maybe I was lucky. I wasn't ever going to make a good 9 to 5 man, never going to climb any corporate ladder. So what if all I was doing was junk films, playing blues at a small time bar and getting old. I wasn't exactly happy, but nobody's happy all the time. It just wasn't a century for happiness. The best you could expect was a moment or two. Like Paloma. Not the sex so much as the sheer sweet surprise of her honesty. She was the true *enfermera*.

Finally I pulled myself out of bed, and the room steadied enough for me to get my clothes on. I went outside, dropped a coin in the phone box and dialed time. At the tone the time would be seven seventeen and twenty seconds. Dr. Malm might just be getting home. I called my answering service. Dennis, who would soon be transformed into Denise, told me, "No messages, Mr. Dancey." I made the same round of calls I'd made with Paloma and came up empty. Then I tried to get the number for Roger Trevelyan, but it wasn't listed. I'd have to wait until nine when Agnes got in. We'd dicker over price, then she'd try and track it through her mysterious sources.

I went back inside and sat on the bed. If Paloma had happened to still be there I would've said, listen I've got a check for five hundred and one credit card with a couple of hundred left on it, what do you say, let's go for a long ride and be happy for a while. But she wasn't and I realized I was scared. He'd hit me hard and I still didn't feel right. I reminded myself that tough guys are at least six-three, press three hundred and don't succumb to fear or concussions or half fall in love with whores named Paloma. Tough guys lived in the movies.

Still, it's good for you, Dancey. It'll make you a better actor. A taste of real life pain. What a laugh. Art. A big word. Joanie could bring it down to size, make it unpretentious, make it real. Still, it wasn't a word you used in Hollywood. Art: skill in performance acquired by experience, study or observation. Webster's definition. I liked it. It could embrace my artist-nurse Paloma who would never be seen in any theatre or museum other than the VACANCY Motel. My quote to Sabrina about being undermined by thought came scuttling in. I still wasn't sure if it was Camus, but I'd read him once. A long long time ago. Now where did that fit in? Everything fits, even if you don't know it, is how Joanie used to put it. Why bother to force it all to fit anyway?

I stopped undermining myself, at least for the moment, and drove toward Hollywood. After a while I wasn't seeing the ghostly double images any more. I was keeping a lookout for a place where they wouldn't sneer if you only ordered coffee and didn't leave a tip; then I decided that kind of place was just the kind where I'd want to leave a tip, so I gave it up.

Coming down Western, I passed the College of Intercourse. Somehow seeing the place set off a quivering in my legs that made it an effort to brake and clutch. It wasn't the place itself; it was Sally Swann. She was one more innocent Larry Loper had involved in whatever it was he was up to. And George, who was so defenseless he'd bought my shabby tough-guy act lock, stock, and barrel. I'd have to apologize. It wasn't far out of my way. And I had a roll of film to pick up.

The Cadillac was still where it had been parked, the scratch still on it, the pistachio shells still in the ashtray, all of it just the same. I went up the overgrown walk and rang the bell, but it was still out of order. I knocked, then knocked again. After waiting a while, I went around to the alley and hauled myself over the shaky wooden fence. A black cat, fat with kittens, scooted off one of the rotting wicker chairs and disappeared in the rampant vegetation. The door to the darkroom was padlocked.

I looked around for something to pry the lock off, then I remembered that when George Paskus had led me through the house, I'd noticed spare keys, each neatly tagged, hanging over the laundry tub. The back door turned out to be a cinch. Just slip in the credit card and bingo. A rare success, but sweet. I was smiling, the sun flitting through the Chinese elm. Life was grand. I undid the lock and as soon as the door swung open my brief euphoria collapsed.

Underlying the familiar pungency of hypo was a rancid stench. The safe-light was burning and there was bleached-out print of a couple in ecstatic embrace floating in the fixing bath. All I could hear was quiet. A deadly quiet, then a muffled, swarming buzzing.

I felt my way through the light trap into the office. It was pitch dark, a buzzing, stinking blackness that grabbed at my throat. I felt out the switch. George Paskus was there, sitting in his chair. I blinked and saw a very small neat hole in his left temple. A dark, dried trickle of blood ran past his ear, down his neck, under his shirt, a mass of feasting flies following it the entire way. There were flies in his nose, flies in his eyes, flies crawling into his mouth, flies swarming around the chair where his bowels had released. A rattan swatter with a wire handle hung over the spout of the bottled water dispenser. I swung the swatter, and the shroud of flies lifted, then almost immediately began to resettle. His eyes were open, his face set in a look of surprise. No anger, no hatred, no particular sadness, only surprise.

On the floor six inches under his left hand was the instrument that had made the neat little hole. A .38 Beretta. I'd used one once as a prop, and even filled with blanks, it had given me the chills.

I thought it'd be odd for a right-handed man to shoot himself with his left hand. Perhaps the mistake was deliberate, but how was doing a bad job going to mislead anybody? In fact, why poor George? Because he knew your game? Because he'd been so quick to try and sell out? It wasn't enough, but then it never was.

The flies resettled on George's face. Even in death he had kept his look of innocence. Larry Loper had to be sick. You can't kill somebody like George Paskus without being mad. Very mad. Then again, maybe it hadn't been Loper. I was in over my head. Just as George had been.

A little quick money and suddenly you're dead. If I hadn't

snooped around, if my curiosity hadn't gotten the better of me, if he hadn't believed my tough guy act, none of this might've happened. Then again if I'd had a little more luck fishing, or if Sabrina hadn't had that twitchy little mouth. . .

I remembered the face, the beard, the glimpse of what seemed an expression of pleasure as he watched me go down, a slightly remote pleasure, the aesthetic joy of a sadist.

I couldn't imagine George Paskus could've been thrilled about this rapping people over the head. His voice must've been even more panicked than with me. Larry Loper was a real tough-guy. He followed through. He even seemed to take a certain pride in his work. And what a sense of humor. Let's drop this guy Dancey off in Forest Lawn and leave a chunk of hash on fire in his ashtray, then we'll jinx his car and see what happens. It didn't make sense. It was pure mad embroidering.

I imagined Loper driving the Buick and George following in his old Cadillac. On the return trip George might've let his jitters get the better of him and Loper maybe decided the cops weren't likely to break their butts over the murder of a two-bit photographer with a lot of pornographic negatives lying around. If he had even bothered to think it out. Maybe he killed out of sheer impulse. Presuming. I was doing a lot of it, and it didn't prove a thing.

The big old safe stood open, negatives and prints scattered over on the floor. A convenient motive: some enraged blackmail victim. Plenty of clues leading into a labyrinth of dead ends.

I was glad I'd missed breakfast. By the time anyone discovered George, they'd have to break his legs to make him lie down. And they'd probably have to wear masks to get close. He was cooking in better than a hundred degrees. I decided the least I could do was to turn on the air-conditioner. At this point, the extra on his bill wasn't going to matter.

My roll of film was still on the desk where George had carefully set it down. Which probably meant he hadn't had a chance to mention it to Loper. Everything must have felt completely unreal. Poor George had been in a dream until the end. He'd died in that same dream, a very nasty dream that had started off as a shabby piece of work on an ordinary Saturday night when I'd had hard luck fishing. On the way out I noticed a strip of negatives left in one of the enlargers. I hit the timer. Half a dozen frames of black and white 16mm film appeared on the easel. Two figures, one male, the other female, stood beside a bed toasting with plastic champagne glasses. The entire scene was framed in an oval. In the foreground was the corner of a television screen with what I could imagine was Hulk Hero and The Arab blurred in mad circling. I pulled the strip slowly through the carrier. There were twenty frames in all, and in the last, the man was lying back, and the woman was sitting beside him. There wasn't enough detail for me to tell much more about them. It seemed conceivable the girl was Sally Swann, but I didn't think so.

I tucked the strip of negatives in my pocket and went back outside. The smoggy Los Angeles air had rarely smelled so fresh. I had just pulled my chin over the shaky fence, when suddenly I remembered George had taken a couple of portraits of me free of charge. I'd had my tough guy face on, and I was standing beside his old black Cadillac. If I was lucky they were still latent images inside his Nikon, which was sitting on a square of maroon velvet on his desk.

꙳

I GOT TO THE STAR MOTEL, put the undeveloped roll and the strip of 16mm negatives into an envelope, and told Felix to hold it for Jamey Stuz. No, Sally wasn't back. Yes, I was more or less alive.

I made the round of calls: the *Corlinda*, no answer; Sabrina's apartment, no answer. I called Agnes: no messages. I asked her to dig up Trevelyan's number. She said she'd need a few hours. It'd be ten bucks if she didn't get the number, fifty if she did. Then I called Peter and left a message on his machine that I had some film waiting at the R&R. It seemed like the whole world was operating from answering machines.

I drove to the marina and deposited Sabrina's check and cashed out what funds I had clear in my account, then I drove down to Pier 6 to see why the answering machine there was off. I didn't see Sabrina's van around, or Fitzgibbons' brown Jaguar sedan. I stood gazing through the locked gate looking out at his boat, vaguely surprised it was still there, although part of me knew better.

I stood a long time. Nobody came and nobody went. I didn't plan on scaling the chainlink fence with the razor-wire on top, so I tried my pick. After five desperate, losing minutes, I made a frustrated move and broke off the tip. It wasn't that tough a lock, and shouldn't have been too good for me, but it was. I was in a slump.

Sweat trickled down my back, phosphenes danced in my vision. I ducked my head between my legs to avoid the faint, and it dawned on me that I couldn't remember the last time I'd eaten. I walked over to the Lair on Lincoln Boulevard and ate the house special, taking my time, although it wasn't food to linger over. I was trying to decide whether to call the cops and mention Larry Loper. The anonymous homicide tip — just what they love. After an hour of procrastination my only decision was further procrastination. I knew it was time to bail out; it had been for a long time. Call it curiosity, call it a certain obsession with completion, riding the wave all the way to the beach, staying until closing. Whatever it was, I could only curse it, acknowledge it and follow it around the next bend.

I sailed there in a shoebox sailboat I rented from a garrulous once-upon-a-time chiropractor to the stars named Herman, proprietor of Herman's Sassy Sabots.

It took me almost half an hour to maneuver around the chainlink gate with its welcome sign for "Owners & Guests." I could've rowed faster, but I was in no hurry. I adopted a fatalistic view: I'd get there when I got there. It was nice on the water, nice to be out with the other fortunates of leisure. Like the UCLA boys intent on ramming that wooden hull over the water. It rooted up memories of when sweat and muscle had earned me a few brief moments of glory. The sabot bumped the dock and remembered glory faded. You can still bail out, I told myself. But the wind had died, and I didn't want to row. And there was the mystery of the silent answering machine. A man like Hal Fitzgibbons didn't like to miss a hot date.

The *Corlinda*'s cabin door wasn't locked. At first glance everything seemed just as we'd left it the previous morning. But the air had an odd feel: the feel of something missing. The mystery of the answering machine was easy: someone had turned it off. I took out my handkerchief and switched it to play. Only an empty hiss. I left it in the answer mode and continued to prowl.

The sink in the master cabin contained a pair of white cotton shorts and pink underwear, both damp as if they'd been left to soak and the water had seeped out. An inchlong roach decorated a ceramic ashtray on the counter. Beside it lay a handful of change and a fresh-cut brass key I recognized as the one Sabrina had used on the gate to Pier 6. I decided to help myself, then I found myself scouring the boat for red pistachio shells.

After a while everything seemed to shimmer with implications, turning into a baffling conglomeration of clues concerning the fate of Sabrina Trevelyan. She'd come back to change her clothes, then what? Maybe she'd run off with a gang of surf-bums and forgot all about Elton Dancey, dirty pictures, and playboys with fifty-foot yachts.

I returned to the little sailboat, glad to see that the breeze was now with me. On the way back I began to come out of the dream enough to realize that I *had* to call the cops and let Sabrina take her lumps. I had an eight-year-old daughter who would soon be eighteen, and maybe she'd want a live daddy to see her on graduation day and maybe even a few bucks to help in the quest of the higher education the Dancey clan had always dreamed of and never achieved.

I checked in the boat, gassed up the Buick and headed up the Coast Highway towards the local surf spots. It had always been where to find me when things got too tight, but somehow, this last year, something had changed. It didn't sit right when the kids called me "Wild Papa." Sabrina must've been a newcomer, or I would've run into her.

I pulled off at Malibu and found a parking spot amidst familiar vehicles. I stepped out and stood looking out at the waves curling and foaming. Christ, time really did pass. And when I was dead there'd be fresh young bodies enjoying the ephemeral pleasures I was already beginning to grasp at with a quiet, insidious desperation. It killed me. I wanted to be part of it. Always. But you couldn't, and maybe that's what made it good. Deep down you had to know that, but it usually didn't sink in until most of it was squandered.

I trudged across the sand and eyes that seemed to have been born in some other epoch stared out from impossibly tanned faces. The surf was desultory two-foot breakers, which meant lots of young bodies, mostly male, were sprawled on the beach amidst the handcrafted boards and black wetsuits. They appeared to be amphibious beasts waiting for waves to carry them on brief liquid dreams. An elite few had a lush female creature to nuzzle, but most had to kill time with talk of mythical rides. Some simply baited each other into brief sandy skirmishes, expending their excess energy like antic puppies. Half a dozen wallowed on their boards fifty yards out as if trying to conjure the big ones from Hawaii with some sort of savage prayer.

"Anybody seen Sabrina around?"

The question seemed to ripple with implications. Was "Papa" really making it with the chick? Who *is* this little rich girl playing surfer queen?

"She wasn't around today, Papa," one said. "Haven't seen you out here. Hanging it up?"

"Got a job," I said, wanting to leave the door open.

"Hey, when you get to be a fuckin' movie star, don't forget your buddies."

"What's with that chick anyway?" another asked.

"If you see her, tell her to get in touch," I said.

A few wise remarks about robbing the cradle fluttered

through the warm sea air. A joint floated my way. I remembered the tempting dislocation of time, how the sun and water would take over, how everything became the wave, the quick ride worth a half a day's wait. It was a simple hunger arising from some primitive impulse to be a part of the world, a hunger dependent on luxury for its satisfaction. I found myself with a handful of empty beer cans by a trash barrel on the edge of the highway that mauled the coastline with nonstop traffic. The day seemed to wobble on ancient legs. I wasn't even in love with her, but for some reason I couldn't call it quits. Hell, who was I kidding? Maybe that Saturday night had left some kind of resonance, and maybe, just maybe, I wanted to see if it'd work better a second time.

ᵧ⸴

THE PARKING LOT of the general store at the mouth of Topanga Canyon held vendors of imitation Oriental rugs, fruit, Indian jewelry, and a phone booth that had doubled as a public latrine. Agnes gave me the bleak news. She hadn't had any luck procuring the Trevelyan number; Sally Swann hadn't returned to the R&R; Sabrina hadn't left a message.

My head was throbbing again. I looked out over the intersection, a crossroads for healthy young flesh. All the cars seemed to share a larkish destination resplendent with hope. I stood there sweating and remembered Mifune as he threw up a stick at a crossroads in the opening shot of *Yojimbo*.

It pointed to a town where he performed a matchless samurai ballet in his triumph over greed and petty ambition. Mifune was prepared for such forays. He had a director named Kurosawa and was one of the few action actors in the world possessed of genius.

I had no stick, nor a director, nor genius of any sort. Only a vague desire and a hand-drawn map. The one Sally Swann had made in that jasmine-scented nightmare several lifetimes ago. If her map was anywhere close to accurate, it meant I was about a quarter of a mile from Larry Loper's trailer. I told myself it wasn't worth it, I should be grateful just to be alive. I wanted to kick the guy in the crotch before I called the cops, but it wasn't revenge that pointed the stick. It was an obvious thought that should've occurred to me a long time ago: maybe Larry Loper had gotten to Sabrina.

It seemed like the longest quarter of a mile I'd ever walked in my life. I had to trudge up the canyon a hundred yards, then cut north on an unmarked gravel road with a steep downgrade into a dry stream bed. I passed a bank of mailboxes sitting just above normal flood levels. A tattered pedestrian suspension bridge hung over a river of baking boulders waiting for rainy season. Katydids hummed. Further away, the Coast Highway hummed. Another dizzy spell came and went. I told myself to forget it, then ignored my advice. I was in that dangerous state, skirting along the edge of obsession. It was bringing me close to Larry Loper in more ways than one.

I climbed the opposite bank of the stream bed and cut down the lower fork of the lane. A fine dust puffed around my shoes, and I swore I could hear my own heartbeat. The ramshackle houses were scattered willy-nilly, one every fifty yards or so, variations on the expendable canyon shack. A few had obviously rambled; the ones spared by the two-headed canyon ogre—one spewed fire, the other mud.

A dog got off its haunches, barked once and decided it wasn't worth it. Further down, a swaybacked mare in a makeshift corral moved her tail through the flies. A billygoat stood in the fork of a live oak and stared out at nothing. Lush green ivy entombed an abandoned car. The lane narrowed, the ruts shallowed. A furious hissing of flies erupted from a patch overgrown grass. It came from a kidgoat, its head wrenched back, its neck broken.

A hundred yards further, in a bamboo brake, sat an old aluminum clad, wood-framed trailer, right where Sally had drawn it. Maybe she'd missed her calling. Sally Swann, cartographer. With a reliable husband, a geologist perhaps, and a couple of kids, a big backyard in a small Minnesota town. I stood there listening to the flies. There were no cars around, and no noise, producing a flawless impression of desertion. The door wasn't locked, so I stuck my head in and heard only the pervasive insect hum. I took a step up, then another inside and nothing happened, nothing at all.

The trailer consisted of three rooms with a chemical toilet in the back that needed emptying. There was no water, no gas, no electricity. A windup alarm clock that didn't work lay on its back on the floor. Ants feasted on a chicken carcass discarded beside a blackened kerosene lamp. On the rear door, a lone, black rubber swim fin hung beside a diving mask missing its glass. A fatally wounded surfboard stood in the shower stall. It was all decay, decay and lostness, and by the time I emptied the brown bag that served as a trash bin, I wanted to give up again. The trash didn't help: the remains of meals from various fast food joints, more ants, and about a pound of red pistachio shells.

I went back to the bed. Unmade beds were getting to be a habit. This one had no sheets, only striped ticking on a soiled double mattress. I ran my hand across and picked up a long fine almost transclucent strand of hair. It could've been Sabrina's, and it could've come from any of a thousand others. I couldn't tell unless I had a microscope and a matching one. It was time to get out. Maybe past time. I cut back through the kitchenette and something stuck to the sole of my shoe. A thin gold medallion. An engine noise penetrated the insect hum, a big engine panting down the lane, sucking a lot of air. I pocketed Sabrina's lucky charm, ducked out the back door and dove into a wall of bamboo.

Car doors opened and voices, low and serious with authority, spoke, but I couldn't make out the words. Then a knock, followed by a demand for anyone inside to come out. The door of the trailer opened. The voices stopped, then started again. Two sets of footsteps went from one end of the trailer to the other.

Finally I heard the slam of their doors and the engine moving away. I circled out onto the lane. The heavy car came backing up on the tear and skidded to a stop. They wore plainclothes, shortsleeved golf shirts pulled over their belts to hide the short-barreled colts.

"Hey you," the driver said. "You know a guy named Larry? Big husky guy with a beard, real friendly."

"No," I said with a faint Boston twang, "but I'm new around here."

"You seen anyone in that trailer?"

"Always looked sort of abandoned to me."

"Where you been, buddy?"

"Down the creek."

He snickered. "Checking out the action at the nudie beach, huh."

"There isn't much," I smirked back, and they both

laughed. The big engine revved, and the car thumped over the dead goat leaving me in a cloud of talcum-fine dust. I fished out the medallion that had stuck to my shoe. It was about the size of a nickel and the thickness of a dime. It looked the way gold is supposed to look. I swore I could feel her lingering warmth.

T HE PHONE BOOTH STILL SMELLED like a urinal. I left the door open and battled the traffic noise as I made my round of calls. No Sabrina. No Fitzgibbons. No Sally Swann. But I owed Agnes fifty dollars. She'd sharked out Trevelyan's home number.

It rang three times before a latina voice informed me it was the Trevelyan residence. I asked for the señor. He was in Washington, D.C. I asked for the señora. She was out. *¿Donde esta la señora?* Who was calling? Hal. *¿Quien?* Hal Fitzgibbons. She is making a bath, *señor*. May she call to you back? I gave her the number.

Then I called back myself. This time I was Elton Dancey, and I couldn't speak a word of Spanish. I asked if Sabrina was there. She said Sabrina no longer lived there. I asked to speak with Mrs. Trevelyan. The *señora* was out. No bath—just out.

On the way into Santa Monica, I stopped by Sabrina's apartment. It was on the second floor of an old two-story brick building next door to a place called *Les Deux Chats*, one of those exclusive pseudo-dives that caters to the monied artistic set. Very casual, very expensive. There was no sign of her van and no sign she'd been there. I made a feeble attempt at the locks, but there were two of them, and there wouldn't have been much point other than to try and beat my slump. A couple of weeks of mail was flowing out of her mailbox.

I went into the deli-liquor store on the ground floor and the counterman confirmed that she hadn't been around for a while. I bought a pint of brandy, refilled my flask and I arrived at the Trevelyan's eighteen-room, mock-Tudor palace fifteen minutes later. Such a modest place made the Buick feel right at home. I wasn't quite drunk, but a couple of shots on an empty stomach had done wonders for my tough-guy act.

I parked on the street, let myself in through the door in the wrought-iron gate, and took the long walk up the vaguely familiar drive. The house had been empty then, the landscaping different, the realtor's sign still up. Sophia Trevelyan had appeared very happy that afternoon, utterly carefree.

I pushed the bell. Her uniform was the crisp traditional black-and-white of servitude. I arranged my grin and asked in my best kitchen Spanish if I could talk with *señora* Trevelyan. She knew then I had been the guy on the phone. She told me to wait, she'd see if Mrs. Trevelyan could see me. I told her to save her legs, I was going to see the *señora* anyway. I pushed past her into a foyer the size of my entire abode.

She stammered, "*¡Pero ella se baña, los perros, señor!* Please, *señor!* The dogs will bite you.*"*

It was only a two-minute walk through a few rooms worth at least fifty grand apiece to the screened-in patio that opened to the pool where Angie Trevelyan was indeed taking a bath.

She was stretched out on a chaise longue, wearing cotton pads over her eyes, a headset over her ears and nothing else. The maid was still stammering behind me, pleading and warning. When I slid open the screen door, she trotted off toward what was probably the kitchen to hide.

As soon as I stepped out, two yapping Dobermans sent me diving back behind the screen. Mrs. Trevelyan bolted upright, blinked and cursed while her guardians threatened to tear down the house. She took off her headset and whistled. The two dogs backed off and sat, leery growls still rumbling in their throats.

"Olivia!" she yelled. "Come here! *¡Venga aquí!*"

Olivia didn't answer. Mrs. Trevelyan slipped on what I supposed could be called a robe.

"Olivia!" She practically screamed this time.

"Sorry to intrude, Mrs. Trevelyan." I stuck my head out. "My name's Dancey. I'm looking for Sabrina."

She exploded, and the shrapnel informed me I was in violation of everything, that she'd have the cops on my ass, I'd better have a damned good lawyer, and so on. Then suddenly her tirade petered out as inexplicably as it had begun. She went back to her chair and lit a cigarette. When I tried to step outside, the dogs leapt to attention. She laughed, smoke billowing from behind perfect teeth. It was a deep throaty laugh, and I could guess why she'd once had ambitions to be a singer.

"What'd you say your name was?" She'd apparently decided to appear calm, maybe even ladylike; it was as if she'd flipped some internal switch.

"Dancey. I'm sorry to barge in, but Sabrina's in trouble. I thought someone might like to know."

She picked up a riding crop, swung a sedate little snap, and the dogs backed off again. I edged around to where

I could see her face. A breeze opened her robe, and she didn't make any attempt to close it. I looked, and she let out a smokey giggle that told me it was quite all right; she would've been insulted if I hadn't.

She had a beautiful body, but I didn't like her voice or her dogs or the way she enjoyed that whip. Even so, she might've had a sort of perverse allure if she'd moved with some sort of grace instead of quick jerky rushes. Although it was as perfect a body as I'd ever seen outside those idealized paintings that appear in men's magazines, there was something unhealthy about it. And unreal, as though its youthful lines had been earned through false alchemy. Even my post-marriage dementia and extremely versatile lust hardly registered a twitch of interest. She might as well have been one of those blow-up dolls with real hair and battery action.

"So you're looking for little Sabrie?" Her whip tapped a nervous little tattoo against the edge of the table. "Just what kind of trouble has she got herself into this time?" I suddenly felt cagey. Maybe it was just the brandy working overtime. "I'm not sure," I said. "But I think the police are going to have to become involved. Sabrina didn't seem to want that to happen."

"Police? Boy, that's something. Well, her Daddy's out of town so she doesn't need to worry." She laughed again, it felt forced and inappropriate, and made me believe Sabrina's report that her stepmother was hooked on something besides money.

"What worries me is she should've been in touch. . ."

Angie Trevelyan laughed again. She was stringing out some private joke.

"Come on—is it Elton?—what a charming name. Please,

sit down," she said, suddenly seductive. "It's a simple matter. You've been stood up. It's just like her to do that." She
yelled for Olivia again and cursed when the maid didn't appear. Her right hand brushed a fly from her navel, then remained resting in her lap. The nest of pubic hair fluffed
around her fingers was just as blonde as the fashionably
feathered cut framing her face, only it had a neat heart-
shaped trim. Everything about her was manicured. She'd
probably taste like lemon-lime.

"How do you know she stood me up?" I asked.

She sighed and shook her head. Everybody in the family
seemed to be reading lines. "Because she told me to relay
a message to her father that she was taking off on some
grand surfing tour. Hawaii, then Fiji. Apparently you
weren't included, Elton. But she's a little young for you,
don't you think?"

"When was that?"

"Yesterday evening. Called from the airport. Said she'd
be gone three weeks. Nice to be young and have money of
your own, isn't it?"

"I wouldn't know on either count, Mrs. Trevelyan."

She laughed again. I figured she couldn't have ridden the
amphetamine train too long. Maybe she went for a bit of
this, a bit of that, looking for the answer that never comes.
But the crumbling was on its way. I could see hints around
the corners of her mouth and in the way her eyes seemed
to fall back into her face.

"You're quite a cute little wiseguy, Mr. Dancey," she said,
switching into her seductive mode again. "Care for a drink,
now that your mystery is solved?"

"I'm not sure it's quite that easy."

Those beautiful teeth again, that strange grin. "Come on

now, you don't need any excuses. We're very much by ourselves. What do you say we both relax? I'm sorry we got
off on the wrong foot."

The riding crop continued punishing the edge of the table. I was witnessing a war: part of her knew that her body
was her only asset, the other wanted desperately to escape
it. The war had caught her a long way back, and it had made
her sick. I could imagine it taking a few people down besides herself.

"Do you have any more information on this tour, Mrs.
Trevelyan?"

Another impatient sigh, then a dramatic pause as she lit
a fresh cigarette. "Our little Sabrie isn't in the habit of con-
fiding in me, Mr. Dancey. Maybe we can drop the formal-
ity? My name's Angie."

"Well Angie, maybe you could help me find Hal Fitzgibbons then."

Her knuckles turned white, and suddenly she looked closer
to fifty than thirty. Her canines perked. Little stabs of
adrenaline worked around my heart, just the way they
worked around hers.

"Get the hell out of my house," she said. Her voice was
quiet, but her body was shaking with barely controlled rage.

"I have it on good authority he just called," I said.

She expelled a sneering hiss and cracked the whip. Before I could move one of the dogs got his jaw around my
wrist. My fist swung into his windpipe. The she-dog leapt,
and somehow my foot connected and sent her sprawling into
the pool. By then the male had its wind back. He dove for
my leg and got a mouthful of pants as I scrambled inside.
Mrs. Trevelyan wailed threats of lawsuits, castration, and
the Santa Monica cops, punctuating her tirade with a vicious volley of lashes as I showed myself out.

※

I GOT TO THE CAR, PULLED OUT THE FLASK and dumped an ounce of brandy over my left wrist, then bandaged it with my handkerchief. The brandy stung like hell and didn't stop stinging. I took a pull, and the warmth hit my stomach about the same time as the front door of the Trevelyan place opened and slammed shut. A minute later, Olivia came out the gates, all hunched shoulders and downcast eyes, her walk a trudging lament. I offered her a ride home, but she walked by, headed straight for the bus stop three blocks away. I got out and followed, pleading in broken Spanish. She remained unmoved all the way to the bench, where she sat, neck rigid, eyes fixed on the space where the bus door would open.

I'd lost her a bad job that wasn't any worse than all the other bad jobs, and she'd have to go home and tell the others. I was one more strange and pushy bird in this country full of strange pushy birds. I probably had some bad motives. Possibly I was a pervert, or maybe some sort of police that would make trouble because maybe she or some brother didn't have papers. She could've been thinking anything.

I used up my repertoire, except for the ultimate slapstick. By then the second round from my flask was beginning to take effect, and my wrist wasn't bothering me anymore. Neither was my head, or even my ankle. At any rate, I put my hands on the grass and kicked up into a very formless handstand. I rapped my feet together and chanted something to the effect if the kind lady didn't allow me to ride her home I should surely cut my heart out. A shy giggle trickled out, then she remembered all the trouble I'd made and muttered something about my being *loco*. I stood up and explained in flowery terms that I was a gentleman despite all appearances, and would pay for the privilege of transporting her home. It wasn't meant to be a bribe, merely a sort of bouquet. Finally she gave a resigned shrug and said, "If you insist, *señor*," Then she added, "*señora* Trevelyan is a bad woman."

I ran back and got the Buick to the bus stop just ahead of the bus, and we set off for the other side of the freeway to a corner of Santa Monica that hadn't been made nice and neat and white. A perfect ghetto for servants, so close and so far away.

Whatever it was that had made Olivia accept the ride kept working. She spit out stories about Mrs. Trevelyan's escapades that gradually emerged into a sort of disjointed mosaic of the Trevelyan marriage. The *señora* combined pill-popping with a little gallivanting, but apprently the *señor* didn't mind. Maybe because he didn't notice. He was always away. At home, he was quiet, always locked in his room. But one night the *señor* had beat up his wife, although it sounded almost as if the *señora* had enjoyed it. For certain, the *señora* was crazy, but maybe the *señor* was too.

I kept seeing Angie Trevelyan's face when I'd asked for Hal Fitzgibbons, the way it had twisted and scattered and become old. I asked Olivia what had happened on Monday, my day at the Sunset Palms. She remembered how the minute she'd gotten to the house she knew it was going to be a bad week. There'd been a phone call from some man who spoke excellent Spanish and he'd asked for Mrs.

Trevelyan, had insisted that he had to talk to her, that it was news that concerned the family. Olivia didn't remember the man's name. I asked if it sounded anything like Loper. Yes, she thought so. Loper, like *lobo*, she remembered because he had sounded a little like a wolf.

Mrs. Trevelyan had talked to this man a while before she'd become angry and cut him off. The man had called back. She'd talked to him again and she'd written something down. Then she'd told Olivia to prepare her bath. Mrs. Trevelyan was always taking baths.

After the bath she'd started drinking. Then she'd called somebody else and had yelled and argued for several minutes and after that she'd driven off in her little white Alfa Romeo. The next time Olivia had seen her was on Tuesday. Mrs. Trevelyan hadn't gotten up until three in the afternoon.

There were too many things to wonder. A thousand if's I could twist into a demented tangle of speculation. A blow-up of those negatives I'd picked up might make one of the speculations gel. I thought of entwined pubic hairs and tired grey sheets and shook my head.

"How did the *señora* look when she woke up?"

"*Nervosa, muy nervosa*," Olivia said, and then she spoke as if to herself, very softly and rapidly, something about the bad luck of the Trevelyan family, how she didn't understand them. She could tell it would be bad, she could see such things, and I was mixed up in it, but I wouldn't die.

I asked who would die.

"I cannot say, *señor*," she said, and again she spoke in English. Maybe her native tongue was too close, in danger of contamination. Maybe she thought I wouldn't believe her unless she spoke in mine.

"No, *señor*, it is nothing. Just superstition. I talk too much. Maybe you are a good man in a bad business, *señor*."

I told her I appreciated her telling me all this, and then I asked her if the *señora* had a gun.

Olivia's eyes widened. "Yes, I see a pistol, *señor*. I am not sure if it belongs to her."

"And this chauffeur — Mr. White? He's around all the time?"

"Not now, *señor*. He leaves for vacation today."

She gestured and I turned left onto a street two blocks long that came to a dead end against a chain-link fence that guarded eight lanes of freeway. Her house made the Trevelyan garage look like a mansion. A crumbling set of concrete steps laced with graffiti led up a tiny hillock, and at the top of the steps a broken walkway led through bare patches of dirt to a front door hanging on one hinge. The yard was full of dark-eyed children from about ten down to still in diapers, only they didn't have any diapers to wear. I slipped fifteen dollars into her purse. It was more than I'd promised so she tried to return the five. I gestured toward the children staring down at this monstrous car that had brought their mother home at two in the afternoon, a time that meant bad news.

"*Gracias, señor.*"

"*Buena suerte,* Olivia." I opened the door. She wasn't much over thirty, but age was already creeping in, the kind of hunching age that constant struggle brings. "You'll find a better job," I said.

She turned and gave a little nod, "I know, *señor*."

"Give me your number, I'll look around."

"No telephone now, *señor.*"

"Then I'll remember the address."

Maybe she believed me and maybe not. Her eyes were ancient with resignation.

M Y PULSE BEAT IN MY EYES and paranoid thoughts of rabies beat in my mind. Of course the dog was pedigreed and pedigreed dogs were free of disease, weren't they? It was nothing but a nip anyway. Still, I'd have to report it. Damn right I would. Then she could nail me for trespass. What the hell, let her. But what I really wanted to do was to forget. Forget the fly-shrouded face, the gold medallion I'd found in the trailer, the blonde ex-singer with the nasty dogs. Forget the dozens of inferences and connections I could make, none which were apt to make me happy.

It was good getting back to Venice. It was run down, overrated and ugly, and the money-hounds had pulled down all but the last vestiges of what had been ersatz charm in the first place. But endearingly ersatz, and it was still home. The wounded beast feels better on home ground. I thought of brandy and Billie Holiday. In a few hours the sky would deepen over the skylight, I'd put clean sheets on my bed and not even care it was empty except for me.

I turned down Speedway, idling along between condominiums constructed to project an impression of instant quaint. I was still a couple of blocks from the shack, when something made the hair stand up on the back of my neck. Another of those eerie notions. Like the one that'd led me back to the darkroom. Which reminded me, I still hadn't been a responsible citizen. I had to call the police and make an anonymous report.

Then I saw a light grey Plymouth of the type preferred by the plainclothes boys, and it occurred to me they were idling directly across from the shack for a reason. I braked and eased into reverse. Somebody in the Plymouth glanced in his rearview, and the car started to move. I gunned it, and the Buick lurched back. I jacked it around and took off down Topsail and halfway down the block I stopped. I heard them peel out, heading for Pacific where they could block the only route off the peninsula. It would take them about thirty seconds to realize I hadn't gone anywhere.

I pulled back onto Speedway, drove into the underground garage of the Windjammer Apartments and parked in space 33. I stripped off my clothes, climbed into the trunks I kept under the seat, and took an easy stroll down the beach to the pay phones on the fishing pier. It seemed the right place to perform my long overdue act of responsibility but nobody on the switchboards seemed to care. After a symphony of "will-you-please-hold's" and two broken connections, somebody figured out that I needed Lieutenant Dmitri, would I please hang on.

The Lieutenant didn't sound like a happy man. He probably needed a pint of Jack Daniels, an understanding woman and a six-month all-expenses-paid vacation. He needed solutions to a dozen unsolved murders, and he didn't want any funny business, which was about all I had to offer. I started off playing it cagey, but he broke me down, and in the interest of credibility I gave him my name. I told him about Tunney Ray Mackey, which was not news, and in exchange he explained the grey Plymouth.

"Miss Swann gave us the rundown, Dancey. I'd advise

you to get down here within an hour. If you do, I won't throw the book at you." His voice had a reasonable calm, beyond worry.

"How'd you get her, Lieutenant?"

There was a sharp click; our connection broke and then was miraculously restored.

"I'd be glad to tell you in person, Mr. Dancey." Static blasted my ear. I asked if Sally had gone back for some cash she'd left in the freezer. Dmitri grunted, his patience already frayed, "You're in the file, Dancey. Got yourself into some clever scrapes. Even tried playing private eye before. And I don't mean in the movies. You may be a hotshot, but I'll keep you staked out and generally harass anyone that knows you. So why don't we cut the crap and get this cleared up."

I liked him. I liked him quite a lot. I told him I was looking for someone in trouble, and I didn't mean to come off as a wiseguy, it was just a role I played for self-protection. I suggested I had as much contempt for Hollywood arrogance as he did, which was probably part of the reason I wasn't gainfully employed and why I was trying to help somebody out of a jam. I needed to pay my rent.

"It's a good spiel, Dancey. Anyway, come down, and if you're as innocent as you say, no hassles. I guarantee it."

He almost had me convinced. "You have superiors, Lieutenant. You can get everything you need from me on the phone. I didn't lift any evidence. By the way, your boys were awfully quick to shoot the other night."

"They weren't my boys. Don't make me wish they hadn't missed. You don't amuse me, Mr. Dancey."

"You sound like you could use a little amusement, Lieutenant."

"All right, we've had our fun. Now tell me about Loper and Tunney Mackey and this Swann girl."

I told him everything I knew, with a few adjustments to keep my list of indictable offenses down. He didn't interrupt. I figured there was a tape running that maybe he'd forgotten to tell me about. I told him about Sabrina Trevelyan, that I thought Loper had her stashed somewhere, that I hoped it wasn't in the ground or under water. Finally, I told him about George Paskus. I said I'd made the discovery late this afternoon.

"And you were just rushing to Venice to phone us, but just as you arrived at your front door, you decided it'd make better sense if you did it from a pay phone."

There was another blast of static. "Something like that, Lieutenant. You know nobody's going to report that girl missing but me."

"It's a little crazy, Mr. Dancey."

"Do you believe me or not? I'm just curious."

He laughed. It was a low tired laugh followed by a sort of staccato sigh. "I'm still going to haul you in. Your attraction to homicides is unnatural, Mr. Dancey. This department could use someone like you."

I wasn't sure if he was kidding back or not, so I played it as neutrally as I could. "I doubt Mr. Mackey's case is going to cost you much sleep. George Paskus won't either."

"I'm not like that, Dancey. Murder's murder. I treat the scum and the debutantes the same."

"You're a classic, Lieutenant."

"So they tell me. They say I went out in the Forties. Maybe I never existed."

"Your problem is you're not the whole department and you probably still do your job, so they give you a lot more scum than upper crust."

Dmitri grunted and let out a little laugh that was cut short. "I half like you, Dancey. By the way, I forgot to inform you this is being recorded. So it can't be used against you. Strictly for posterity. When you're rich and famous, I'll cash in."

"What about Sally Swann? I'd guess she stands a better chance."

Dmitri put me on hold. I stared out at the waves, the long slant of evening light. Then his voice was back, picking up exactly where we'd left off. "I'm not holding her, Dancey. So she's available. Very available by the looks."

"You have anything on Larry Loper?"

"Charming," he muttered, then added, "No, there's nothing on Loper, Dancey. The Swann girl looked over a couple a thousand mugs."

"I get the feeling he's not dumb. Twisted, and sly as hell. I'm just afraid Sabrina Trevelyan's in real trouble."

"Have her Daddy call us. By the way, I caught you at the drive-in the other night. Some motorcycle time-warp thing. My kid thought it was great."

It took me a second to remember why he'd sounded so familiar. Dmitri had been on what was loosely known as the Hollywood Squad, and I'd met him when he'd been the resident cop on a couple of low-budget pictures a few years back. A "consultant," they'd called him. He'd been a very funny man who didn't seem like a cop at all, and was apparently taking a rest cure from real murders by supervising play ones. I didn't know if it was good or bad to have Dmitri rather than someone else on my tail, but at least he had a sense of humor, and I always felt safer with people who could laugh. Laugh and mean it, that is.

"You've been playing me for a fool, Lieutenant."

"It's not that hard, Dancey."

"What can I say?"

"I'm sure you'll think of something. So long. I've got a family to keep happy."

I reminded myself that cops have nervous breakdowns, and cops are actors too. Maybe Dmitri was desperate. Why not play along, then nail me for leaving the scene, resisting arrest, playing detective without a license, whatever he could make stick. Maybe he'd call off the heat or just let it die on its own. Maybe not. My life had always had too many maybe's. Somehow that led to the fact that I'd better call County General and consult the only doctor I could afford.

The switchboard told me Dr. Malm would be a minute. It was a long minute. The wait cost me my last two quarters. Then he was there, hale and hearty. "Dancey, you old son-of-a-gun, you bring back Turkish amoebas, or something more exotic?"

I told him my health had been perfect until I'd arrived back in Los Angeles, and gave him the number of the booth so he could call me back. Thirty seconds later he was saying, "Damn, I can hear the LA death rattle even over the phone, Dancey."

We batted that around a while, kicking the dog as Malm would say. Eventually, I spilled my tale. He apologized for laughing, then ordered me to get down to County General. I told him I was tired and the cops were on my tail. He accused me of not trusting him, and I said I did, I just didn't like hospitals. Then I asked if he minded if I stayed aboard *The White Plume,* and that was okay with him but first he had to give me a medical clearance. He'd pay for the cab. I told him I wasn't dizzy, I'd stopped vomiting, my head didn't even hurt that much. He wouldn't buy it. I had to come pick up the key anyway. He was on an eighty-hour shift and there was a woman he had to tell me about. I tried to beg off, saying I couldn't call the taxi but he told me he'd call one for me, so I gave up.

꿈

THE CABBIE WANTED TO KNOW what was wrong with me that I needed to go all the way to County General in my bathing suit, why not Marina Mercy. I told him I had something rare, very rare, and if I didn't get there quick I might go into convulsions.

"Into what?"

"Throw a fit. Froth at the mouth."

"Hey, buddy, give a guy a break, okay?"

I reminded him it was six months and a suspended license for refusing a medical emergency. He scowled over the back seat and I thought he looked familiar. "Christ, you're a gem," he muttered, but got me there in just under half an hour. At County, they'd seen it all and then some, so a man showing up in his bathing trunks didn't rate a second glance. I asked for Malm, and after ten minutes or so he whisked me off to an examining room. He poked and probed while interrogating me with his usual medical ruthlessness, and concluded that he wanted x-rays of my skull. I refused to sign.

"There could be a hairline fracture, Elt."

"I'll live, right?"

"Probably, but weird things happen. People walk away from major trauma they don't even know has happened and two days later drop dead."

"Thanks."

"Anytime. Besides it's *The White Plume* for a hide-out or the cops'll be leering over your pitifully decadent life, right?"

I accused him of blackmail. He cheerfully agreed and held out the key to his boat, dangling the carrot. I signed. Half an hour later he brought me an extra pair of jeans from his locker and invited me to examine my skull. I shuddered with mortality. Thinking too much had me undermined, but this was worse. There, serenely clipped to the lightbox, was what I would look like in a year or twenty, maybe even fifty if I was lucky, But I wasn't feeling lucky, not even when Malm told me my head looked in one piece. "On the outside," he added, then handed me the key and told me not to worry about the geese or a girl named Leiko who might show up this weekend. She needed a place to stay until she found an apartment and since July 4th was a big weekend in the Emergency Room, it was unlikely we'd be seeing much of him. I could feel the set-up. Malm had been playing matchmaker ever since Joan had gone to New York. He justified it on medical grounds. He said being without a woman was bad for my health. I reminded him that it was a woman who had led to my current malaise.

"I mean the right woman, Elt. And Leiko may just fit the bill. Japanese-Hawaiian, but she doesn't fit any of the stereotypes. Sophisticated, excellent nurse, smart as a whip and great mental health. Plus, she's a violinist. Plays jazz. You two could jam."

"She's got to be frigid, overweight . . ."

"Try around ninety-eight with her clothes on, and as for frigid, when I say great mental health, I mean it."

"Better marry her quick, Malm."

"I tried, old boy. She prefers you wild artistic types, not

us slogging surgeons. Sees us every day with our makeup off." Dr. Malm slipped my skull back into a brown envelope. "If anything changes, any more nausea, pain, dizziness."

"I'm okay, Malm. All I needed was your medical assault. Instant cure."

We shook hands, then he was being paged on a code blue to surgery. As I watched him sail down the hall, I unfolded the fifty he'd slipped into my hand.

I was surprised the cabbie had waited. Probably dying of curiosity. Or maybe he wanted to get paid. "You okay buddy?" he asked and sounded like he meant it.

"I owe you. Just in the nick." I gave him the address of the Buddha Disposal Corp. and handed him the fifty.

"I'm not sure I got change. You read the sign, five bucks is all I carry."

I told him to keep it and he thanked me profusely. We got caught in the rush, so we chatted our way down the freeway at ten miles an hour. After a while it came out we'd both worked on a film called *Boulevard Nights* about five or six years back. So we talked movies and acting and trying to stay alive and half-human in Los Angeles until the big break came. Ray Smith was still trying just the way I was, only he worked at least a hundred days a year. Just as an extra, he said humbly, then listed all his credits for the last six months. By then we were outside the chainlink fence that enclosed a dozen garbage trucks and mounds of compressed refuse. On the far side of the compound the silhouettes of three boats were visible against a hazy mauve sky. They seemed magnificent and forlorn, like beached sea mammals. One of them, a sixty-foot steel trawler in a state of perpetual renovation, was *The White Plume*.

"Spooky kind of place," Ray said, and we shook hands

over the seat. "Don't forget your buddy when you make the 'Big Time'. You need a driver, I got a sure hand. Sober, reliable. . ."

"More than I can say for myself, but I doubt I'd be the chauffeured type, Ray."

"Hey, just don't forget is all."

"I won't."

"I believe you, man. Not many actors I believe."

He drove off and I stood there, stunned by the same aching sense of waste I'd had in looking at the x-rays of my skull. "Fuck it," I said aloud, then walked along the fence to the side gate. It took the geese about ten seconds to announce my intrusion. They accompanied me across the lot taking stabs at my legs, finally giving up when I got to the stairs that took me to the deck of Malm's boat.

The same wonders he performed on ravaged human bodies, he seemed capable of performing on a twenty-ton heap of scrap iron. It was hard to believe he'd been living on her since before he'd gotten out of medical school, ever since I'd met him. Christ, eight years, eight years gone just like that. He'd delivered Angelina and tended her through the usual childhood maladies. Watched her grow, watched my marriage fall apart, and my rumor of a career hit a thousand dead ends. He'd never lost faith. Maybe he was right to try and set me up. I was going to have to get over it. What was that formula? Three months for every year to untangle the threads? Was that what Sabrina was all about: untangling threads?

I showered, fixed supper, made up the bed in the forward compartment and picked up yesterday's paper. The world was, by all accounts, coming apart as gracelessly as I was. Men shook hands in high places and others starved. Trains derailed and peaceful little towns were immersed in toxic fumes. I read through the litany of disasters and took them with the relative calm of a human who's been through the assault for so many years he's learned the dubious art of maintaining distance. Then, for some crazy reason, I checked the obituaries. There it was, in stiff, black Gothic, making the whole nightmare come to life again. So much so the paper rattled in my hands. Here was a very minor disaster I had experienced first hand, and now, long after the actuality, it was hitting home. Tunney Ray Mackey, light heavy-weight title holder in 1957, survived by his loving wife and thirteen-year-old son. Burial tomorrow at Forest Lawn, Glendale. I switched off the light.

❧

I WOKE UP AT SEVEN and sat with the news and coffee for an hour. Then I took three hundred in cash out of Malm's stash and left my IOU. I figured another day before Sabrina's check cleared, and cursed myself for not driving to Beverly Hills to cash it. I borrowed an undershirt to go with the jeans and jogged the half mile to the Rath Towing Company, the outfit with the beach concession. Sure enough, the Buick was there.

I bailed it out and drove to St. Matthew's Thrift Shop and picked up a fairly respectable funeral wardrobe for less than the price of a fast-food meal. An hour later I cruised past the cornucopia of angels being showered with

Waters of Hope, wondering why I was showing up for the burial of a man I'd only known dead.

The guard at the gate answered my inquiry with something called an "Interment Guide." A blank for the name of "The Beloved," rapturous with calligraphy: services were to be held at Patriot's Hall in the Flag Chapel from 11:00 to 11:15 a.m. Interment was in Freedom Hill, row 28, site 14, at 11:18. A blue "S" for Service and a red "X" for Interment marked the respective spots. I followed the map up to the same parking lot where Larry Loper had left me a lifetime ago.

Everything happened on schedule. Cars arrived with what looked to be solid citizens who might be members of the Rotary or Elks. I hoped there were at least a couple of fans who had come because they remembered Mr. Mackey's brief moment of glory in 1957. I recognized Mrs. Mackey and son, a middle-aged woman accompanied by a big gangly kid with long arms and a vicious case of acne. They all plodded through the portals of the windowless cathedral with the stone faces of history-book Americans. At exactly 10:55, a hearse cruised past to some secret entrance to unload.

I wondered if Mackey had planned this little event himself. It seemed odd to come all the way to Glendale. More than likely some slick salesman had helped paint the final view a little rosier, and Mackey had signed, ten bucks a month for the rest of your life, no worries, think of all the trouble you'll save the loved ones left behind.

A big procession of limousines moved solemnly by and stopped at a canopied gravesite within the fenced garden of Patriotic Hall. This was someone who had made it big. There had to be a hundred and fifty mourners. Further down the hill was the spot marked by the red X on my map. In Los Angeles, status could always be equated with elevation, even in the final resting place. Mackey's grave was at the bottom of the slope. Maybe his son would do better. He had the build, but he'd need luck, smarts, persistence. If his father had left him enough money to get into one of the baseball colleges, some scout might discover the kid and sign him for a farm team and maybe he'd make the majors and maybe he'd be good enough to last.

A system. It was all a system. And Mackey's place in it had determined his position on Freedom Hill. There it all was, the green polypropylene mound cover, the burnished aluminum mechanism that would lower the casket into the grave scooped out by a yellow backhoe the day before. Only a dozen white folding chairs for Tunney Ray Mackey.

At 11:10 a pink Thunderbird convertible, just shy of being a classic, circled around the lot. The driver was a classic: a fortyish blonde on the brink of over-the-hill, jabbering over her shoulder at a pair of miniature poodles perched on the back seat. She didn't look exactly like the picture in Mackey's wallet, but she looked like the sort who would be Mackey's babe. She took two turns around the lot before she finally parked a couple of cars away. She primped in the mirror, then started glancing around. She caught my eye and winked. As I walked over, she remembered her sorrow and heaved a highly audible sigh. I asked her if she was a friend of Tunney's. There was a catchy little growl in my throat.

"Listen," she said, "I just came to pay my last respects. You work for Sidney Landis?"

I didn't know who Sidney Landis was, but the name rang a vaguely sinister bell and something told me I'd better not be Elton Dancey anymore. And somehow she looked as though she expected someone a little hard at the edges, someone who would feel at home with the man about to be laid to rest. "Depends on the situation," I tried, and it seemed to work.

"I got something of interest for him, but it's going to cost."

"Most interesting things do. My name's Lime. Harry Lime."

The solid citizens, including Mrs. Mackey and Tunney Ray Junior, came out and drove a half mile around and parked again down the hill nearer the gravesite. They lined up and stood in the heat and waited.

"Poor old Tun," Doris said. "He really was okay. Maybe not too smart, but generous. He always worried about his wife finding out. Not that I gave a damn. Funny, I actually do feel bad."

That was Doris's funeral oration; probably not much less eloquent than the one that was being paid for. Not that Doris hadn't been paid.

"Yeah, not a bad guy," I said and we both stood in silence as the hearse arrived, the pallbearers lifted him out, and the procession proceeded to the grave.

"Christ," Doris said. "I think I'm going to bawl."

"That's the whole point."

"He was so kind," she sniffed.

"At least he died happy," I said, for no particular reason.

They set the casket over the grave and we could hear the distant voice of the funeral director intoning the usual platitudes that probably had no more to do with the man in the casket than what the president says has to do with the real world. But everyone listened, and, for the moment, everyone believed.

"Oh god," Doris bawled, and chewed on her scented handkerchief. "He just pushed the button."

The casket slid down. Flowers were tossed in time to catch

138

the slow ride underground. The requisite handful of dirt thudded on the polished mahogany and it was over. There was a moment of communal hesitation, hunched shoulders, tearful embraces, then the mourners began to scatter. Doris buried her face against my shoulder, "Christ, the big lummox was in love with me."

"Listen, Doris," I said, patting her with dubious sincerity, "I think I need a drink. I got to get outta this christly sun."

She lifted her face. The tears had eroded twin troughs in her rouge. She choked back a little sob, "See, I was the only one he trusted. That's why I got this info."

"I know this nice quiet bar," I said, and she followed me out on San Fernando Road to the cantina where the mariachi band played on Saturday nights.

It was too early for Paloma, which was just as well. In fact it was too early for anybody. We had a nice big booth all to ourselves where we performed a beautiful duet over a mysterious piece of the Mackey estate that might be of interest to a certain Sidney Landis. It was a duet of resigned compassion, but then Doris Daly and Harry Lime were two practical people. We downed a couple of get-acquainted drinks, and exchanged brilliant innuendos over our deluxe triple burgers Mexican style. Doris passed tidbits under the table to the two poodles. On the set over the bar, a golf tournament displayed acres of smooth lawn that were naturally reminiscent. Every few seconds Doris would exclaim, "All that money for hitting a little ball into a hole." Harry replied, "Yeah, there's a lot of money in holes all right. Look at Forest Lawn."

Christ, I was drunk, and Doris suddenly started getting friendly, then just as suddenly she started to bawl. We finally settled on two hundred cash for Tunney's little notebook.

I just hoped Sabrina was as flush as she pretended to be, because I'd just played a long shot. Hell, she could afford it. We hadn't talked expenses, but two hundred: nothing — absolutely nothing to a Trevelyan.

Doris had the book in a safety deposit box at a savings and loan, and she wanted the money just outside the door. I counted out four of Malm's fifties, then went inside and sat in a chair that had cost at least that much, while Doris went into the vault. She managed not to break into laughter until we got back outside. I thumbed through my two-hundred-dollar notebook. All but three of the pages were as blank as the day they'd cost 29 cents at the Pic & Sav.

"This is it?"

"He was real nervous about it. Said if he ever got caught with it on him, he might end up in a pair of cement shoes on the bottom of Santa Monica Bay. See, poor old Tun didn't remember things too good anymore. He got hit pretty hard, I guess. The poor guy thought he was getting that disease everybody's getting now."

Harry nodded in sympathy. "Doris, this is nothing. It means nothing to me."

She giggled and patted my arm. "Come on, I betcha you woulda sprung for a grand, huh?"

"There isn't a damn thing in here we didn't know, Doris. And I doubt there's anyone else who would've dreamed he'd have this stashed with you."

She giggled again, "You don't think I made a bad deal?"

"Shit, Doris, think of it as a present from the organization. This shit is worthless, but you were Mackey's girl."

"Well, he didn't exactly leave me a fortune."

"Hey, Landis is no cheap-skate. No hard feelings."

"Say, you're okay Harry. You got my number. Don't lose it."

She gave me a kiss and a long, meaningful look. Then the pink Thunderbird and the poodles and Doris were gone, another figment fading into the Los Angeles twilight. I put Harry away, but he kept popping up in this funny demented laugh. Maybe it was being close to broke and the prospect of endless scripts like *Bloodbath Blues*. All that and Sabrina's disappearance illuminated by certain nagging memories from that summer job fifteen years before. Sure, the coroner's report had said accidental drowning, but deep down I'd known it had been one of those self-inflicted accidents. And maybe if I'd been smarter I would've told somebody: listen, I think this woman is about to self-destruct. But I hadn't seen it then. She'd been so in control of me, I'd assumed she was in control of everything. I was getting the nagging feeling Sabrina Trevelyan was a lot more like her mother than I'd ever admitted, and that I was already too late.

ℑ

I TOOK THE LINCOLN EXIT, nipped down Pico and found a place to park a block from the beach. The breeze was dizzy with smells, the scent of ocean itself all but obscured by the reek of coconut oil glistening on a host of inanimate bodies. You could almost smell the desolation as the calliope on the pier pumped out its antic desperate merriment. I found a bench and sat looking over Mackey's 29-cent notebook that had cost two hundred dollars I doubted I'd ever recover. Which is what you get for playing long-shot hunches and drinking too many bourbons after funerals.

I read the three pages over and over. Just a list of names and dates and a few figures. Most of the entries were in blue ballpoint, others were in pencil. They were printed in tortured, erratic capitals that were always running off the page. None of the names rang any bells except R. TREVELYAN. Beside it was an account number and another name: D. CISCO, BANK OF BAHAMAS, NASSAU. $150,000, JUNE 25TH—$250,000 SEPT. 25TH.

There was the name of a freighter with its docking and departure dates: SALASSIE BERTH C PIER 27 LONG BEACH—ARRIVAL JULY 2ND—DEPARTURE JULY 5TH. ARRIVAL BEIRA, SEPT. 8TH.

There was a circled notation: AL MERGEL $5,000 JUNE 23RD, 8 PM ROBERT D. LEE, MARK TWAIN ROOM, ST. LOUIS—$5,000 JULY 4TH, 9 PM, PIER 27 INTERCONTINENTAL SHIPPING, WAREHOUSE 11B.

There was a note regarding what I took to be a shipment: ARMCO INTER. PLANT 5, ST. LOUIS BLACK BALL LINES JUNE 27TH 8 AM TO SANTA FE SPRINGS, CA ARRIVE JULY 4TH, 9 PM. LOAD APPROX. 9 PM.

There were other names and addresses scattered from Lusaka to Paris. None of them meant a thing to me, and some of it didn't seem like the kind of information a man like Mackey would normally be keeping track of.

A large orange and green beach ball bounced into my lap and knocked the 29 cent notebook onto the dirty pavement. A girl about ten with two golden braids and a face full of freckles stood frozen with one hand to her mouth. I spun the ball on my finger and tossed it back. She caught it, and her giggles faded into the rinky-tink of the calliope. Christ, ten or twelve years ago that might've been Sally Swann.

People were starting to meander home. I tucked the notebook into the inside pocket of my thriftstore funeral suit, walked over to Al's Kitchen and ate their fried clam special. Every so often, I felt at my pocket to make sure the notebook was still there. I ordered another beer and tried to think of some lyrics for a song about the Taoist nature of Coronas consumed at Al's Kitchen after the funeral of a forgotten fighter. I thought and thought and nothing came. The effort reminded me of the puzzle crowding my head. Maybe I was forcing pieces never meant to fit; pieces to different pictures. The one conclusion that kept coming up was that Larry Loper had to be the keystone. I could connect him directly to Sally Swann and George Paskus and, if Sabrina was right, to Angie Trevelyan. And indirectly to Tunney Ray Mackey and Hal Fitzgibbons. And the medallion meant Sabrina had been where he lived, or had once lived.

You're in over your head, Dancey. Way over. Too many pieces. Now there was Landis. And Roger Trevelyan. What about those pictures of Sabrina that had started it all? And a freighter called the *Salassie*. Way over, Dancey.

I polished off my fourth beer and remembered Beira was a seaport in Mozambique. I paid the tab and walked back to the merry-go-round. The music was still too merry. I stood and listened a while, then drove back to the Marina and parked in the public lot nearest Pier 6. There was no Hawaiian-sunset van and no brown Jaguar. When I got to the gate, I took out the virginal brass key I'd swiped from the *Corlinda*, but before I used it, I had to torture myself for about thirty seconds with my broken pick.

The sink in the master cabin still held the white shorts and pink underwear, the ashtray with the half-smoked joint. The dollar or so in change was still on the table and brackish harbor water still made its lulling rhythm against the hull.

As soon as I switched the machine to playback the phone rang. I let it ring again, then picked up and answered in my imitation Hal Fitzgibbons.

It was Lieutenant Dmitri from the homicide squad. He wanted to ask a few questions in regard to Mr. Tunney Ray Mackey. I told him I didn't believe I knew the chap, what was it all about? He informed me a Mr. Elton Dancey said Mr. Mackey was employed by Mr. Fitzgibbons. I said, "Mr. Dancey must be mistaken, whoever in hell he is. What's this all about?"

"Just routine, Mr. Fitzgibbons. I could tell you a lot more if you could come downtown."

Dmitri was such a reasonable man. He wanted everyone to come downtown for a little talk. I wondered why he was using the telephone, and why in hell I'd answered.

We dickered and after awhile I agreed to meet him at ten the next morning. "It'll be nice to see you, Mr. Fitzgibbons," he said, and I knew he didn't expect anyone to show.

I punched up the playback and listened to the messages. The first was from the Baron Cleaners saying the shirts were ready. The second was from someone named Suzie who'd been stood up. She explained all the trouble she'd gone to getting rid of Ronnie and how she'd waited at the Oceana Motel and how Hal was a no-good bum. She elaborated for some time, then broke into tears. The tears subsided into an odd whimpery sound: a sort of pleasurable whinnying which gradually built into little ecstatic cries. They may have been exaggerated, but it was exaggeration with an authentic base. If she wasn't a porno star, she should immediately apply. Top billing as Suzie Succulent. Very succulent. Someone held the receiver; an auditory closeup. John the expert diver, Suzie a very wet ocean. Suzie kept talking, her voice tight and thrilled. She was thrilled with John and thrilled with taunting Hal; telling him how good John was, indeed, how much better. The words stopped, and there was only her breath. Spasms of delicate whimpers that broke into a climactic wild shrieking. *Oh god,* Suzie cried, *put it in, put it in deeper, oh god . . .* And apparently he did and after a few more seconds of agonized encouragement, John expelled a subdued grunt that seemed almost embarrassed. Suzie breathed one last taunt: *It was good, Hal, better than you could dream of being.* Quite a performance. I was tempted to rewind and go for a curtain call, but the next message had already captured me. It was masked in long distance hum, and the caller didn't identify himself. He didn't need to, that insistent confident drawl with its perpetual hint of peevishness was unforgettable even after fifteen years. Sabrina's father, Roger Trevelyan. Very formal, very cool, very remote.

I didn't receive your call, Hal. Nor the expected draft. Shipment was made to Intercontinental, June 28th. They have orders to hold the shipment until the balance is received in the Nassau account. I will expect a call between 8 and 8:15 my time tomorrow. 202-714-2100, Room 113. That's eleven your time, Hal. It's essential this matter be cleared up ASAP.

I listened to the message three times, then pocketed the cassette. I fished around in the desk, found a blank, and stuck it in the machine. I kept on fishing but didn't find much of interest, except an envelope stuffed with polaroid snapshots of Hal's harem: half of them were in the throes, many with Hal included. He looked athletic and confident, not giving a damn if anyone saw or knew, but with the one female Loper had caught him with, he was concerned enough to send his muscle to fetch the negatives. Why? Because Daddy might be offended enough to scrap whatever deal they had working? Maybe, maybe anything.

Through the window I noticed a couple of klieg lights crisscrossing beams against a clear sky. Another Hollywood hangover in a town that still tried to conjure the good old days when the studios were glamorous factories drunk with dough. The moon chipped in with a big orange crescent rising through the smog over LAX. The beams crossed, then swept apart, shooting up from the shopping mall where the Baron Cleaners had Hal Fitzgibbons' shirts waiting, all neat and clean and wrapped. I had an inkling he might end up that way himself. A man doing business with Roger Trevelyan wouldn't forget to make a call and he wouldn't fail to collect his messages. Fitzgibbons may have been loose with women, but I had a feeling he was tight when it came to business, if for no other reason than it kept the carousel of debauch on its merry whirl. Maybe I played Fitzgibbons so well because there was part of me that was dangerously like him.

⤳

I OPENED THE GATE that welcomed "Owners and Guests" and let it slam. A man leaning against the seawall fence dropped a lighted match, turned and struck a stance in the middle of the walk. Then something heavy appeared in his right hand.

"You Harry Lime?"

He was well dressed, a few inches taller than I was and probably fifty pounds heavier. I put him around forty. Somebody else poked something equally convincing into my back, and his breath slammed my ear, "Or you Mr. Elton Dancey?" The breath in my ear gave me a quick, thorough frisk.

"I believe you gentlemen have the wrong guy." I sounded nervous. My tough guy act would be lost on them. I tried to pretend it was just a movie, that the guns had their firing pins removed, that in the end Dancey the underdog would come out unscathed.

The man in front said, "Well, that'll be embarrassing, won't it, Tullie, if we have the wrong guy."

The man in back grunted. "Okay, Mr. Dancey, let's take it easy and just start moving smooth and natural."

"You guys mind telling me what this is about?"

Our feet fell against the concrete in heavy haste. I heard every nuance, felt every breath. "Just an interview, Mr. Dancey. We don't want trouble."

"You guys from the Chamber of Commerce?" I couldn't believe I'd said it, but the one named Tullie actually laughed.

"Yeah, that's it, Mr. Dancey. As a matter of fact Mr. Landis is a member of the Chamber. And as such, he gets a little upset about people misrepresenting him."

Tullie nudged my ribs to underline his point.

"Who's Mr. Landis?"

"Keep walking, Mr. Dancey."

A muscular paw gripped each of my arms. They were firm but not quite surly, and I was beginning to feel better. They were professionals, high class thugs who had guns but probably wouldn't use them frivolously. They were tools of the trade, not toys. Mr. Sidney Landis had to be big to afford this kind of muscle.

"I guess he didn't say what this was about," I said, babbling in a pitiful attempt to be affable and harmless. But I was hating myself, hating the piece of poor George Paskus that was in me too.

"I told you, he don't like people misrepresenting him."

"Listen, maybe we could make it in the morning. I'll give you my card."

The only answer was a synchronized nudge against my ribs. There wasn't even a break in stride as they guided me toward a black Lincoln limousine hulking in a remote corner of the parking lot.

The slender man, the talker named Tullie, took the wheel. The other sat in the back and kept his gun on me; the gun that had the firing pin and real bullets. I kept thinking how it had crossed my mind to drop Mackey's notebook in the mail, addressed to the office, just for safekeeping, but it had seemed a ridiculously paranoid impulse. Now I'd have trouble even ditching it. I wondered how they knew about Doris. How they knew my name. If they'd been on my tail ever since Forest Lawn. I wondered and watched the scenery go by, trying to look composed as we circled the marina and eased into the underground parking of four round highrise complexes called the "Marina Towers."

Only the successful lived here. Lots of stock and bond money, lots of lawyer money. This was wealth made from wealth; parasitic money that took a long time to seep down. The basement was full of gentle echoes. The private elevator to the penthouse was so quiet I could hear myself breathe.

The room was what they call modern. The furniture was the latest and pleasant to look at, in the same way a perfectly built, completely frigid woman may be pleasant to look at. The lamps were large globes suspended on curved chromium limbs sprouting out of Oriental carpets I figured at a grand per square foot. There was an interesting hodgepodge of what's called abstract art. All very tasteful, all of it looking more bought than loved. A high-class interior decorator's stale dream.

My escorts ushered me to a big chrome-and-leather sofa opposite a matching chrome-and-leather chair that pretended to be a throne. I sat down. The guns were no longer in sight.

Sidney Landis appeared so quickly and quietly that I hardly noticed him until he spoke. "Sorry to inconvenience you, Mr. Dancey." His voice was a soft, gravelly baritone that reeked of power, a man who no longer needed to pull the trigger himself. He was just under six feet and thickset, but there wasn't any flab. He looked about fifty and might've been a CEO of one of the Fortune 500, except he was in better shape. More serene, more vacation time. Crime *did* pay. Paid very well thank you. If you did it right. Just like anything else.

"No real inconvenience so far, Mr. Landis. I'm just a little beat, and I'm standing up a real nice girl." Why was I trying to be clever? I was never going to impress this guy, not in a million years.

"Funerals are tiring, aren't they, Mr. Dancey?"

Two large freshly manicured Afghan hounds came and sat down on either side of the chrome-and-leather throne.

"I suppose it depends whose it is," I said. "How do you know my name anyway?"

Landis let out a dry laugh. The laugh was tight and pitched higher than his voice — an eerie ventriloquist act.

"You're a regular character, Mr. Dancey."

"Too bad we aren't president and premier." There I went again, pure out-of-control fear straining to become wit.

Another polite empty snicker, "I'm not really in the market for any comedians at the moment, Mr. Dancey."

I blundered on relentlessly, "I'm not usually for hire anyway. If you paid a man to make love, he'd probably learn to hate it." Stop, I told myself, stop.

"You're quite a philosopher, Mr. Dancey. Can I offer you a drink?"

I heard a strange voice that was mine say much too carefully, "I've had more than my quota already, but thanks anyway." Then I was watching a large aggressive hand scratch the thin bony head of a fancy dog. The dogs seemed an oddly feminine choice for someone like Sidney Landis, or maybe they were meant to represent refinement in the interior decorator's scheme.

"I think we're beating around the bush, Mr. Dancey."

"You're the one who invited me to this interview, Mr. Landis. I got lots of questions myself, but I didn't think you'd let me in on any trade secrets."

The big hand stopped scratching, the grey metallic eyes held me in a cold steady gaze. All very traditional. Almost formal. We might've been bluffing over a two-grand pot.

He reached in his suit pocket and pulled out a small hand-rolled cigar. I shook my head as politely as I ever had in my life.

"You have something that belonged to Mr. Mackey," he said. "Why are you so interested? I presume two hundred dollars isn't pocket change to you, Mr. Dancey."

I figured it was pointless to try and bluff. His muscle had got to Doris, and she had no reason to lie; in fact she had every reason to want to see me nailed seeing I'd taken her for a ride with my Harry Lime act. So I told him how I was looking for a friend who'd been hanging around with someone named Fitzgibbons, and that Fitzgibbons had disappeared, and my friend had disappeared with him. And since Mr. Mackey seemed to be working for Hal Fitzgibbons, I thought there might be a clue as to Fitzgibbons' whereabouts in the notebook.

"You've got no interest other than finding this girl?"

"I've got my curiosity, but I wouldn't risk my neck for the sake of curiosity, Mr. Landis."

I couldn't tell if he believed me or not. He extended his right hand, and the bitch hound stretched her head to meet his fingers.

"Where's the notebook, Mr. Dancey?"

I kept thinking maybe I could get the jump on Landis, and somehow get out of there without encouraging his high-class muscle to lose their tempers.

"What notebook?"

Landis laughed his tight high laugh that seemed so at odds with his serene baritone voice. "Do we continue the charade, Mr. Dancey?"

"Just a feeler, Mr. Landis. Nothing serious."

"I'm doing my best to believe you about chasing this girl. Please don't make it difficult."

"I was hoping you'd at least be willing to turn one card up. . ."

The male Afghan suddenly started to scratch himself, whacking his head violently with a rear paw. Sidney Landis didn't appear to notice.

"Did Trevelyan hire you?" he asked.

"You know him?"

"He used to be in the city attorney's office, didn't he?"

"Until he found an easier way to make a buck."

His left eye twitched again. His hand stopped working the dog's head. Both the dogs lay down as if on cue. I felt movement behind me. Tullie and his friend. Without a word they gently lifted me and removed my jacket. One of them nabbed my wallet. They weren't rough, just very firm and businesslike almost as though they respected my inherent fragility.

They placed the notebook and the cassette on the glass and chromium coffee table in front of the sofa. Landis made a gesture and Tullie put two one-hundred-dollar bills in my wallet and slipped it back into my pocket. The whole process went off like a well-rehearsed routine. It took about thirty seconds.

"It's a pleasure doing business with you, Mr. Dancey."

"It is, isn't it?"

"If you happen to be working for Mr. Fitzgibbons, I'd advise you to hand in your resignation."

"I take it you don't like him."

"It's nothing personal," he said with a quick wincing smile. "Just business."

"I guess Fitzgibbons didn't give Mackey the same advice, or at least Mackey didn't take it."

"Mackey spent too much time in the ring. It left him foolish. And he had an expensive mistress. Hard to be a fool and play both sides in any business, Mr. Dancey."

It seemed good advice: you couldn't do it in Vegas, in a marriage, or in a racket. "About that cassette, it's kind of personal."

His left eyelid began to show a slight tremor. I was pushing for no reason. I might pay for a few cheap digs with a carved-up face. "If the tape is anything personal, Mr. Dancey, we could certainly mail it back if you'd care to leave an address."

It was my turn to laugh. "By the way, were your boys on me all afternoon?"

Landis couldn't hold back his grin. Like any executive, he took his pride in efficient underlings.

"Why'd you wait so long? Did you think I'd take you to Fitzgibbons?"

"We didn't know. No hard feelings, please."

"Of course not," I said, and oddly I felt warmth bordering on gratitude as Tullie and his partner lined up on either side of me.

"They'll give you a lift."

"I'd just as soon walk."

"Very well, Mr. Dancey. They'll escort you to the lobby."

Sidney Landis stood up, and his dogs stood up with him. I could feel those grey eyes ride my back all the way to the elevator. I was curious what a man like Landis dreamed about at night. Maybe perfect cold blondes to match his furniture. Maybe just business.

The elevator stopped. The doors opened onto a very expensive lobby that reminded me of funerals. I stepped out, and they tipped their hats goodbye.

W HEN I FINALLY GOT OUT OF BED it was two in the afternoon. Dr. Malm had gone. Twelve hours of sleep that somehow hadn't been sleep had left me groggy. The time to have called Roger Trevelyan was long past.

I showered, dressed in my thrift-store suit and walked to my useless office to make calls. I stuck my key in the door and the phone rang. It was Agnes with messages. No word from Sabrina. Sally Swann had left words of thanks but no number, Jamey Stutz would deliver the developed film and prints to the R&R at around seven p.m.

My hand actually started to shake as I dialed the number Roger Trevelyan had left on Fitzgibbons's answering machine. I took a deep breath and listened to the line play its distant computer song. The phone buzzed. The buzz echoed. Finally the switchboard of the Willard Hotel informed me in a bored nasal twang that they believed Mr. Trevelyan had checked out, but as a big favor they'd try and catch him. He picked up on the first ring.

"Yes?"

"I believe you were expecting a call, Mr. Trevelyan?"

"Hal? Where in hell. . ." He realized and cut himself short.

"My name's Dancey. It's pure coincidence, but I happen to have worked for the Egleton Detective Agency quite a number of years ago. You may remember me."

There was a pause; not a very long one.

"Thirteen years, Mr. Dancey. Now, if you'll excuse me, I've got a plane to catch. What do you want anyway? And how in hell did you get this number?"

"Your daughter's in trouble, Mr. Trevelyan. She hired me to help her out, but I haven't been able to get ahold of her for three days."

"Frankly, I don't like talking to you and I don't know who told you where I was."

The cool, peevish voice was getting on my nerves. I liked Sidney Landis more than I did Roger Trevelyan. Suddenly I felt a sort of sordid glee at my indiscretions with his wife; a feeling I had never entertained at the time.

Roger Trevelyan was still talking, his voice still cool and controlled. He was interested, very interested. But not in Sabrina. He wanted to know what had gone wrong.

"Maybe you ought to shut up and listen, Mr. Trevelyan. I've got more than just a feeling your daughter's been abducted by someone pretty crazy, someone who's committed a couple of murders. It looks like it has something to do with Hal Fitzgibbons, which may have something to do with a lot of money in the Bank of Nassau." I could almost hear the sweat break out. He started to fire questions, the old cross-examiner fighting back. I didn't know what he expected, if he expected anything. Maybe it was pure nerves, just the way I'd been trying to crack jokes with Sidney Landis.

When the questions finally ran out, I gave him a quick rundown on what had happened since Sunday. I couldn't tell if anything had gotten through. All he said was, "I've got to talk to Fitzgibbons."

"He isn't around, Mr. Trevelyan. Otherwise he would've gotten your message. I suggest you ask your wife about Hal, and I suggest if you give a damn about your daughter you report her missing. The law isn't going to take it from me."

"Are you suggesting my wife is lying about Sabrina?"

"Listen, none of this is much of my business. I've had my head bashed in, gotten hit by a car, threatened by some very smooth thugs, and I don't know why I bother. Your attitude stinks, and I'm mad enough to cause you a couple of problems more serious than mere embarrassment. There's a tape-recorded message, for instance. Your name in a certain notebook for another. If you care to believe Sabrina's surfing in Fiji I guess that's up to you. More than likely she's in the same place Hal is. Maybe some canyon or stretch of desert or deserted beach. This isn't a joke and it isn't a shakedown. There's nothing in it for me other than some peace of mind in the knowledge that somebody cares enough to help get her out of the trouble she's in."

There was a long pause filled with a faint hum of voices. Trevelyan cleared his throat. I had to give him points for poise. A very big deal had probably just been shot to hell, and he had to have at least vestiges of paternal concern, no matter how deeply buried.

"Listen, Mr. Dancey. If you keep this quiet and if you find her, I'll make it worth your while."

I didn't answer.

"How much do you want? A thousand? Ten thousand?"

"How about twenty?" I said, just to see what he'd say. There was another pause.

"I think that can be arranged."

"How do I know your check's good?"

"Okay you've made your point. There's a nonstop in about an hour, it arrives at 6:15. I'll take a cab, call you as soon as I get home. Tomorrow we can go to my bank." I wished I could see his face. Lawyers like Trevelyan lied so well they could even slip one past themselves. "Dancey, I've got to go if I'm going to make that flight."

"Just a minute, Mr. Trevelyan. You know anyone named Loper, Larry Loper?"

He didn't answer right off. I could hear his breath, short, quick, erratic. A man with tightness in his chest, a man wracked by guilt and greed.

"Ring any bells?"

"Nothing."

"Is there anyone who might want to get at you?"

"I could fill the Manhattan directory."

"Didn't you have a son?"

He hesitated, and his voice seemed to crack, "Matthew's gone," he said. "MIA in Laos. Years ago. Many years. Now if you don't mind."

"If I don't hear from you by seven Mr. Trevelyan, I'm going to start getting nervous."

"Don't worry, I'll be there. Just hold your horses, Dancey. Please."

"One more thing. Your daughter has some sort of trust fund. Maybe somebody's after that."

"That trust was left by my former wife. I've got nothing to do . . ."

"Come on, Mr. Trevelyan. We're supposed to be co-operating. We're trying to help Sabrina, remember?"

"Call a lawyer named Ronald Doak. In the Roosevelt building, downtown."

"Thanks."

The connection broke. The receiver was slippery with sweat. I'd done a good job with Roger Trevelyan, gotten a few personal jollies. Somehow it didn't matter.

❧

NATURALLY RONALD D. DOAK, Attorney at Law, was out with a client. Could he return my call? I stated the urgent nature of my business. Mr. Doak had a brilliant receptionist, just enough snip and sass to discourage without being rude. I was straining. "Listen, I don't give a damn what his orders are, I'll be down there in half an hour and see if he's out."

"Goodbye, Mr. Dancey," she sang, and hung up very gently.

I waited a few minutes, stopped spitting curses, called back and managed to tell her without yelling that I'd keep calling back all day.

"Mr. Doak will speak with you now," she said with perfect equanimity.

He announced himself with a voice so slickly polite it could've greased most any judge right off the bench. He was oh-so-understanding of my predicament and the urgency of the situation, but unfortunately his hands were tied.

"Okay, Mr. Doak. Let's do it the hard way. Let me play the insistent little investigator. Let me inconvenience your phone and do burlesque in your office. Better yet, the homicide boys have a talk with you when Sabrina turns up in the morgue. Maybe they'll let you break the news to her father."

"You're telling me you're working for Roger Trevelyan?"

I hedged, "He's the man signing the check, Mr. Doak."

There was one of those pauses fraught with the busy whirrings of professional evasiveness.

"You understand this is highly irregular, Mr. Dancey."

I decided to play a long shot, "So is extortion. It didn't surprise you when she suddenly shows up on her birthday and wants the whole damn wad? You want the cops bustling around your office?"

The long shot worked. "You knew all along."

"Exactly when did she come in, Mr. Doak?"

"Tuesday afternoon about one-thirty."

"And there was somebody with her, a guy in his late thirties, six foot, a beard?"

"No beard," he said.

"Did he say anything?"

"He introduced himself as Lawrence Jaspers. He claimed he was an art dealer."

"Did Sabrina say anything?"

"Just that she was going to Europe, something to do with buying some old paintings. That's why she wanted the money. She seemed to know what she was doing."

"She didn't seem nervous?"

"She was in rather a hurry, Mr. Dancey. The papers were waiting, and I only saw her for two or three minutes altogether."

Doak paused. I was pumping a reluctant well. I was tired, losing my concentration, and my private investigator act was ragged at the edges. In fact, it was falling apart.

"So where'd she go to pick up the money?"

"The trust department of Great Western."

"How much?"

"$25,000. Now Mr. Dancey. . ."

"Pistachios," I said.

"What?"

"Was he eating pistachio nuts?"

"Yes, as a matter of fact. Now I'm really going to have to say good-bye. I've a very important client."

Something vile tried to gallop up my throat and into the plush, remote importance of Mr. Doak's ear.

"If it's any consolation, Mr. Doak, the man Jaspers fits the description of a guy wanted for a couple of murders. You might be helping keep the body count down. So thanks, Mr. Doak. You're a man of infinite grace. Truly infinite." I hung up. Dr. Malm was right, I didn't like much of the world, and it was burning holes in my gut. So Dancey, start liking it, or turn the blind eye, or go ride a wave breaking on a remote tropical shore, say Samoa or Tonga. . .

I scavenged the refrigerator and came up with a half pint of blueberry yoghurt and two slices of salami. I had the feeling that Larry Loper hadn't appeared arbitrarily out of the blue after all. He was someone who'd known the Trevelyans for a long time and had a grip on their strings. I kept seeing Olivia's face when she was talking about bad luck. Maybe it was all just superstition, but she didn't believe that it was and neither did I.

No, Larry Loper wasn't out of the blue, and he was far more clever and far crazier than I'd given him credit for. I racked my brain to figure what he held over Sabrina sufficient to make her hand over twenty-five thousand dollars. It had to be more than just the pictures of her and Hal. Then again, maybe not. Maybe $25,000 didn't mean that much to her. Maybe deep down she wanted to be the good little girl in Daddy's eyes.

I couldn't help thinking how twenty-five grand would set Olivia and her family up for life. Or it could just buy some dirty snapshots. Or it might end up nowhere. I punched up the Trevelyan's Santa Monica number and a female voice with an easy drawl that shrugged off the weight of the world answered on the fourth ring. With a subtle hint of satire it announced, "Yes, this here's the Trevelyan estate."

"Mrs. Trevelyan there?"

"No, she ain't here, and I got no idea when she be back."

"I've got to leave a message. This is Hal Fitzgibbons. . ."

"Hold your horses, Mr. Fitzgibbons. Got to find me a pencil."

She was a long time finding the pencil, and she had me spell out Hal Fitzgibbons and *Corlinda* letter by letter. I said I'd be on the boat from eight o'clock on. It was essential that Mrs. Trevelyan call. "Okay, Mr. Fitzgibbons. I'll leave it somewhere she be sure to find it. I take off at six no matter."

"Did she take the dogs?" I asked.

"Them mean hounds? I wish."

"You sure she's not there?"

"Listen, mister, I got no reason to lie. I'm strictly temporary."

"That might not be a bad idea."

"You tellin' *me*? This is one crazy house."

The line clicked dead. A double set of footsteps hit the stairs and sent little quivers through the floor. I eased the receiver into the cradle and eased myself to the door. The peephole gave a nice wide-angle shot of a pair of clean-cut mugs meaning business. In the harbor behind them, sailboats meandered back and forth in the late afternoon light.

I slunk to the far corner and sank into the old overstuffed sofa where they couldn't get a glimpse of me through the mail slot. They knocked and waited. They announced themselves as the law. Maybe they were official law or maybe some other kind. I slunk down further.

One of them walked out onto the roof and tried to peer around the avocado window shade with the silly black fringe on the bottom. The other one rattled the doorknob.

I closed my eyes. My left eyelid trembled. Not so different from the tic I'd seen on Landis. We both paid the dues. Two egotists, each with his microcosmic kingdom. Mine was dirtier, crawling with liabilities, but sometimes it danced and almost seemed alive. Or maybe that was illusion too.

I hoped it was just a question of waiting them out, but there wasn't much choice. I twiddled my thumbs, I tried not to think, I avoided glancing at the photograph of Angelina sitting on the desk. Finally the men went away. It was 6:25 p.m.

꙳

THERE DIDN'T SEEM TO BE ANY REASON to move, so I just kept sitting there in the corner. If I was lucky, Roger Trevelyan might be getting his luggage and hailing a cab. It would still be an hour before I might get even luckier and have a shot at worming out of him why a shipment of something from Armco Plant #5 was worth so much to so damn many people. And why his own daughter might be in the way.

It would've been nice to have an ear with a live human attached. Someone who'd listen and nod and pat Dancey on the head and say, poor dumb sap, it's okay, you're just slow, old boy, a real slow learner, just like your daddy.

I finally dragged myself up and let the sun in under the cut-rate avocado window shade. A stream of light fell on the picture of Angelina, caught mid-stride, her hair flung out by the seebreeze, a wave just curling behind her, her feet above the sand, the toes reaching, a trail of footprints fading behind her. There wasn't much of me in her except the eyes. Intense and dark, not like her mother's which were full of capricious light and color. I said a brief prayer; not a very religious one. It wasn't addressed to any particular deity. It was a sort of general request to whatever was out there that Angelina's eyes might not have to see the same world mine did. I called downtown. Lieutenant Dmitri picked up, working late as usual. Perhaps saying some prayers of his own, maybe asking that the boys in the grey Plymouth would deliver me with my hands behind my back. We dispensed with the growling banter and I spilled how the Mackey case had suddenly been adorned with a number of interesting sidelights: extortion, kidnapping, throw in possible hijacking, and maybe an international arms deal. I told him it might earn him a raise, but he didn't even snicker.

"Dancey, let's get serious."

"I am, Lieutenant. How'd you get caught anyway?"

"What do you mean caught?"

"Being a cop."

"I forget. What's it to you?"

"Maybe I'll get to play a cop sometime. A smart one."

There was a weary grunt. "You never get us right anyway."

"People don't want it right. Even if they did, the producers wouldn't or the directors or even most of the writers. No money in it. Getting it right scares people."

"So, what do you say we get down to business and scare little old you and little old me."

"We ought to get drunk sometime, Lieutenant."

"Let's hear it, Dancey. About the Trevelyan girl and this Loper character and extortion, I need something juicy."

I gave him what I had about Doak and Sabrina and her escort named Jaspers who was Larry Loper in his latest guise. Even the psychopaths were actors these days, along with the CEOs of the semi-legal syndicates. I wondered if even Dmitri had a bit of the ham in him—'something juicy,' he'd said, and I gave it to him, though hardly believing it myself. I told him about Hal Fitzgibbons and Roger Trevelyan. I told him to check out a darkroom at an address in West Hollywood, where the key to the padlocked door was hanging in the back hall over the washtubs.

"You mean George Paskus. We got him. You already told me, remember?" He sounded as though he were waking from a long sleep.

"Yeah, I remember. Sorry Lieutenant, I'm a little fuzzy."

"Happening so fast you can't keep track, huh, Dancey? Can't remember what you told who—or is that whom?"

"I got hit on the head, Lieutenant. How do you put it together?"

He laughed. It was a low, tired laugh that broke into an equally weary sigh. Finally he said, "We've got to get ahold of how Loper fits into this. Who is he and what's running him?"

"Maybe he's just another crazy who thinks he's doing noble deeds."

"We've got to nab him to find out." I decided I had to tell him. "You may have a chance, Lieutenant. Tomorrow night at nine, Pier 27, Warehouse 11B, Long Beach. Fitzgibbons was supposed to meet somebody who'll probably be driving a rig full of automatic weapons."

I could almost feel Dmitri doing a slow burn. "Yeah? So where'd you get this one?" I didn't say anything. "Your problem, Dancey, is you think all cops are alike, and they bungle everything."

"What's in it for me?" I asked.

"Okay, I'll pull the heat."

It was worth it, and there was no reason not to tell him anyway. I sketched out the Doris Daley episode, and the sequel starring Sidney Landis. When I'd finished, Dmitri's voice came in an exhausted rasp. "So you're implying Landis might have some shadowy representatives?"

"You got anything on him?"

"We can't touch him. We suspect, hell, we *know*, but it's the hard evidence. He slips it. Just like Teflon."

"Part of the job requirements, Lieutenant. You get that big, you acquire a Teflon coat."

"Sure, I'm working on one myself. Was Landis alone, or has his partner resurfaced?"

"I didn't know he had one."

"Well, let's say associate. Guy by the name of Harlan Flannery or O'Flannery. Smart, good-looking guy about thirty-five. Con artist, businessman, womanizer, charmer of many talents. We almost nailed him. He had a nice, lucrative cocaine airline between Lima and LA before it got popular."

"What happened? Deregulation?"

Dmitri cleared his throat. "Funny as hell, Dancey."

"I'm serious. I'd like to know why he quit."

"Who knows, it got hot and he disappeared. Apparently he skipped the country with plenty in a numbered account."

"So it's conceivable he took a sabbatical in Zimbabwe?"

"Sure, why not?" He sighed another long weary sigh.

"You sound tired, Lieutenant."

"I've only been up since six. It's past my suppertime. I'm trusting you not to make a fool out of me, Dancey. Pier 27, Warehouse 11B, nine tomorrow. Christ, it's the Fourth."

"Think of it as the spirit of independence."

He expressed his appreciation of my humor by hanging up. I began wondering if he really existed, this frustrated man in an office with a file cabinet full of slime; this man who'd gotten fascinated with a job because maybe he'd seen it as a chance to do some good. Maybe he'd seen it in some personal light, then discovered that light didn't illuminate a thing. He might be bucking for early retirement or the funny farm. I hoped he didn't have a big family. I hoped he owned some good stocks, or a secret patent. I hoped he found a way to stay honest and still make a living.

ン

THE CLOCK TURNED and I watched, waiting for the telephone to ring with news of how to put the pieces together. None of it felt real any more, and I wondered if it ever had. It was like that plunge into unreality that happened in a film. The whole world got to be a movie. Now the world had become finding Sabrina Trevelyan, and I knew I would've done it even if her father hadn't offered me a cent. I no longer knew or cared why it was important. It was like the role you took that seemed completely natural at the start, that begins to unravel as the weeks wear on and exhaustion sets in. But you kept on, you'd keep on even if they stopped paying you.

I searched through the pint-sized refrigerator next to my desk and found a semi-petrified grapefruit I'd missed in a back corner. I managed to remove about a quarter of the peel before running out of ambition. I set it down on the blotter and stared at it. I called the morgue and pretended to be Lieutenant Dmitri. I had him down pat, and it kind of made my day.

A cordial lady who didn't sound dead, just faintly dragged-out, ran through the roster. There was no Hal Fitzgibbons, no Sabrina Trevelyan. There were three John Does that were possibilities. One was in his late thirties or early forties and had died of gunshot wounds to the head. He'd turned up in Latigo Canyon. He was relatively fresh.

There was only one Jane Doe young enough to be Sabrina. She'd died of multiple knife wounds and had washed up in Malibu. I asked how long they figured she'd been in the water and when she told me a week to ten days, I breathed a sigh of relief.

I hung up and the grapefruit told me I was in a bad way. I needed a drink. I measured a timid shot and started calling airlines to see who had a 6:15 flight due from DC. I got it on the third try. The flight had arrived right on time at 6:23.

I called the Trevelyan house and nobody answered. I watched the clock again. It was close to eight. Where in hell had Trevelyan gone? Why hadn't he called? I picked up the grapefruit and set it back down. I called the Trevelyan house again. I let it ring once, hung up, then called back.

This time someone picked up. I waited. Whoever was

there waited. After a minute of silence, I said, "Is that you, Mr. Trevelyan?"

The connection broke.

I called back and did the single ring trick again. Nobody fell for it, so I made one last try. I called Agnes and told her if a man named Trevelyan called, to make sure he called the *Corlinda*, that I'd be there for the next hour.

"Anyone chasing you, Mr Dancey?" Agnes always smelled trouble a mile away.

"A couple of shady dreams. Nothing to worry about."

"Someday they're going to lock you up."

"In a little pine box. And you'll still be sitting on your millions."

"Ah, shush," she said, and I was alone again with a dead telephone in my hand. I locked the office and realized I still hadn't gotten around to taking down the brass "Phoenix Productions" sign. There were shapes running peacefully through the harbor. Far beyond the twinkle of lights on the Santa Monica mountains a glittery stream marked the freeway over the pass. I stuck the key in the gate to Pier 6 and noticed there was a view to the penthouse suite in Marina Tower 4. Sidney Landis could watch anyone come and go. As I walked down the pier, it felt like a jaunt I'd been making for years. It was dead quiet except for the soft slap of water and a occasional halyard striking an aluminum mast.

A quick inspection of the *Corlinda* told me nothing had been disturbed. I turned the answering machine to playback. The Baron Cleaners reiterated their message about laundry being ready. They said it would be held for thirty days before it was sent to the Midnight Mission. All I could think was a month from now somebody was going to be spilling cheap wine on some expensive hand-tailored shirts.

❧

I T WAS ALMOST TWELVE by the time I parked on a side street three blocks from the Trevelyan's wrought-iron gates. I'd called the house for two hours, and gotten nothing but a busy signal. Then I'd armed myself with a few shots of brandy and $3.49 worth of ground beef liberally laced with tranquilizers, courtesy of Dr. Malm.

The two wads of ground meat made obscene bulges in my side pockets. My inside pocket was stuffed with a dozen 5 x 7's folded lengthwise. The photos were grainy, and a bit out of focus but somehow sordidly appropriate. I took out the flask and uncapped it, but put it back without taking a drink. I got out and started walking.

The fog hadn't reached this far inland, only the anticipatory chill. A block from the Trevelyan place, a private patrol car cruised by, its spotlight flicking over dark windows. I waited for it to pass, crossed Channel Road and peered between the bars up the long drive. The house sat like a cardboard set in the diffused streetlight. Pausing for a brief second, I reminded myself I didn't love her, this wasn't a movie, I'd never see a penny of Roger Trevelyan's money. Then I rattled the door in the gate and the two dobermans came bellowing around a corner of the house, terrifyingly three-dimensional. I heaved the packages of meat like live grenades. The dogs froze for a few seconds, confused between the duty to guard and the call of the meat twenty-five yards up the drive. Then they went for it.

I walked back to the Buick. In fifteen minutes, if it worked the way Malm had said, the two dogs would be dreaming dog dreams for at least six hours. I pulled out the flask and took a long pull. Then another. Enough, I said aloud. Then I took one more.

Twenty minutes later I rattled the gates again, and no dogs appeared. I rattled some more, and when there was still no response I walked west along a brick wall. It was about ten feet high, well grown over with ivy and sheltered by a line of tall eucalyptus. I'd gone about fifty yards when the fog draped a damp blanket into my lungs. I waited and listened, then leapt and caught the top of the wall. I pulled myself up and sat there: no dogs, nothing but fog-dampened silence. I put on my gloves and dropped.

There were two lights in a rear wing of the house, one on the first, another on the second floor. The swimming pool glowed an eerie green. I was headed toward the back door; the house suddenly vanished. I stumbled around for what seemed an eternity before I found it. Through the window I could make out a vestibule lined with cupboards, and beyond that the kitchen, illuminated only by a small light on the stove. For five agonizing minutes I worked at the lock with my pick. Finally, I gave up and walked around to the sliding door I'd used when I'd caught Angie Trevelyan in the midst of her poolside meditations. This lock was in my league: a simple catch any kid could jimmy by his fourth birthday.

The silence inside was full of vague noise, as if the house was short of breath and trying not to show it. I walked around until I found the door that had defeated me. I turned the lock open and unhooked the little brass door chain.

No smell of cooking lingered in the kitchen. Everything

was put away. Not even a glass in the sink. The clock on the stove read 12:25.

I heard a faint electronic bleating. The receiver of a white wall phone dangled against the wall. I held the button to remake the connection, but the line stayed busy.

Down a hall in the main dining room the lights were on. The room had a wide entrance way with sliding doors open about a foot. I poked my head in and something screamed, and I slammed myself back against the wall, my heart jumping in my throat. I smiled. A coward and a fool. But I didn't feel drunk anymore, not in the least.

It stood, one leg chained to a perch in a rock garden that sported a miniature waterfall. The bird kept on screaming: *"Hello . . . hello . . . hello . . . Wanna cracker? . . . cracker? . . . cracker?"*

I started to leave. *"Don't go . . . Hello . . . don't go . . ."*

"Hello," I said.

"Hello . . . hello."

"Got no time," I said.

"Wanna cracker?

"No thanks," I said.

"Hello . . . hello . . ." it said.

I started to back slowly out of the room. The bird shuffled back and forth beseeching me to stay, asking if I wanted crackers. As soon as I was out of its sight, it stopped. I stood listening. Nothing but the impression of something giant and alive holding its breath.

The stairs swept in a long curve to the second floor. As I went up, I had the sensation I'd been up the stairs before. And I had. A long time ago. He'd just bought the house and it had been completely empty. Sophia had been dizzy with laughter, a queen in her new palace mansion.

And on the bare hardwood floor with the afternoon light streaming in. . .

A crack of light leaked under a closed door at the end of a dark corridor that seemed too long. I didn't remember the corridor. Only the room, the sunlight falling over her pelvis, her hands there, parting the hair. *See, Mr. Dancey. Do you like, Mr. Dancey? Kiss me there, Mr. Dancey.*

I walked down the hall and set my ear against the door. After listening a long time to nothing more than what I'd already been hearing, I tried the knob. It was made of black marble. The cold seemed to seep through my gloves and snatch at my fingers. The knob turned. Even fully furnished, I recognized the room and my eyes locked on the precise spot that we'd left our sweat on the polished oak.

The room was furnished now, heavy and dark, reeking of virility: hunting and fishing trophies, leather-bound volumes, rifles in glass-fronted cupboards, a big four-poster, an equally massive dresser. The master's bedroom. I stood looking, my legs loose, my teeth grinding each-other to dust.

The only light was from a small lamp on a large antique roll-top desk in front of which stood a high-backed stuffed chair that didn't look like it would belong at a desk. There was someone in the chair, slumped onto the desk, one arm dangling free.

Finally I walked over. There was no sign of blood, no sign he'd been hit. His face was faintly blue and appeared swollen. His eyes were cloudy brown, distant, wide open, looking less alive than the eyes in the twelve-point buck staring down at him. He wasn't hard to recognize, even after fifteen years. No, it was thirteen, as he'd reminded me with that controlled enraged precision. But it had only struck me then that Roger Trevelyan must've known about his wife's indiscretions, no matter how many times she had assured me he hadn't.

His face rested on a slew of 8 x 10 black-and-white photographs. I pulled them out from under him and stared at the blaring white figures caught against a dark background. The first flash had taken them completely by surprise; by the fourth, Sabrina had her hands over her face and Hal Fitzgibbons was lunging toward the camera. Snapshots of a bad dream. The last paying job for a skinny, anonymous photographer who'd been afraid of his own shadow.

On the floor was a note typed in capitals:

DEAR MR. TREVELYAN,
    IF YOU'D LIKE THE NEGATIVES OF THESE IT WILL
COST YOU $5,000 CASH. PLEASE HAVE IT IMMEDIATELY
AVAILABLE. I WILL CONTACT YOU BY TELEPHONE TO
ADVISE. OTHERWISE IT'S IMPOSSIBLE TO SAY WHO
MIGHT RECEIVE COPIES.

Somehow the photographs didn't seem the sort of thing that would kill a man like Roger Trevelyan. I dropped the note back on the floor. There wasn't much left to do but make the appropriate calls, then get the hell out.

The telephone was one of those that hides in a box. The lid depicted a man shooting ducks done in plastic pretending to be ivory. The box was closed but the receiver wasn't inside. The cord led to Trevelyan's right hand. There was a faint high bleating telling him to hang up.

Maybe when he'd started to feel whatever it was that was going to kill him, he'd tried to call. Maybe all he'd gotten was a busy signal because the phone was off the hook downstairs. Maybe he'd never gotten a number punched. Or maybe he'd never opened the box at all. I eased the receiver out of his hand. He hadn't been dead for long. I was calling the paramedics when a voice behind me said, "Put it down, Mr. Dancey." It was a low, sultry female voice with a hint of tremble, but it meant business. I did just what she said, very slowly, very carefully.

She was already dressed in black, a very elegant widow ready to mourn. Make-up carefully done, glossy red lips, platinum blonde hair, all of it perfect. Even the small chromed revolver seemed appropriate. She held it in her right hand and the barrel didn't shake. She held it as though there was nothing in the world more comfortable than a gun.

ஃ

I ALWAYS SEEM TO BE BUSTING IN at the wrong time, Mrs. Trevelyan."

Her lips rolled back over perfect teeth. A wily, nervous snicker floated across the room. "Still the wiseguy."

"Where's Sabrina, Mrs. Trevelyan?"

"You shouldn't have come nosing around, Mr. Dancey. It's too bad, plain too bad." A cat growling the initial soft warning.

"Was it really those pictures that killed your husband? A coronary, is that what it's supposed to look like?"

She took another step. She wanted to be close enough to be certain. I kept watching her eyes and that crimson mouth and the tendon in her wrist, looking for a little flicker of movement.

"I don't think it'll work," I said. "The Los Angeles homicide squad knows too much. Did our friend Larry ever show you the candid shots he took at the Sunset Palms?"

She took two quick steps towards me.

"Like to see the results? They're right here in my pocket, Angie."

I didn't like the sound of my voice. It was dry and thick and far away. Someone like Angie Trevelyan might squeeze the trigger without even knowing she'd done it.

"Don't," she said, and now her voice began to tremble ever so slightly. "Don't you dare."

"Listen, nobody's going to care about Hal Fitzgibbons because he's likely to turn out to be a gangster named O'Flannery. Could be you didn't have anything to do with your husband's death. What's all the fuss? He already knew you and Hal had something going. He can't hurt you now, can he? Look at him, Mrs. Trevelyan. He can't hurt you."

She slunk another step towards me. Her face was a mask of equal parts terror and hatred.

"How did Sabrina get mixed up in all this, anyway?" I was babbling, operating under the dubious assumption that it's harder to shoot someone engaged in conversation.

"Listen, Mrs. Trevelyan, all I really want to know is where Sabrina is. I'm not interested in justice or going to the cops. You do what you have to do, and I'll just leave and you can forget you ever met me. But if you know where she is. . ."

The mask moved. It was almost imperceptible, but I caught it and was already on my way to the floor when she fired. Two sharp cracks within a second. The first one threw a steel fist into my right shoulder. The second smashed a Tiffany lamp.

The quiet was filled with humming reverberations and a delicate tinkling of falling glass. Then pandemonium, as she fired into the darkness over and over until the hammer clicked on an empty chamber. I scrambled towards her legs, embraced them, and took her down just as another gun fired from the doorway. A tremor raced through her body. Whoever was there fired again, and she slumped into my arms.

Downstairs a door slammed. An engine roared and tires squealed. Then everything stopped except Angie Trevelyan's moans. She tried to make words. She was telling me not to leave her. She was afraid, terribly afraid. She couldn't feel her legs.

"Was that Loper?"

She'd been hit under her left breast. The blood flowed through my fingers, pulsing, alive, startlingly hot. I pressed my palm against the wound but it wouldn't stop.

"I'm going to call an ambulance, Mrs. Trevelyan. You understand?"

Her eyes were wide. She was too heavy to hold, but I held her. She was like anyone who didn't want to die. Her beautiful body wouldn't do her any good. Her money, her dogs, none of it.

"Water," she whispered, and began to repeat it over and over. She called for Olivia. "Olivia, *agua, por favor. Agua . . .*"

I told her to take it easy, but she didn't seem to hear me. I eased her to the floor and unclenched her fingers from my arm as gently as I could. I crawled to the phone, dialed the paramedics, gave the address, and said there'd been an accident with a gun. Then I called the Santa Monica police. They wanted to know who I was. I told them about the "accident," gave the address and hung up just as Angie Trevelyan stopped moaning.

She still had a pulse and was still breathing. Her face felt cold and clammy. I tore open a pillowcase and tried to staunch the wound. I raced from door to door, finding everything but what I needed. By the time I'd reached a bathroom, the air was being torn by the wail of converging sirens.

I ran downstairs leaving a trail of lights. The paramedics had made it before the law just as they usually did. An ambulance was stopped outside the iron gates, horn blaring. The parrot was screaming *"Hello . . . hello . . . hello . . . dont' go . . ."* I threw the switch to open the gate, and ducked out the back. I skirted the pool and headed for the wall, a low, throaty growl trailing me through the fog.

T HE DOG LURCHED, made a feeble lunge at my leg, and collapsed on the manicured lawn. I reached the wall and made my jump, just as it revived and locked its jaws around my right ankle. I kicked and it fell backward, staring at me in abject canine sorrow. I scrambled over and dropped to the sidewalk.

Squad cars were closing in on the front gates, shredding the foggy quiet with tire squeals and the wavery decelerations of half a dozen sirens. I waited until Channel Road was clear, and followed the streetlamps that hovered in the fog like dim moons. After a roundabout fifteen minutes I found the Buick, got in and took a long pull from the flask before checking my shoulder. I peeled off my jacket and opened my shirt. There was a small neat hole, oozing a little blood. Between the brandy and the shock, I hardly felt a thing. Which helped me decide I didn't want to answer any questions. So I'd skip the emergency room and as much as it would embarrass me, I'd have to call Dr. Malm and take his lecture on living dangerously along with my medicine. It would be a reasonable lecture and I would agree.

I headed back to Venice, and by the time I reached Buddha Disposal, I was having second thoughts. The shock was wearing off and my shoulder was beginning to burn. I hoped that by some miracle Malm would still be there.

The geese came out of the fog and surrounded me with demented honking. Then they seemed to recognize I was only another wounded beast that'd come crawling home. All I heard was the muffled shuffle of webbed feet leading me to the stairs.

Dr. Malm wasn't in. I turned on the galley light, sat down and felt the pain throb. I tried to get up, but nothing seemed to work. I heard a familiar but oddly distant voice, a voice that was tired and afraid, say, "Fuck it."

Then a face with large, dark eyes and brown skin framed by hair so black its highlights shimmered blue, peeked out and squinted against the light.

"You're Elton?"

"Yeah, I am."

"I'm Leiko, Gordon's friend. He told you?"

I nodded, "Sorry I woke you up."

The sleep evaporated from her face. She looked puzzled, then startled.

"My god," she said.

"Listen, it's no big deal. I don't think it is. If you wouldn't mind taking a look."

She already was. A pair of scissors materialized out of nowhere and were slicing through my shirt.

"This is a gunshot, isn't it?"

"Nothing. A twenty-two. Just a toy."

"We've got to get you to County. Gordon'll take care of this."

"Listen, I can't." I couldn't remember her name. "I don't think it's serious."

She actually smiled. "Ever hear of infection? Gangrene? Happens all the time, believe me."

"I believe you. Just patch me up for tonight."

"He said you were crazy. You've been drinking."

"I drink. I get shot. But they're not habits. I swear. I'm steady, responsible . . ."

Her glare of disbelief was softened by the grin. "You're also an actor is what Gordon tells me."

"More or less."

"This is a real bullet, my friend," she said with professional severity.

"I'm beginning to notice."

"Jesus, you are nuts." I couldn't tell if the idea turned her on, scared her, or just plain bored her. She kept working as we argued about going to County. Finally, she agreed to call Malm but he was in surgery. We argued some more as she boiled water and got out Malm's little black bag. I kept sipping quietly and looking at her face, keeping away thoughts of Angie Trevelyan's blood pouring through my fingers. I was drifting out of the chair. Somehow she caught me. She couldn't have been five feet tall, but she was strong. There was a long way into her eyes. I hoped she saw the small part of me that still consorted with life. The gentle

part, maybe even the wounded part. Okay, I was drunk.
It hit me fast. My tongue had amnesia. Finally I got it out.
"You're nice to do this," I said.

She wrinkled her nose. "You're no fun to argue with. No
common sense."

"That's what my wife said."

"Poor her."

"Conflicting bloodlines is my theory."

"Gordon also mentioned you were something of a
wiseass." Her mouth lingered pleasurably over "wiseass."
What a lovely thing to be called. I wished she'd do it again.
I smiled, and said, "Maybe he also mentioned that we might
play some jazz together."

The original meaning of "jazz" flashed through my mind.
I doubted that it flashed through hers, yet she smiled a tiny
smile that seemed full of implications before she tried to
cover it up. I was drunk and getting lyrical. There was something about a woman digging a bullet out of my shoulder
when I'd had close to a pint of 86 proof that tended to make
me lyrical. She picked up a swab and her voice tickled my
ear with a crazy hot caress. "This'll burn, Mr. Dancey."

I laughed, then she hit me with it, and I yowled. She took
the tweezer, pushed her rear end against my chest and held
me. "Don't move, please."

I hissed through my teeth, and a second later she dropped
a neat little lead orb into a saucer.

"It looks nice and clean." Her voice sounded a little shaky.
I didn't ask if she'd ever done this before, but I didn't have
to. We were both putting on our best act.

She swabbed and bandaged; I kept looking straight ahead.
She was lecturing again, dissipating her nervousness. I didn't
mind listening. Finally, she sat down and picked up the flask.
I thought she intended to take it away, but instead she tipped

it to her lips. When she wiped her mouth with the back of her hand, I could've kissed her. We sat there for what seemed a long time, not saying a word. I had a dumb grin on my face, and she a lovely one. We just sat and then I was falling off the chair again.

🦢

I T WAS AFTER FOUR in the afternoon by the time I woke up. I tried to remember how I'd gotten into bed. I lay there, my head swarming with demented wasps. Finally, I gritted my teeth and rolled out.

They were both sitting on the wheelhouse deck, looking very fresh. I told them I felt great. Dr. Malm and Nurse Leiko shook their heads in unison, reminding me I'd never been much of an actor in front of friends.

Malm looked my shoulder over and complimented Leiko on a job well done. Then he shot me full of antibiotics and told me to stay put. We had a round of drinks, from which the doctor abstained. Half an hour later, as the first firecrackers and rocket whistles began to sound, he took off for County General to confront the rush of weekend disasters. Leiko whipped up chicken with mint leaves while I sat watching her culinary choreography with what was probably a sappy look of delight plastered on my face.

"You scared me," she said.

"I hope I didn't say anything too wiseass."

Her eyes glanced down, then she shook her hair back, to offset the idea that there might've been anything demure in the gesture. "Let's say you got a little disoriented . . ." She didn't go on. I was staring too hard.

"Thanks for not leaving me on the floor," I said.

"I hope I didn't lecture too much. Gordon says I'm a terrible nag."

We indulged in another grin, then we ate, and didn't find anything to say. Or maybe we thought we'd find too much and thought it was better not to start. I looked at my watch. It was 7:50 p.m. I wanted to forget all about Long Beach and a freighter called the *Salassie*.

"Now you've got to tell me about it," she said.

"I've got an appointment. How about later?"

"Oh no you don't. Doctor's orders. Seriously, you've got to stay put, Elton."

"Malm tells me you play the violin."

"Now please."

I stood up. She lifted her face, and I was looking into her eyes. It was all I could do not to sit back down.

"Later. We'll get together. Play a little."

"It's very foolish," she said with resignation.

"In a couple of hours I'll tell you the whole damn story, and you'll swear I must've made it up."

As I walked across the yard with the geese clustered around my legs, she yelled "good luck," and I felt her eyes follow me to the gate. I waved over my shoulder and jogged down to the Buick.

I pulled onto the San Diego freeway and blended into the stream of taillights that seemed to bleed in the dense damp air. Traffic slowed. By 8:30 the fog had closed in, and I couldn't see more than a car length ahead. Dancey and a hundred thousand other maniacs sat there growling in their machines, slowly dying. Every so often a Roman candle shot a dim orange trail up from the tract houses below. At 8:45

I exited to head south on Avalon. The fog opened for a few seconds, then became impenetrable again. A signal light, flashing crimson, jumped out of a dense white wall. Amber foglights bore down, then swerved away. A billboard displaying the Statue of Liberty loomed out of the fog, telling me of a beer made the American way.

It was a long ride to Long Beach. There were too many dead ends, too many red lights, too many streets curving in circles. My shoulder complained and my Forest Lawn headache flared up again. I thought about Roger Trevelyan and the twenty thousand dollars I'd never get. Somehow it all seemed to have started with what was left on those oak floors thirteen years before. Of course it was crazy. What happened then had nothing to do with anything. I'd had plenty of chances to get out, and I hadn't taken them. Sabrina had had a few chances too. Sometimes you simply didn't see them, and sometimes you pretended not to.

It was 9:15 when I got to Pier 27. The vague shape of a freighter was etched against a white backdrop. Rust, black paint and fog; a monochrome world. Lights appeared and disappeared, erratic, meaningless orbs. I cut the headlamps and crept along by the diffused radiance. The tires sputtered in a soft vibrato against brick, then squished over rails. When I reached Warehouse 10, I cut the engine. A chorus of foghorns bleated in forlorn conversation. I left the Buick, backtracked on foot, and got close enough to the freighter to make out the name on her rust-stained stern: *Salassie/Beira*.

I headed back out the pier. Behind me I saw a pair of close-set headlamps with amber parking lights set wider. Not the configuration of any law-enforcement vehicle I knew of, but very much like a Jaguar. The lights veered away, and all I could hear was a vague rumble of engines turning the oil well pumps. Then a different sound intruded, an undefined clacking. It grew closer, becoming foot treads. Two or three men moving with brisk purpose.

I crept to the south side of the pier and hunkered behind the wheels of a rolling derrick. A hole in the fog let me read a sign above the mammoth doors of Warehouse 11: INTER-CONTINENTAL SHIPPING, INC. The footsteps stopped and the men spoke in low muffled voices. The northern sky lit up with a strange radiant pink, then green, then blue. A second later the sound arrived with a remote whisper of thumps and booms; the San Pedro fireworks display climaxed and died.

I waited. I couldn't hear the men or see them, but they were still out there. My mouth got dry and my head throbbed and my shoulder pulsed, but none of it seemed to matter anymore. I heard a low diesel grumble different than the periodic revving of the engines on the oil wells. A few seconds later, I saw the headlights, set high and wide above a pair of yellow fog lamps. A big rig. Maybe the shipment from St. Louis that Tunney Ray Mackey had so torturously set down in that little spiral notebook. A well-run show, all happening on cue, just as someone had planned. I wasn't sure who that someone was. Maybe Roger Trevelyan or Hal Fitzgibbons or Larry Loper. Maybe Sidney Landis.

Three shadows crossed the diffused beams as the rig crept forward. Now the shadows were moving beside it, a walking escort. One of them seemed to resemble Tullie, another his silent partner. The truck kept on, apparently unaware of the three men flanking it.

Then another set of headlights burst out of the fog, the same pair I'd seen earlier. They flashed on and off twice and the truck eased to a stop with a muffled sigh of air-brakes. The car door opened. It was a Jaguar, a brown Jaguar, but it didn't look like Hal Fitzgibbons opening the door.

Nothing told me what to do. It was none of my business and I didn't want to be there and I didn't expect to find Sabrina. Maybe I'd just been afraid to stay with the strong little nurse on Dr. Malm's eternally stranded boat. Maybe I thought I'd get stranded myself in one of those forevers that's always ending.

I kept low and watched the three men reach inside their coats. They all reached together and they reached very calmly, as if they were going after cigarettes. But they weren't. I'd known that all along. Boy, I was smart. I could die there hit by a stray bullet. Damn, I couldn't get much smarter.

Just as calmly as they'd reached inside their coats, they took aim. It was so perfectly choreographed and timed that it didn't seem real.

Whoever was getting out of the Jaguar dove back inside and rammed it into gear. Tires spun on the wet brick, then caught and the car jumped forward, running straight at the three men. They fired simultaneously. The Jaguar plowed ahead. Two of them dodged, but the man in the middle was sent slamming against the truck's chrome grillwork. Figures poured out of the fog, a dozen or more, their guns going off like firecrackers, the noise abstract, remote, meaningless. The Jaguar pitched and fishtailed around the big rig. In a second it was gone, its taillights swallowed by the fog.

I was already running. Dmitri had believed me after all. The armed mob that had come out of nowhere had to have been police. But I wasn't sure, all I knew is that they were men with guns. And those guns were still firing. They seemed to be behind me, then suddenly in front. I kept on running.

I realized I had circled back, but the sporadic shots were closer. I stood panting, unsure, the fog opened, and there it was, the dull grey faithful beast called a Buick.

꙳

THE ENGINE CAUGHT, and I experienced a great rush of affection for a machine. I pressed the accelerator and breathed in damp plush, bakelite, and steel. I talked to her and she listened, sympathizing completely when I cursed the fog and the cops and Larry Loper and Sabrina and, for good measure, myself. I said to hell with moral obligations, to hell with my word, to hell with the whole messy Trevelyan clan. To hell with chasing bad dreams.

By the time I'd worked my way north to Marina del Rey, the big fireworks displays had long since petered out, and the streets were all but deserted. The parking lot nearest Pier 6 was empty. I drove on to the next. It was deserted too; containing only a yellow pick-up and a rusty old wagon that had been there for weeks.

The next closest lot served the night restaurant trade at the phony fisherman's village where I had my useless office. It was half full, a slow night for a weekend holiday. I cruised up and down looking for brown Jaguars. There were dozens of Mercedes, plenty of BMWs and Porsches, a smattering of Rolls-Royces but not one Jaguar.

I parked and stared out at the fog. The only way to stop muttering to myself was to get up and move. I jogged over to Pier 6, and this time I didn't challenge myself, I just took out the key. I couldn't see the *Corlinda*, and all I could hear was the soft chug of a marine engine between the bleats of foghorns out in the channel.

I walked down the dock feeling the damp cling to my throat. For some reason when I saw the outline of that lovely wood-hulled cutter, I had a momentary flash of almost proprietary pride. I had to admit Hal Fitzgibbons or Harlan O'Flannery or whoever he was, had taste in boats. And in women too. Yes, he had an eye for beauty, all right. And he probably had an intuitive sense of a certain fragility. But instead of being drawn to protect it, he recognized opportunity. The mystery was how that kind of fragility seemed to welcome exploitation with open arms.

I stepped on deck, eased into the cockpit and thought, hell, Bogart would've liked this boat. He would've certainly liked Leiko, and maybe Sabrina did have a little of that youthful cynical sophistication that had made Bacall so appealing. I stood lost in indulgent fantasy as the reverberations of the big foghorn on the jetty faded. Then I heard a heavy muffled thudding from somewhere forward. The big foghorn let out another long mournful hoot. There were three more thumps, something heavy thunking against wood.

I crept forward to the bow, listened, tapped my foot twice. Two responding thumps answered from under the forward hatch. I stuck my pick in the heavy brass lock and fiddled. In ten seconds I knew it had me outwitted, but I kept trying, hoping I was overdue for some sheer blind luck. After a while, I tapped again, and whoever was in there responded.

"If you hear me, hit once," I tried. Nothing happened. I raised my voice and a single thump answered. I concocted a quick code: once for "yes," twice for "no," three times

187

for "uncertain." I asked if it was Sabrina and there was a thump of affirmation. I felt myself smile and something warm and joyous moved inside me. It was over. The nightmare was over.

I continued to fumble with the lock, yelling out questions. She didn't know if Loper was in the neighborhood. He hadn't been there for several hours. There was no other access to the compartment except the one I was standing on.

I gave up tinkering with the lock. I jumped, kicked, stomped, then pulled and pried with a boat hook. I told her to hold on, I was going to the car and get my tools, it'd take about five minutes.

The dock seemed to grow longer with every stride, and it took forever to get back to the Buick. Forever to get the key in the ignition. But it was over, this madness that still baffled me was finally over. Sabrina could go back and be the object of pretty surfing visions. Lieutenant Dmitri could wrap up the loose ends and get a commendation. Dancey could sleep and mind his own business forever.

I pulled into the empty lot adjacent to Pier 6, grabbed my toolbox and tire iron, fumbled with the key, and skidded down the ramp, losing all control at the end of a long race. Everyone had been ahead of me, but it didn't matter anymore, and it didn't matter that there was no one at the finish line to cheer. I just had to pry her out, and then sleep. Christ, sleep . . . Billie Holiday and my own sweet bed.

I stepped on board. A foghorn hooted. Then I felt him, felt movement, felt his breath. Instinct told my body to duck, to scramble, to run, but my body was exhausted. It tried but it was too late. The first blow hit the side of my head. I felt an exquisite movement of imbalance, my tool box flying, my feet searching for anything solid. Something inside me wanted to give up, to tell him, hey, its over, let's end it right here, curtain time, I'm tired, friend, my head aches, everything aches. I'm a coward, I'm no damn good at violence, not even in the movies.

A foot came towards my face. I rolled and took it in the back and every cell in my body begged for air. Something hard and unforgiving smashed against my cheekbone. The foot found my groin, my back, my head.

Later, much later it seemed, he was sitting on top of me breathing too hard to speak. I mustered a feeble defiance and he pushed the muzzle of a gun against my nose. I heard someone say, "You won't get away with it, Loper." He responded with a calm, insolent grin. Suddenly he got off. Maybe he'd believed me, I thought wildly. I started to get up. I wanted to thank him for seeing the light at last. Sure, we're all reasonable human beings. Civilized. We had problems, but they weren't worth getting nasty over.

He stood watching. His arm began to move. He was going to help me. The arm kept moving. I heard a hiss of expelled breath. I fell forward, my head exploding with light, an agonizing light that flared briefly before collapsing into darkness.

⁊

I T WAS A VISCOUS DARK, damp and empty with no sign of an exit. My ankles and wrists were bound, my feet and hands numb. I lay face down and gagged. With every heartbeat, a hot needle plunged between my temples, a continuing case of deja vu. Compliments of the man who'd signed a gloating piece of doggerel *LL*. He'd been calmly breaking my skull ever since I could remember. He never said why. He always seemed to know where I was, and he always outwitted me.

Wherever I was wasn't spacious, and it stank. The needle plunged. Sweat dripped in my eyes. I could sense her, but I couldn't see her. There were gurgling sounds, like boiling water amplified. After a time, I distinguished her breathing. Somehow she was asleep, maybe drugs, maybe exhaustion. But I'd found her, I was free to resign. Perhaps we'd have a good laugh. I lay there for a while feeling dangerously close to prayer until I foolishly let myself slip into thinking about Joan and how I might've done a lot of things differently. Like accepting roles I didn't want to play and making enough money so we needn't always have been scrambling. But that wasn't it, at least not all of it. It wasn't money and it wasn't sex. The sex had been fine, more than fine, until the end.

I forced my thoughts away from what I couldn't change, what neither of us could've changed or we would have. I listened to the water, thinking it might tell me something. Certain Melanesian tribes could navigate whole oceans by the direction of the waves, without the aid of sextant or compass. It was a dying art, soon to be extinct. The corrosion of instincts. I tried to use mine. They told me we were running south with a good wind. There was no sound of engines. South. Yes, south.

Inevitably, the question I'd managed to keep at bay knifed into my mind: how was Loper going to dispose of us? There weren't any pleasant answers. None that gave us a chance. I began to think of Angelina. I remembered her first trout, the squeals, the pure glitter of the stream, the sunset. Boy's stuff, trout-fishing, but at seven you didn't have to worry too much about being a girl. At seven you didn't have to worry period.

The boat heeled and rolled me across the compartment. Sabrina awoke, and almost instantly her body convulsed with sobs. I wrenched myself around until my fingers could work at her gag. It took a while, a long while, but I finally managed to get it undone. I could hear her spitting and coughing, and she cried some more before she tried to say something and couldn't.

I started to work on the ropes binding her wrists. That took longer, a lot longer. I rested, and made my hands work again, digging until my fingertips were raw. Finally a single strand began to give. Then another, then layer after layer, and at last her arms came free.

She clung to me, still unable to speak. I knew it was going to be hard to keep her afloat. When she calmed down, I coaxed her with nudges and gestures and at last got her to work at my knots.

"He's insane." Those were the words that broke the silence, the first words I had heard in hours. "Insane," she repeated. Her voice was small and lost and far away. The Trevelyans had had everything, and it had all come to nothing for no reason I could fathom. I made a noise to remind her I was still tied and gagged. When she finally removed the gag, I tried to shape words, comforting words, but my mouth no longer worked.

"He's going to kill us," she said. She didn't sound hysterical anymore; her voice was flat, almost dead.

"He's crazy, but not that crazy," I managed to say. I tried to keep her talking, thinking the only way for her to stay sane was to get it out. She did, though at times the flat monotone of her broken narrative faded and stopped. Once or twice she seemed to come back to life, and that sassy smart-alecky girl I'd fallen for was momentarily resurrected. But the voice always fell back into desolate flat despair.

As she talked, I tried to grasp the slippery unreality and make it whole. I saw her again on the bright Tuesday afternoon, skipping down the stairs as she left my office on her way to surf at Malibu. I could picture how the eternal watchers sat in summer indolence, how their eyes turned when she came across the sand, this mysterious little rich girl who seemed so remote, yet went through all the motions of being a member of their tribe. The waves had failed to materialize. Her period had started. "A week early," she said. "And I'm always on time. Always."

She'd gone back to the *Corlinda*. She'd tried to call me, but I was somewhere in Hollywood, still chasing those senseless pictures while she was rinsing the stains out of her underwear. She'd heard someone come aboard and, thinking it was Hal, hadn't bothered to dress. She'd hidden to give him a little scare, a cute little joke, both hostile and seductive. It seemed a Trevelyan trait. They were all driven by some hidden rage, though they twisted it into something else. With the women it was sex. Even Sophia's suicide had seemed a sort of demented joke and her nudity, the clothes left on the wheelhouse deck, a sort of last erotic taunt.

Sabrina had leapt out and was almost in his arms when she realized it wasn't Hal at all. The man had a beard and terrifying eyes. He had a gun and a voice that seemed strangely familiar. He'd stared at her, and she was certain he had one intention. It was the funny smile on his face and the way he pushed the gun against her ribs. She'd begged him not to kill her. She'd even hinted at cooperation, if he promised to just do it and not hurt her. But he'd only laughed. Then his voice had become easy, and he'd started to ask questions about Hal Fitzgibbons. He asked if she knew about the deal Hal had with her father. She didn't understand. She'd never suspected Hal even knew her father.

Then he'd told her she'd have to go for a ride. She wouldn't get hurt if she behaved, but he wouldn't hesitate to use the gun. He'd had to use guns too many times. He didn't want to, not anymore. He was tired of guns, tired of everything. That was when she'd decided he wasn't going to rape her. That was when the real terror had begun. Rape she had thought she could survive.

At first he had refused to say what he wanted. He seemed to enjoy the game of terror. Then suddenly he'd become apologetic, telling her over and over he was sorry to put her through this. He berated himself, cursed himself, almost wept. I have to, he told her. I have to. You don't understand what he's put me through.

He'd taken her off the boat, and by then she had felt as though she had no will of her own, almost as if she didn't exist. He made her drive Hal's Jaguar to a trailer at the bottom of Topanga. He said if she didn't tell him everything, Hal was going to turn up dead. In a panic, she offered him money if he'd just let her go. He said, sure why not, its rightfully mine anyway. It seemed a strange remark, but everything he said seemed strange. He'd taken her up the hill to the telephone booth, the same one I used a few hours later. It was from there she'd called Mr. Doak. She had made the offer, and he had jumped at it, but he didn't seem to really care. It was almost as though he was more interested in the game of getting away with it than the money. He had shaved his beard. He had bought a suit and practiced an English accent. I shuddered; another actor who'd lost track of reality.

After the phone call to Doak, they'd gone back to the trailer. He had changed again, become rougher, scarier, even more erratic. She was sure that if she lent a sympathetic ear he'd eventually let her go. The money and sympathy, she had thought. A minor in psychology, I recalled. He had told her the whole twisted tale in that trailer with the dead goat festering twenty yards away, while half a mile down the lane, sunbathers lay on the beach listening for the Highway Patrol helicopter that occasionally landed and handed out tickets for public nudity. It was a crazy world, and it was almost understandable why Larry Loper didn't give a damn anymore. He'd been sent to an even crazier world, a world he couldn't handle, a world few would believe and most had forgotten, a world where medals were handed out for killing or being killed.

He had described the war in vivid detail while smoking big smoldering chunks of hashish. He didn't seem to get high, his bitter thoughts had just kept coming in a crazed insistent stream. It was as if he was talking to himself and at the same time talking to nobody. Then suddenly, and she couldn't understand why it had taken her so long, she realized who he was.

She had remembered the long vigils, the letters, the MIA bracelets, the memorial service for the brother presumed dead. Larry Loper was Matthew Lawrence Trevelyan, her half-brother from her father's first marriage.

Matthew had never been a major part of her life. He'd always been away at some private school or military academy. Her last memory was from when she'd been around five. He'd taken her to the merry-go-round on the pier and told her he was going away and that he might not see her for a long time. He had joined the Marines and had been in one of the last battalions to be sent over. Just before Saigon was overrun. He'd become separated from his platoon in Laos and ended up in Thailand. When he'd discovered he'd been reported missing, the idea intrigued him.

He wanted his father to suffer. The father who had taunted him, had almost told him to go and prove he was a man.

He'd stayed in Thailand a few years pretending to be a German named Loper. There he'd concocted a new dream. He wanted to become an entrepreneur and return to show his father that all his predictions of failure were untrue. There was a long hazy history of life as a soldier of fortune in Turkey, in Morocco, in Greece, in Rhodesia before it became Zimbabwe. He'd met a man named O'Flannery and they'd teamed up on various enterprises. What a moment it had been when Matthew Trevelyan realized Hal Fitzgibbons knew his father.

She couldn't remember any more. Mostly she recalled how intensely he wanted her to know everything, as if he'd chosen her to bear witness to his life. She'd tried to placate him, to remind him that they were, after all, brother and sister. She'd agreed with him that their father deserved to be taught a thing or two. She even agreed she'd been wrong to fall for Hal. She pleaded her case and expressed all the sympathy she could muster. He appeared to soften again. Then suddenly he'd lashed out. She was nothing but a manipulating bitch like her mother. When he'd left her, she'd been a pure little girl riding a merry-go-round — and now that purity was gone and everything pure in his life had been taken away. Roger Trevelyan was to blame. They were all to blame.

By the time they had entered Ronald Doak's office, Sabrina was numb beyond terror; exhausted, limp, without will. She'd believed that once Matthew had the money, he'd no longer have any need for her. The papers were probably being signed about the time I'd found her medallion in the trailer.

After they'd picked up the money and driven to the

Corlinda, she presumed he'd leave her there. But no, not yet. He would let her go as soon as they reached Mexico. He had the money, what else did he want? Matthew had smiled, then he'd grabbed her wrist, pushed the gun against her throat and forced her to swallow a pill. She had pleaded, but when he had threatened to simply shoot her, she had acquiesced. At least the pill wouldn't be messy.

"He'll kill us," she said blankly, when she had said all she could say. "He doesn't care anymore."

"We won't let him." Maybe it was the hint of diffidence in my voice that set her off. She began to beat against the hatch. This wasn't the girl who'd slept with me one Saturday night, certainly not the haughty girl who provided visions for the surf boys. This girl was a fragile effigy about to break. I held her and tried to muffle her cries.

꒰

L IGHT BARELY ON THE THRESHOLD of human vision leaked into the darkness. I reached up and touched the hatch. The wood was faintly warm. I ran through my pockets for the thousandth time, but they were still empty of anything remotely resembling a means of escape. And for the thousandth time I told myself it was crazy to wait for his next impulse to strike and for the thousandth time I agreed. I had to think, but there was nothing to think.

Hours passed. Sometimes her mouth moved in her sleep, the words shapeless whispers of terror that belonged to no conscious language. Little by little the compartment cooled.

The darkness that was always darkness appeared to thicken. The sea calmed. There were faint sounds of music and periodic bursts of gaiety. I smelled food. Muffled words filtered through the heavy planks of the back wall. The words stopped. A rhythmic drumming sent faint vibrations through the wood, and after a time I heard muffled ecstatic yelps ending in a single prolonged cry. I swallowed a curse as the needle pushed between my temples and my shoulder throbbed, reminding me of those almond eyes I knew would never think I was sane enough, maybe not even for a sweet month-long affair. She was too smart to get mixed up with somebody coming off a ten-year marriage. I listened to the water. The needle stopped. Maybe the water could tell me. I kept listening, and eventually the gentle slap of waves put me to sleep.

꙳

SHE WAS SCREAMING as if screams could break walls. I held her and pleaded, but it was like asking a tortured creature to stop running from its torturer. I got a hand over her mouth and an arm around her waist and let her thrash until she was quivery and slack. In the midst of it, a slurry voice yelled a sarcastic invitation to shut up, or he'd make us shut up.

A thrumming vibrated through the hull and our compartment filled with watery sounds. Her body suddenly arched out of my arms. I caught her scream in my hand, and her teeth sank into my thumb and held for a long minute before she let go, completely unaware she'd bitten me. After a while I said, "You ever see that Chaplin movie where he's lost in the north and boils up his shoe for dinner and his buddy, this big burly guy, imagines Charlie's turned into a chicken?"

"I want out of here. Please, I want out."

"You might turn into a chicken," I said. "Then we could fool him."

"Don't," she said. "Don't joke. Please, Dancey, I'm hungry."

"Try not to think about it," I said thinly. The engines thrummed. Our prison stank of urine and fear, of stale breath and hopelessness. A time passed I couldn't measure, a time of no thoughts or thoughts so vague they were forgotten before they formed, a time listening to water and my own breathing. I snapped out of it and hurriedly unscrewed a cap on one of the water tanks. Taking off my shirt, I lowered a sleeve in, pulled it up and wrung it into my mouth. Even stale water bearing hints of stale sweat can seem a sort of miracle. I kept dipping and wringing, and after a while I had something to sweat back.

"I'm sorry," she said. Her voice made me jump. I was sorry she'd had to say it, sorry all I responded with was a bad joke. "There's Perrier a la sleeve, if you're thirsty."

She actually laughed. Then she crawled over. I dipped and squeezed. She made little gulping sounds. For a moment I thought I could see her. As I kept dipping, I remembered waterwheels, oxen pulling the Nile into ditches, a well in India, a small girl's brown face offering a tin cup, a pump on a Utah ranch splashing freezing water on my face. All the simple miracles. Sabrina's hand stopped my arm from its automatic motions. "Let's lie down," she said.

I was a lean mattress, getting leaner, and as she stretched

over me we might've appeared to be lovers. Her breasts were firm against my chest, her breath warm against my neck. I recalled how she had moved, the feel of being inside her, the sounds. But there wasn't a spasm of desire, barely the ability to imagine it. We were like the African tribe that after years of drought stopped reproducing, their language transformed until the words for fornication and defecation had become the same.

My thoughts buzzed aimlessly as I tried to avoid the admission that I had no plan. Without a plan there was only the chance of blind luck. I didn't believe in blind luck. But at least it could hold out a kind of hope, and without hope there could be no resistance. Suddenly a plan materialized. A thin plan, a plan so desperate it might as well have been a knife carved of soap. It was as simple as it was fragile: I would bury Sabrina under the sailbags, then wedge myself into the space above the water tanks where I'd be invisible from the hatchway. He might bend over far enough, and if he led with the gun . . .

"I don't want to die," she said flatly. She sounded like a lost child. I didn't blame her. I felt lost myself.

"Don't even think it. We won't let it happen."

She asked if I thought it would hurt. I answered with my thin plan, mustering as much enthusiasm as I could.

"It's hopeless," she said in that listless, frail voice all the sass and spunk had been leached out of.

"Sabrina, they've been boozing, doping, and lying in the sun. They don't expect a fight. It's our one chance."

"But if it doesn't work, he'll kill us, won't he?"

I manufactured a desperate logic to deflect her despair. I tried to believe what I said. But the having to try was itself the giveaway. I was grasping at straws. "He's had plenty of chances. Maybe he needs us. Not in any rational sense but just to keep it all real for him. Like with you, he made you the enemy, not because you are but because he needs one to stay alive. Another part of him is looking for a way out, a way to self-destruct. He's looking for a way to die, Sabrina."

"But he's afraid to go alone. That's the way they are, people like that."

The maturity of her insight struck me as an abject truth without rebuttal. Still, I clung to the clumsy knife-carved-of-soap melting in my hand. Anything to stop the darkness.

The thrumming of the engine stopped; the rush of water died. Somebody moved forward. I pushed Sabrina into the crotch of the bow, covered her with sailbags, and wedged myself above the water tanks. The footsteps stopped. A faint command came from the stern, "Heave-ho!" The anchor splashed. Cable sang against a winch. The footsteps lurched away.

ᵧ⸲

I T WAS ALWAYS NIGHT, and it always stank. Now it was night for them, too. Time to put the music on, time for smoke and booze, time to ride intoxicated thighs.

I wondered how long we'd been in the stinking night and if the waters under us were Mexican. I wondered when and if Loper would stumble out of his stupor long enough to remember the unfinished business in the forward hold. I kept asking questions, as if questions had become prayers.

I couldn't remember when the music stopped or when the

orgy died. Sabrina was still sleeping when the darkness thinned. I touched the hatchcover and felt the sun. Somebody stirred. There were giggles, a short playful scream followed by a splash. She swam around the bow, yelling coy taunts. The voice seemed familiar, that innocent coquettishness I always tended to fall for. Perhaps she was our amorous companion in the forward cabin, whose muffled cries we'd been hearing for days. Days that were lifetimes. I imagined I smelled bacon, but I'd imagined a lot of smells. Now I could hear her clearly, her gaiety transmitted by the water. I was assailed by the thought of freckles and red hair. I wondered who these people were. Other borderline crazies? Innocents pulled along by Loper's charm, the chance for easy adventure, a free cruise to Mexico?

We listened to the day pass. The *Corlinda* rode her anchor, a lazy bird on lazy swells. I imagined a big lazy afternoon, the ocean a liquidy plate, hardly ruffled, the sky an irridescent blue such as only Hollywood makes. A nice day to lie back and drink and smoke and slip a hand inside a bikini. Just lie there letting the sun take you until you can't stand it any more. Can't stand the heat, can't bear the glitter off the water. You're about to break open, but the big blue afternoon goes on like there's no such thing as law or money or death.

Two of them came below. The big blue afternoon was so still that it was hard not to hear them. Sabrina wasn't enjoying it. Again I pondered who they were, this crew Loper had rounded up. He might've had a few Sally Swanns in tow and a drinking buddy or two, military dropouts, mercenary buddies or leftover lost souls from Baba Ridiculoso's troupe. It didn't matter, there were always a few loose dreamers, careless people who'd overlook almost anything for the chance at a little adventure.

"How can they lie there fucking? How can they?" Her anger had lost its force, but I was glad to see even a tiny spark.

"They don't know we exist," I said.

She kicked the wall. She said she'd make them know. I tried to smother her fury. She clawed and kicked, melting our silly soap-knife. Finally she collapsed into whimpers. I prayed the lovebirds hadn't heard, or, if they had, that they were too far into it to bother. Their sounds stopped. Maybe they had finished, maybe they were just taking a rest. A new voice was speaking to them in the tones of an envious chaperone. The lovebirds invited the newcomer to join, but she declined. Everybody was going to the island, perhaps they wanted to go along. The lovebirds decided they did. The music stopped. Somebody marched forward and yelled down at us.

"You awake down there?"

I buried Sabrina and wedged myself above the tank. My heart seemed to pound against the deck. There were more footfalls; heavy, the gait hesitant.

I heard exultant nervous laughter, then someone stamped on the deck. The vibrations stung my face.

"Maybe we ought to check?"

"Sure, what the fuck. Get the key."

The hesitant feet moved away. The other one stayed, tapping his toes against the hatch. The tapping stopped. There was a faint distant drone. An engine. A boat, a patrol boat I thought wildly. The drone increased little by little. It wasn't a boat. A plane, a small prop-driven plane coming in low. The plane swooped, then circled. I could make out voices, frantic footfalls. The plane was coming back, diving, the engine whining. There was a burst of gunfire. Planking splintered inches from my face. The plane turned and dove again, the engine whine nearly drowning out the clatter of automatic weapon fire. Then total pandemonium, an infernal chaos of engines and guns and screams. I pushed Sabrina under the sailbags and rolled on top of her. The plane returned, the fierce whine coming straight at us; then suddenly it veered away, the sound of its engine diminishing until it was lost in the soft slap of water and a faint tortured groaning.

I called out, but nobody answered. I kicked against the hatch, but nothing gave way. Sabrina began to moan. She was hunched in a fetal ball, rocking in a steady relentless rhythm. I touched her, feeling for wounds, but felt nothing except the dampness where she'd wet herself. The moaning continued, comfortless and low. Finally, she exhausted herself and we lay huddled together in slack resignation. Our only solace was the frail stream of air slipping through the bullet-riddled deck. And there was light now. Delicate spines of light revealing fragments of her face, her tense twisted mouth, a hank of matted hair.

The sea became still, stiller than the calm of the afternoon, the frail spines of light faded. The *Corlinda* swung on her anchor. Waves slapped the hull. We were inside a drum. The rhythm intensified, filling with complexity and menace. The hull lifted and fell and heaved. The waves grew gigantic, pitching us against the ribs, the frail oak ribs that were our prison. A prison we now prayed would hold us through the storm. Sabrina's fingers dug into my face and I felt the dark despair of her breath against my throat. There was nothing to say, and if there had been, we would have had to scream to be heard above the howling of the storm.

༯

I T WAS FEAR TO MAKE BONES freeze. Sobbing screaming fear. Fear beyond hope, beyond prayer. My nerves
were burned away, my mind useless, the ashes of hope
swirling in a sort of deranged gaiety. I asked the bilge not
to rise, the planking not to give way. I asked for a sandy
beach and no reef. The *Corlinda* didn't feel big anymore,
but she was bigger than her anchor. She dragged it for hour
after hour. Waves hammered the deck until the hull itself
seemed to groan and beg for mercy. The drag gave way and
for a moment we were airborne. When she came down, timbers broke with wrenching cracks and squeals as if the craft
were some living thing screaming under torture.

The seconds were endless, stretching until even the no-
tion of seconds was gone. There was only the engine of the
storm ripping the *Corlinda* apart plank by plank. There
must've been moments of something resembling sleep, some
state where the last cell ceased to care, knowing it couldn't
prepare. At some point I felt a hot sting of urine against
my leg. How lovely it seemed, the warmth, the sheer wonder of animal function. Then there was only the ceaseless
drumming, clenched teeth, a last desperate clinging.

There was no indication that morning had come, no les-
sening of darkness. But something in the fury seemed to
acknowledge the earth had turned to face the sun. We were
wedged in the bow, almost standing, the ribs forming a pro-
tective cradle. The *Corlinda* shuddered, shaking from stem

to stern; as insignificant as a mouse in the jaws of a cat. It was tossed and landed with a roar of splintering timbers. Another wave struck and she heeled onto her port side. The waves continued to pummel, working her further onto whatever rock or shore she had come up against, pounding her with ruthless force for hour upon hour.

The miracle must've materialized gradually, though it felt instantaneous. In an eyeblink it seemed, the relentless drumming had given way to lackadaisical tremors. Light sifted through cracked planking. I stood and my shaky legs held me. I heard myself laugh. Sabrina stood and clung trembling against me. Water sloshed around us gently as though it meant to console and apologize for what we'd been through. There were eddies around my ankles and sand between my toes. A wave broke and suddenly there was more light and a line of land. I watched the hatchcover float away in the foam.

"Sabrina, you hear?"

A faint smile flickered on her lips. I could see her now, every detail. It wasn't the same face I'd seen on that Tuesday that she'd skipped down the office stairs. There was no insolent gaiety, no frivolous arrogance. This face could never again be mistaken for sixteen or even twenty. It was still a lovely face, but it was no longer in balance. Especially the eyes; they seemed veiled, permanently lost to some private world no one else would ever see.

I called out and listened for a return call. Maybe the voices were only gulls. I put my head through the hatchway and was momentarily blinded. I saw white bluffs, sky, surf, and there were men, five or six men climbing over the rocks. On the shore another fifteen or twenty people had gathered, women, children, dogs. A double-ended boat was being launched. I waved. *"¡Buenas dias, mis amigos! ¡Gracias, amigos!"* I sang out the salute again and again.

※

D EATH MAKES FOR RED TAPE even in countries where red tape is kept to a minimum. Especially death that is violent, unexpected, unexplained. When it comes out of nowhere like the vague buzz of a fly. A fly that you ignore because it's a calm afternoon, the water glittering, you're lulled by a feast of sunlight and sex so a fly is no bother. Except this fly has a machine gun and there's no place to hide, there's no time to understand.

Maybe one of them had understood. The one who'd fired back. The one who'd crawled inside and sealed the cabin and ridden out the storm, eating red-shelled pistachios. They said he was still warm when they'd found him, so he'd probably died slowly. Maybe he'd known that was what he deserved, or maybe he was just the sort to stay stubborn to the end. As far as I knew, he was the only one I'd seen face to face, and that had only been a matter of seconds.

The ones I hadn't seen kept washing ashore. Mysterious gringos with .45 caliber bullets lodged in vital organs. It was a messy business, not at all like Forest Lawn with the blue "S" and the red X and everything on schedule. The authorities wanted a neat explanation for why this gringo mess had invaded their country. Of course they knew, they were absolutely certain that it had to do with drugs.

I shrugged and told them what I could. I had the benefit

of a double language barrier, their English and my Spanish. We floated in a sea of imprecision between the two. I told them about a man named Landis and a shootout on a California pier. How Landis had a grudge against an old partner named Fitzgibbons. This was pure speculation, but it sounded good. They understand grudge blood more instinctively than business blood. I figured that it was more than likely that Landis had simply wanted that truckload of merchandise. Guns always fetched a nice price. Especially if you could get them to a center of violence where they were in short supply; Angola, say or Mozambique.

I told them about Matthew Lawrence Trevelyan, a/k/a Larry Loper, the guy they'd found on the *Corlinda*. How he'd gone a little berserk and had apparently tried to take over the deal he and Fitzgibbons had been working. The deal the man named Sidney Landis wanted for himself. They liked the image of Landis, so I elaborated a little, explaining that he was a kind of emperor of hijacking. It all made perfect sense to them. They especially liked the image of the fight over a truckload of guns, although they still wanted to know about how the drugs fit in even when I told them it wasn't drugs, it was just a kind of greed.

They fed me decently and offered me cold beer in clear bottles. I talked some more. By now it was just a story I was telling to please them. I enjoyed their smiles and the way they seemed to take it all in stride, as though it not only made sense, but it had all really happened. At times I even thought they liked me. I was a gringo, but at least I tried to speak their language. They seemed to take such a personal interest in me that I came to tell them how I'd started chasing Larry Loper and how this Loper was a character who liked to assume identities. He had slipped right into playing Hal Fitzgibbons. Landis hadn't known this, so after his boys were ambushed at Long Beach, he assumed Fitz-gibbons had done it. When the *Corlinda* left Los Angeles, Landis probably had an inkling it'd be charting a course to the closest haven from U.S. law. Naturally, that was south. If someone cared to check, they'd probably come up with a connection between Landis and a twin-prop plane, possibly equipped with pontoons. Of course, this was just a guess, I'd been locked in the forward hold, but it'd sounded like a Cessna 150.

They never tired of hearing it. Maybe it was the exotic pidgin language we'd developed, or the fact that nothing else was happening. Life sometimes beats the imagination, don't you agree, *señor* Dancey? Yes I do. I very much do. The girl *señor*, this Sabrina, you sure you do not protect her? No, she really had nothing to do with it. Sabrina was gone, long gone. The morning after they had picked us up, she was on a flight from Pasa San Robles to LAX. There was a call to the consulate, and it just so happened the ambassador was a personal friend of the Trevelyan family. Somebody owed the ambassador a favor and so it goes. It pays to be well connected, the passport of privilege is universal. For once I was glad for it.

They kept finding bodies on the beach. Two of the bodies they knew were gringos only by the quality of the dental work. After three days, they'd picked up three females and one male. All the females were in their early twenties, the male in his early thirties. Finally I agreed to take a look because I thought it might get me a ticket. It didn't make any sense, but I no longer worried about what made sense and what didn't.

Larry Loper's entourage was being stored in a makeshift morgue. The refrigeration had broken down, and they were doing the best they could with bodybags and ice. There was one I knew. I recognized only the red hair and the bracelet. I looked, shook my head, and they zipped the bag back up. I could feel it about to hit me, the whole nightmare I'd kept just far enough away. I was protecting the inner core, the fragile human part that Sabrina had been unable to protect in herself. Nor had Sally Swann. I remembered the jasmine haze, the yellow leotard, how easily she had believed me. But then Larry Loper could tell better stories and he had a fancy yacht and he could promise to make all her dreams come true. Dancey could only tell her he'd try to get her a job slinging hash at the Lafayette.

And after it was over I made my plea, but there wasn't any ticket. Then, by luck, accident, or fate, an Inspector Chavez who spoke elegant, fluent English, came up from Mexico City to ask me the same tired questions I'd already answered. I told him the same fantastic story, and he smiled very politely. I happened to mention a Los Angeles homicide detective named Dmitri. The inspector's face came alive and a big grin reversed all the lines in his face. They'd cooperated on a case a million years back, a very notorious case involving a movie star murdered in Baja. He'd give the Lieutenant a call. The next morning I was on a plane to Los Angeles.

Suddenly Dancey had become a plausible gringo, or it no longer mattered whether he was plausible or not. The one thing worth more than a truckload of dollars was having the right connections. The rules and regulations are whisked onto the shelf, and indestructible red tape suddenly spontaneously combusts. Those little deals in back rooms made a lot of people rich and helped a lot of others stay poor, took some off the hook and put others on. As far as I could tell the whole world was run from the little nooks of privilege. I'd stumbled into one without even knocking, and I snatched it.

The jet hummed with monotonous calm. There weren't any ripples in the flight, but my stomach still churned. I fingered her little St. Christopher medallion that had been in my pocket through it all. I wondered if I could face the other lucky survivor, the one with the wheat-blonde hair and flecks of green in her eyes. The dream-girl who loved to ride a surfboard, the dream-girl who wasn't a dream-girl anymore. Everyone had their breaking point. I wondered at the fragility of things, the fragility that was so easy to ignore.

I tried to sleep, but I was haunted by the image of Sabrina's face as they lifted her into the boat and rowed us ashore. The way her eyes seemed to freeze when the *federales* took us into custody. How she clutched at me before they'd taken her to the hospital.

I began to wonder if my own sanity would crack when the authorities left me alone. Such a strange shell; it seemed built of layers of checked impulse, reason, and habit — the whole mass threaded together by desire. It grew thicker and stranger with each passing year. Every so often, I poked my head out and breathed the heady scent of madness. But I always ducked back inside. In the end, it was worth staying sane, I had a piano to play and scripts to read, and a wind-up watch out on San Fernando Road I was just sentimental enough to want to retrieve.

꒦

L IEUTENANT DMITRI was waiting just outside Customs. We shook hands and exchanged a few tired wisecracks. It was hazy late July. A Saturday, which I hoped meant he was getting overtime. The unmarked chauffered car was waiting at the curb. There was no luggage to pick up. We slid into the back seat like old friends who weren't quite sure if they were glad to see each other.

His laughter came as easily, but it seemed to have suffered some wear and tear; I couldn't help notice how it would start and suddenly die.

The freeway was jammed, the mountains were obscured in smog. He informed me three canyons were burning and added, "Even my gut burns, Dancey. You got any cures?"

He offered me a cigarette. I took it, then gave it back. He lit his with a Zippo fitted with a leather case, the leather black with age.

"Nobody even smokes anymore. The whole damn country's gone on a health kick. We live on fads. Good for the economy, I guess."

"The only fad that ever worked for me was sushi," I said. "And hula hoops. I was a hula hoop champ back in grade school. When boys weren't supposed to do that sort of thing."

"But you're nuts, Dancey," he stated with no particular emphasis. "Besides, you're an actor. What do you know?" He inhaled deeply, then stared at the cigarette, hating himself. He took another breath. "I'm presuming you were there when Mrs. Trevelyan got hit."

I didn't answer. Dmitri sighed. The same old game.

"It's okay, Dancey. There won't be any charges. Not from me, not from the higher-ups. I just want to sleep nights."

I told him I'd changed my mind, I'd take that cigarette. He pulled out his lighter. The smoke tasted bitter. I began to talk and stubbed it out. By the time we rolled off the freeway into downtown, I'd given him the details that were supposed to help him sleep.

The cruiser pulled into an underground lot, and a cop doing guard duty waved us into the windowless interior. We walked down empty fluorescent-lit corridors, rode an empty fluorescent-lit elevator, walked down another empty corridor to his clean fluorescent-lit office. It was furnished with a standard grey metal desk flanked by two grey metal chairs and a swivel chair that didn't match. It was an old oak chair with arms, the varnish flaking off, the wood worn smooth. It looked like it'd taken twenty years of nervous energy to sand it down with cheap discount suits and late nights. It was probably something Dmitri had brought in himself, or hung onto when they'd moved from the old headquarters. The rest of the furnishings betrayed no hint of eccentricity: the two grey filing cabinets in one corner, the grey typewriter on the grey typewriter stand, and a half-sized refrigerator just like the one I had in my office.

There were only two pieces of decoration. One was a framed color photograph on the desk, a good-looking redhead with her arms around the shoulders of a girl about seven, and a boy about ten. On the wall opposite the desk was Dmitri's surrogate window: a poster of the Yosemite Valley in winter photographed by Ansel Adams. Somehow it seemed too sophisticated for a cop, but then Dmitri wasn't an average cop. Average cops didn't exist, anymore than average people did.

"Too bad it isn't a real print," he said. "I almost bought one way back. But $250 seemed more than I could hack. So what do I know?"

"You into photography, Lieutenant?"

"I mess around. Which reminds me. The kid with the darkroom — he's about the only one involved in this freak-show I feel sorry for."

I agreed with him and added another: "Sally Swann. And maybe Sabrina Trevelyan. She got in over her head innocently enough, Lieutenant. We fall for the beautiful exterior, why shouldn't they?"

"Because women are supposed to be smarter. And most of them are."

We sat in silence, Dmitri in his oak swivel chair, me in the grey metal chair. He opened the bottom left-hand drawer and pulled out a pint of expensive scotch. It didn't look like a regular ritual. The seal hadn't been broken.

"Wasn't it you made the suggestion, Mr. Dancey?"

"You happen to have any milk? I'd take it neat, but you got company in the funny stomach department."

He got up, went over to the half-sized refrigerator and brought out a half gallon. "Exactly the way I take it myself. We have something in common."

"Probably more than you think."

"Maybe," he said, then he pulled two tumblers full of ice out of the freezer. He poured a couple of inches of booze in each. *Cutty Sark*, with the little clipper ship sailing. Just like the one I'd opened my eyes on one Saturday night a long time ago.

The milk floated the cubes to the top. The two glasses sweated and smoked. We lifted them and touched the rims in a silent toast. We nodded, sipped, and sat without a word, our minds as heavy as the snows of Yosemite.

"You really think Mrs. Trevelyan knocked off her husband?"

I shrugged.

"Maybe with Loper's help, or under his instigation. She was more than half-crazed herself."

Dmitri swirled the ice in his glass. "Patricide. A big word, isn't it? The coroner's report said coronary occlusion. You think a man really has a heart attack over some nasty pictures of his daughter?"

I'd asked myself the same question and come up empty.

"You have a daughter, don't you, Lieutenant?"

"I'd get mad, not die."

"All I know is that Loper seemed to have come back obsessed with getting revenge on his father. Maybe he found something exotic in his travels that would do tricks with a man's heart. I've heard of such things. Maybe it was just the sight of his son's ghost that killed him."

"An MIA come back to life," Dmitri mused. "Weird. A lot of guys got twisted over there. The amazing thing is so many went over, came back, and carried on like it was all part of growing up."

"You sound like you know."

Lieutenant Dmitri set his glass down very carefully. He didn't like remembering that far back. He had no anecdotes of glory he wanted to polish. All he said was, "I was scared shitless and I'd left the girl I married behind and I played "Rubber Soul" day and night. Looking at me now that's probably a little hard to believe. It's hard for me as a matter of fact."

The Lieutenant made himself another before getting back to business. "The way I see it, Loper was born twisted. You probably don't put any stock in that. Liberals usually think it was some sort of deprivation that made them that way."

"I'm not exactly a liberal, Lieutenant. Just a maverick. And I do buy it. I figure he had the right combination to flip from the start. Maybe the war was the catalyst, but a lot of other things might've been too."

Dmitri leaned back in his chair and I caught a hint of what he must've looked like when LBJ had sent him to southeast Asia to fight for reasons even the president wasn't sure of by then.

"At any rate, it's done. Done except for the paperwork." He drummed his fingers inside the circle of moisture his glass had left on the desk. He seemed to be drumming a song about how he'd seen it all and heard it all. Sometimes even crazier stuff than this, but he still had a hard time believing how little people would kill for. The Lieutenant had a far-away look in his eyes. "War," he said moodily. "Loper was off fighting his own little war trying to solve his private gripe. But he lost perspective. War does that, doesn't it? You start off with reasons and you're sure you're right and pretty soon the only important thing is winning, then nothing's real but surviving. But there's always reasons to begin with. When a bigshot gets a reason it's righteous and necessary and patriotic, when a crazy gets one it's murder. Funny thing is you'd think I'd get used to it."

Dmitri's voice was little more than a tired rasp. He was talking to himself, hoping to make sense of what he hadn't been able to make sense of for twenty years. He suddenly looked as if he'd been caught doing something ostentatious in a public place.

"I thought actors drank, Dancey," he said with excessive boisterousness to cover his embarrassment.

"Yeah, some of us do, Lieutenant. This is good stuff."

"Once in a while I treat myself." He didn't look up. He was staring at the steel desk he must have spent years of his life staring at. He wanted to send me away, but I was the one person who might be able to help arrange a few of the pieces. Maybe not perfectly, but I could at least nudge them in the right direction.

"So tell me, Dancey. How did Loper know about the gun deal? Or did he?"

I told him I thought he did. Sabrina had said that Loper and Hal Fitzgibbons had met in Zimbabwe, that it was Loper who had put Hal in touch with his father about buying the guns.

"Christ," Dmitri said shaking his head. "It's all too damn much. And how did Mrs. Trevelyan get mixed up in it?"

"I never could figure that. I have a theory, but that's about it."

"Run it by."

"Hell, what for?"

"Maybe because I've drunk a little too much and I'm curious about how your mind works."

I grinned. He was liking me again. So I told him I had the idea that Angie Trevelyan was actually in love with Hal Fitzgibbons. She wanted out from under Roger Trevelyan, but she didn't want to be poor. And she had reached that point in her life and in her addiction where she could delude herself into thinking Hal represented a certain romance. Then Larry Loper showed her the pictures that poor George had taken and in some drug-addled idea of revenge, she had shacked up with Loper at the Sunset Palms Motel. Or maybe she just liked him. I wasn't sure. But for whatever reasons it had happened. I didn't have the intertwined hairs I'd found that afternoon, but I had pictures. I told him about the surveillance camera in the closet. Dmitri looked stunned, "I remember the damn camera. But what in hell did he want pictures for. Tell me that."

I didn't know. Dmitri wanted my opinion. I speculated that Loper might have seen this as the ultimate humiliation. He would cuckold his father's wife, then he'd rub the old man's nose in it, shove the proof in his face.

"Nah, it's too damn nuts, Dancey."

I shrugged. "Probably. But maybe that's it. Maybe Angie was turned on by Loper's insanity. After all, it wasn't so different from her own. Hell, Lieutenant, didn't you ever see a woman you knew was half-bats, but just looking at her made you want. . ." The scotch was getting to me too. Two men airing not-so-clean laundry in a little grey room lost in the middle of a thousand grey rooms. No, Dmitri hadn't been plagued by those lusts I was prey to. Experience for its own sake wasn't up his alley. Nor were crazy women. He'd kept his head. A sane man. A man who'd gotten through Vietnam with his soul intact.

There was a silence filled with dust motes and unspoken dreams. I handed him my glass and held up my hand to indicate a light one. He made me a drink and sighed, "So poor old Mackey shows up looking for another set of pictures, the one Paskus took of Fitzgibbons and the Trevelyan girl. He probably thinks he'll just rough up this bearded punk kid, get the negatives and the boss'll be happy. But Loper hits him first, maybe hits him too hard. That the way you read it, Dancey?"

I nodded. I was about to mention I had pictures of Mackey too, but of course the Lieutenant had his own. They would be hard and bright and detailed, illuminated by the police photographer's strobe.

Dmitri grunted. "Too many victims, Dancey. This one is never going to read. The motives aren't clean."

"Are they ever, Lieutenant?"

Dmitri drummed his fingers on the desk. He didn't seem to have heard. Then he said, in that same moody, introspective voice, "Well, Mrs. Trevelyan didn't get her romance, did she? And it doesn't look like she's going to. Not with the best part of her paralyzed. A helluva good looking woman. But twisted. Ruins it."

He was losing himself again, drifting off into a private world. But unlike Sabrina's private world, his would have order and logic enough to keep the irrational at bay.

"So where did they find her romantic delusion anyway?"

"Fitzgibbons? Latigo Canyon. Sent him to the medical school eventually."

"You think they'll figure what made him tick?" Dmitri didn't even smile. He seemed too tired to do anything but sigh. "And the daughter's in the nut ward. A hell of a thing."

"Yeah," I said. I didn't want to think about her. Whenever I did, I kept seeing her face in that bright Baja light and how different it was from the sassy little face I'd watched slide under me one Saturday night.

"Well, I figure the lawyers are about the only ones that are going to see the sense in this," he said. "They'll be chuckling like jackals over a fresh kill." The faraway look had come back into his eyes. He was staring at Yosemite in winter. It was a lot cleaner and saner than Los Angeles in July. The thought struck me this was a man who would never get rich unless he won the lottery.

I said: "I guess I'll be going, Lieutenant."

"So soon? Hell, I'll miss you Dancey. By the way, you're not a bad actor. Give yourself another five years." The advice seemed genuine, without an trace of irony. Maybe Dmitri was the real actor.

"And if I don't make it?" I asked him.

Dmitri grinned. "Join the force," he suggested, and this time he completed his laugh.

I started for the door, then stopped. "One thing, Lieutenant, what happened to Landis?"

"You mean the guy that got away with it all, including the *Corlinda* massacre? Hell, the big fish always eat the little fish, Dancey. You been around Hollywood long enough, you ought to know. Now get your tail out of here so I can go play some golf."

We shook hands across the grey metal desk. I left him sitting there staring at the clean white snows of Yosemite two hundred miles to the north. The snows that wouldn't be there for another three or four months. And when they came, they wouldn't be quite as pure as last year's.

ᕘ

THERE WAS NO ONE TO CALL except Dr. Gordon Malm and a certain nurse that I could half hope hadn't yet found a suitable abode, although I already knew that Leiko and I were a lost cause. Strictly short-term, maybe a week, maybe a month and I didn't want that, couldn't take it. Suddenly I felt alone, crazily alone. A dark creature, soft and ugly, and crawling toward nowhere laughed like a hyena and told me I was finished. I thought of Sabrina and I felt worse. I wasn't up to a visit, not even to a nice, clean, progressive crazy-house for the rich like the Arnold Rush Center. She didn't belong there. She should be out on a surfboard teasing the boys with that pretty little tail, pretending she knew it all and finding out the hard way she didn't.

The dirty air raked my eyes and left a film of grit on my throat. My mouth tasted sour, my nose was dry. Fire season. It came every year and you never got used to it.

I walked up Broadway, not feeling the scotch anymore. It was good letting the crowd rub against me. Most of the faces were dark and most of them owned nothing more than the clothes they wore, but a lot of them were smiling. I found a branch of my bank, stuck my little plastic rectangle into the slot, and miracle of miracles, despite its punishment in the *Corlinda*'s bilge, it worked. It proved I was, after all, an authentic member of society. The computer reminded me the nightmare was real. Sabrina's check had cleared.

I pressed the buttons again and with a soft mechanical whirr, six twenties floated out. I was a late twentieth-century man who'd watched the conquest of the moon and took his money from a machine. I put five of the bills in my wallet and tucked the sixth in my sock, then I was wondering what had happened to Sabrina's twenty-five grand. It had probably gone in the storm. Maybe some poor fisherman would find it washing up on some remote Baja beach.

A wedding party tootled by, led by a red Impala peppered with white crepe-paper carnations. The happy pair was in the back seat all dressed up like the bride and groom on top of a cake. I walked down Broadway until I came across one of those low-budget supermarts for jewelry that's always blasting some heart-rending song from south of the border. The window was cluttered with rank upon rank of cameras and radios hidden in plastic Rolls-Royces and television sets disguised as satellites. I bought their top-of-the-line lady's watch and payed with my one credit card. The clerk kept winking as he etched the inscription on the back. He surveyed his handiwork through a magnifying glass, grinning as though he had his eye to the bedroom keyhole on opening night. I winked back to let him know it was going to be everything he imagined.

I picked up a dozen roses and caught a cab to San Fernando Road. I wasn't sure of the address. There was a tumbledown motel where the VACANCY sign would always be lit, and next door was a loud cantina.

It wasn't too hard to find, although it didn't look quite the same in daylight. Nothing ever does, not women, not cities, not even thirty-six-year-old, no-name actors.

The cantina was empty. The bartender told me Paloma was next door, but she wouldn't be too long. When I asked how long, he shrugged, "Maybe one hour. You like a *cerveza, señor?* Relax yourself. It is better, no? The *señoritas* look better at night I think."

"You're reading my mind," I said. He set down a cold bottle on a napkin with a beautifully understated flamboyance.

"Hot day. Very nasty, the smog."

"You're dead right."I pulled out my wallet.

"On the house, *señor*. I see you here before."

He smiled. He had big square teeth, all perfect, except someone had stolen the pair out of the upper middle. I liked him. He didn't seem to mind that I was a gringo. He took my roses and arranged them in a pitcher of water.

"*Gracias*," I said.

"Always quiet at this time," he said.

The beer tasted good. It came in a clear bottle with a little train running across the label. Chug-chug, the little train that could. I smiled. I'd been mixing too many kinds of booze and leading too many lives, but at the moment it didn't matter much.

There was a golf match on the TV above the bar. Just

like the one Doris and Harry had made jokes about so long ago. It was nice and simple, at least so it seemed. Then suddenly the fairways were gone and a girl with sun-bleached hair, a girl who looked much too much like Sabrina Trevelyan, was telling me men who smelled like such-and-such cologne turned her on. That was simple too. Commerce. I'd never been very good at it. I ordered another beer and thought of the tubes of gravestone rubbings still sitting on the living room floor. I should frame them and take them around. I should also call Max and see if he had any hot properties for me to read. I thought of how Tuss Washington and I might split a pint and drop in at the Sundown to stand in for a few sets, and my heart lightened.

"Later she really swings," the bartender said.

"Yeah, I bet."

"Then you feel much better, *señor*."

He pushed his white towel toward the end of the empty bar. I nodded and brought out the little velvet-lined watch box. Above me, men in clean white clothes walked across perfect lawns hitting tiny white balls for big money. I sipped and stared at the roses and waited.

ABOUT THE AUTHOR

R. B. Phillips has been somewhat gainfully employed as an agricultural laborer, warehouseman, teacher, dishwasher, wedding photographer, ghostwriter and documentary filmmaker. He has published poems, articles and a novel, *TV Man,* under his own name. At present, he is revising another Elton Dancey mystery with the working title of *Snow Fall,* and is completing a new novel, *The Marriage of John Le Beau.*